The Elixir
of the
Green Willow Guard

THE ELIXIR OF THE GREEN WILLOW GUARD

A Kingdom of Ethereal Story

A.D. UHLAR

Unearthing Treasure Press

Cover Art by **Malice and Mayhem Book Covers**
Find her on the web at www.mmbookcovers.com

Character Art by **Peyton Christensen**
Find her on Instagram @sweetpeasketches

The Elixir
of the
Green Willow Guard

DEDICATION

To my family, who listened to all my excited breakthroughs and
supported me through the entire process.
&
To all those who struggle to see the treasure within.

PRONUNCIATION GUIDE

Characters:

Abaddon = A-bu-dawn   **Liam** = Lee-um

Apollyon = U-pol-e-on   **Naamah** = Nu-moh

Durmad = Der-mod   **Shylah** = Shi-lu

Jorden = Jor-den   **Trulian** = True-ly-un

Places:

Baylon = Bay-lawn   **Kyselina** = Kiss-u-lee-nu

Castigation = Cast-u-gay-shun   **Morena** = More-en-u

Dimmet = Du-met   **Typhon** = Tie-fun

Miscellaneous:

Cyanelle = Si-o-nel   **Strobilus** = Strow-by-luhs

Peripatetic = Pair-u-pu-tet-ic   **Vocular** = Voe-cue-lar

Quiescence = Kwy-es-ence

CHAPTER ONE

SHYLAH

Silver-blue light sliced the darkness in Shylah's sparsely furnished room. She should be asleep. Midnight neared, and her distillate ability continued to deplete. Sitting on her bed staring at dust glittering in the moonbeams would not renew her energies for tomorrow. Only sleep would do that, but she couldn't resist the nights when a full moon lit the cloudless sky. It reminded her of Baylon—of home.

On nights like this, when her ability waned, she missed home more than usual but knew it would never be the same. It couldn't be. Not after the fire. Pulling her knees to her chest, she glanced at the bottle of Lull in her hand. She really did need sleep.

Her little sister, Trulian, shifted in the bed a few feet away. Shylah smiled as her sister's gentle breathing brushed her consciousness. Sighing, she tipped her head back and closed her eyes. Trulian's breathing transformed into the leaves that danced in the gentle breeze wafting from the nearby Cerulean River, and for a few precious moments, her small room, with its dirt floor, transformed into her childhood room. The room where her mother tucked her in and pulled back the curtains, giving Shylah a clear view of the forest just beyond their low stone fence.

Trulian mumbled, pulling Shylah back to the present. She really should be asleep. Folding her legs, she sat up and fluttered her fingers through the glittering silver-blue beams inches from her nose. Her fingers stirred the dust particles until the light touched the black feather mark wrapping around her wrist like a permanent bracelet. To most, it appeared to be a simple tattoo, but there had been no ink punched into her skin, and yet it still shackled her. It appeared the moment her feet hit the boat deck that brought her and her sister to Dimmet.

Turning her wrist, she let a moonbeam illuminate the feather tip as it barely kissed the hollow shaft that should have been attached to the bird. The slight bump of her blood vein crossed just beneath the joining point—a constant reminder that her beginning and end were hollow without the Queen's provision and will. Shylah was a Bonded—one of the Queen's many feathers in the wings that beat down the very air around the kingdom of Dimmet.

Had Shylah known stepping on that boat deck would seal her fate, she would have grabbed her sister's hand and ran. They could have survived on the streets of Typhon or tried to rebuild Baylon. She dropped her hand to the bottle of Lull in her lap and sighed. They hadn't run. After three years, dosing herself was still the only way she could sleep without the flames licking the backs of her eyelids, accented by the overwhelming guttural screams of Baylon's people — of her parents.

The cool glass rested against her lower lip, and she exhaled. The pale blue liquid inside glowed like the dust floating in the moonbeams. Her forehead ached at the use of her fading ability. She really did need rest.

Trulian's scream shattered the calm. Shylah's grip tightened around the Lull, keeping it from spilling on the thin blanket draped across her lap.

The dose of Lull she'd given her little sister must have worn off. *Not good*. She'd increased the amount in the last few months, and no matter how much sleeping elixir Shylah gave Trulian, it eventually wore off.

But this was too soon. Shylah's chest tightened. It hadn't even lasted through the night. Holding the bottle up in the faint light, she frowned. There wasn't enough for them both.

Pursing her lips, Shylah flipped the blanket off her lap, and, in a single stride, sat on the edge of her sister's bed. She gently shook her sister's shoulder and whispered, "Tru. Tru. Wake up."

Trulian squirmed, still thick in sleep.

"It's only a nightmare," Shylah said, rubbing her sister's upper arm before whispering, "Please be just a nightmare."

Trulian only screwed her face into a grimace. Shylah sighed and lifted the small bottle still clutched in her hand. Pinching Trulian's nose closed, she readied the bottle of Lull next to her sister's lips.

Trulian arched her back. Lull spilled on her cheek as another scream burst from her throat before she sat up so quickly that Shylah nearly dropped the entire bottle. Staring at something in front of her, eyes glazed over, Trulian's mouth moved as if speaking to a ghost.

Not a nightmare. Trulian was traveling.

Shylah shoved the cork back into the bottle and tossed it on her pillow. Her parents had celebrated when Trulian traveled for the first time on her seventh birthday—at least one of their daughters had a true ability. But their parents weren't here, and traveling would draw the attention of the Queen. No one could know Trulian's true ability, especially the Queen.

Dragging her bed away from the wall, Shylah retrieved a bottle of pink liquid from its hiding place. Lull might stop nightmares, but it only dampened the external effects. It couldn't stop the traveling –only Quiescence could do that.

The first night the girls were brought to Dimmet's capital city of Morena, Trulian traveled. Those with peripatetic ability were sought after, but in Dimmet, they were forced to become tools of its Queen. No one could know the truth. Trulian was the only family Shylah had left. When the guard had asked what was wrong, she had lied and said, "Nightmare." They had seen and heard their parents burn along with most of their village, so he believed her.

Trulian laughed and twisted, placing her feet on the packed dirt floor.

Shylah pressed down on her sister's shoulders and sat across her legs, pinning them to the bed. It took all of Shylah's strength to keep her sister from standing while uncorking the bottle of Quiescence.

She screamed again.

Shylah poured the rest of the thick pink liquid into the cheek of Trulian's open mouth. Holding her breath, Shylah's muscles stayed taut for the ten breaths it took for Trulian's muscles to finally relax, and she laid back down. The first few breaths were ragged and agitated, but with each one, Trulian's breathing became more regular and finally transitioned to the drawn-out breaths of someone sleeping.

Shylah swung her legs off the side of her sister's bed. Trulian's ability was growing stronger, and her traveling was becoming more frequent. Shylah glanced at the empty bottle gripped in her hand. The last dose of Quiescence had only lasted a few weeks.

Pounding shook the door, and the handle rattled.

CHAPTER TWO

SHYLAH

Jumping to her feet, Shylah pressed her body against the door.

"What's going on?" Apollyon's nasally voice made her ears twitch.

"Nightmares," Shylah said. "I just gave her Lull." She glanced down at her sister, lying flat on her bed, eyes darting rapidly behind closed eyelids. "It will take a few minutes to take effect, Sir."

"I know how Lull works," he growled. "If she wakes me again, she will wake in Naamah's dungeons."

Shylah's body shook as he hit the other side of the door.

"Mark my words, Bonded, you can be replaced."

The familiar threat still sent chills down her spine. Not as replaceable as you are, Shylah thought. Queen Naamah exclusively requested elixirs designed by *The Apprentice* for the past three weeks. As far as everyone else knew, Trulian possessed no ability, no value, which meant she was replaceable to everyone else.

Shylah pressed her ear to the door and listened for the click of Apollyon's door. It slammed a few seconds later, and Shylah turned her face back to her sister to see her body shutter before the Quiescence finally overpowered the traveling. It had been unnerving the first few times Shylah had seen Trulian fall out of the peripatetic state, but now she breathed easier. The Quiescence still worked.

She glanced at the bottle haphazardly tossed on her pillow. Lull was the first potion Apollyon had demonstrated, but it was not taught, because Apollyon never taught anything. He didn't want Trulian's nightmares to wake him. After six months, it had taken too much Lull to help Trulian rest peacefully—too much because he quickly grew tired of making it every week; there wasn't much he didn't quickly tire of. He had refused to make another drop. That's when the dungeon threats started.

The one thing he liked more than sleep was control, so he hadn't given Shylah the recipe. Instead, he'd tossed a blank journal at her and said, "If the Queen thinks you are so skilled in elixirs, you can figure it out yourself." She'd been left to her own devices and had to recall all the times she'd watched him make Lull and teach herself, but even then, some ingredients were locked away.

Shylah sighed and slid down the door until she sat on the floor. *Only four weeks.* It was wearing off faster and faster. She held the bottle up. *Empty.* She'd have to get up early and make more before Apollyon sauntered in at his usual midday start time. Closing her eyes, she leaned her head against the door, remembering the first time she'd had to design an elixir behind Apollyon's back.

They'd only been in Dimmet a month. He'd refused to give her the last ingredient for a new batch of Lull until she could name and harvest her own. So, that night, she had snuck up to the elixir shop to either figure out the name or retrieve the final ingredient locked in the cabinet: a small flavorless berry. *Surely his main elixir book had a recipe listing the berry's name.* Flipping through it, she found a page with the word *Travel* scrolled above the description of an elixir.

Quiescence: prevents anyone with a peripatetic ability from traveling, day or night.

It had many of the same ingredients as Lull: chopped fire onion root, heliotrope nectar, linden sap, and powdered snakeroot. But instead of mentioning a berry, it called for honeysuckle nectar and biting strobilus milk. Both were rare ingredients, and both were kept locked in the cabinet.

She'd tried the cabinet, thinking he'd forgotten to lock it, knowing it was a futile attempt. They hadn't budged. Lifting the pestle from the mortar, she'd almost broken the glass doors, but broken glass would raise suspicion, and she couldn't draw any more attention to herself or her sister. But she had to unlock the cabinet.

Rifling through a drawer, she grabbed a bone pick and blindly jammed it into the slot.

Cool metal touched the tip of her nose. *A key.* Her blood froze. She'd been caught.

Hot breath tickled her ear.

"This will make it easier."

She squeezed her eyes shut. Not Apollyon but not much better. What excuse could she give? The idea of being punished had been bearable, almost welcomed, when the chance of being caught was a mere idea, but now, reality chipped away at her resolve. "Lull. I needed the berry juice."

He gently moved her aside and unlocked the cabinet before facing her, his emerald eyes glowing in the workshop's low candlelight. Stepping back, he waved at the cabinet, "I don't know what you need, but I know Trulian needs to sleep."

"Thank you, Sir."

He flinched at the formal nomenclature. "Durmad," he said.

Shylah hesitated. She knew his name, but in the short time since the Green Willow Guard had *rescued* her, thrusting her involuntarily into his world, she had learned Bonded did not refer to their caretakers in such familiar terms—no matter how young or green their eyes. "Thank you. Durmad. Sir." His name grated on her tongue even as his eyes soothed it.

He grinned. "Progress."

"May I continue?"

He nodded, sitting on a stool in the corner.

"Are you going to watch the whole time, Sir?"

Durmad crossed his arms and leaned back against the wall. "Someone has to lock it after you're done. Unless, of course, you want my uncle to know the cabinet was opened. And it's Durmad."

"Fine, Durmad. *Sir*," she said.

That night had been the first time Shylah made Quiescence. It took only a drop to pull Trulian back into a calm sleep the next time she traveled. That first dose had lasted nearly six months. Durmad may not have known what she made, but his uncle most certainly would have. She had to hide it. She'd carved the hiding place in the leg of her bed and slowly squirreled away the easy-to-find ingredients, becoming quite adept at hiding the real reason for additional trips to the market. Apollyon's control of the rare ingredients necessitated her making a copy of the key the night Durmad had left, and Apollyon drank himself into a stupor before the fire.

Durmad had kept her secret, and the ingredients went unnoticed. She'd started relaxing and even had fun learning to design elixirs on her own. Those green eyes became more inviting, at least until the Fire Onion Juice incident.

She leaned forward and shook her head. No time to think about emerald eyes no longer around and that no longer mattered. Holding the empty Quiescence bottle in the moonlight, she frowned. There hadn't been enough time to collect and hide all the ingredients she'd need for another dose, and she wasn't sure Apollyon even had the rare ones. He hadn't gone collecting for the last three weeks.

Sighing, she picked herself up off the floor and returned the bottle to its hiding place, pushing her bed back against the wall. Shylah retrieved the bottle of Lull, uncorked it, exhaled across the bottle again, and took a large gulp. It was the only way sleep would take hold in spite of the adrenaline still pumping through her veins. She was sure she knew where Trulian had traveled, and Shylah didn't want any fire or screams. The only image she wanted to see was the veins of red sprouting across the darkness as her ability renewed for the full day of elixir designing that always seemed to lay ahead. She laid back down and prayed for Lull's dreamless darkness to take hold quickly.

CHAPTER THREE

SHYLAH

The next morning, Shylah's head ached. Not enough sleep, but it didn't matter. She stood on tiptoes and peered out the small ground-level window of her bedroom. Everything lay in the gray pallor of early morning, and no feet passed by. Quickly rebraiding her long red streaked flaxen locks, Shylah glanced at Trulian. The muscles of her face relaxed into a slight smile.

Good. Sleeping peacefully.

Shylah pulled her leather apron from its hook just outside the door but carried her boots. Stocking feet were quieter in the elixir workshop above them. She had to make more Quiescence without waking Apollyon.

Creeping up the stairs and over to the locked cabinet, she pulled the middle drawer free and unfastened the rudimentary copy she had made of Apollyon's key. It had only taken a bit of wax and a few sweet cakes to bribe Aidan, the fires smith's apprentice, into making her a copy. In truth, he had offered to make the key for free, but the bribe provided a convenient cover story. The two had become friends on

Shylah's first visit to the market alone nearly two years ago. There had been something in his demeanor that she could trust. She couldn't put her finger on it and couldn't really explain it, but she knew from the moment they met that they'd be friends. Besides, she hadn't wanted to rely on Durmad to keep any other secrets.

She opened the cabinet and pulled the green jar from its place; her heart sank. The key ingredient, biting strobilus milk, was empty. It only grew in the acidic soils of the Kyselina Desert—a nearly three-hour hike beyond Morena's walls. It was the hardest to collect.

Apollyon had tried to keep her from learning just how to collect it as long as he could. Controlling the elixir ingredients and their collection ensured he couldn't be easily replaced. He kept all the collection materials in a locked box beneath his pillow. A year ago, she feigned illness to avoid delivering an elixir, forcing Apollyon to deliver it. As soon as he left, she found his hiding spot, but knowing the spot didn't make it any easier to get.

She retrieved a black bottle of honeysuckle nectar and uncorked it. It wasn't empty, but there wasn't enough. Returning everything to its original state, a sigh escaped her lips. Not only would she need to purchase her own collection supplies, but it would take her entire Replenish Day. So much for any actual replenishing.

That doesn't matter. Trulian matters.

I need an excuse to go to the market, she thought, scanning the herbs and oils that were low from frequent use in her most requested elixir designs: Fire Onion Powder, Comfrey Root, Nettle, Yak and Rosehip Oils. Each had a little remaining, so Shylah poured the herbs into her boots, trying to divide it evenly between both, and shoved her feet in. She could empty them on the way to the market, but just standing on the uneven shoe sole made her feet ache. Walking even a few houses down would be uncomfortable. She wiggled her toes to get the material to flatten beneath them. It was better, but if she could only get it to the tip of the boot where there was extra room, she could avoid blisters until she reached the alley just outside the market. Bending her foot behind her, she thrust the tip onto the floor. The loud thud reminded her she was above Apollyon's room, and every muscle tensed as she listened for any hint that her haste had woken him.

Satisfied he had slept through it, she returned the empty bottles to their designated shelf. Now for the oils. She looked around. It could contaminate the soil if she poured it into the plants, and Apollyon would blame her. Her eyes scanned the room and landed on the fireplace. Grabbing the fire poker, she moved the wood and ash and emptied both bottles on the bare stone before returning the ash and wood to their original place and tossing in a pinecone in case she needed an excuse for any abnormal flame.

Now, she needed to make sure the empty ingredients were needed and noticed. Shylah picked up the stack of elixir orders for the week and sifted through them. The top one was Resurgence, a youth serum for one of the regulars that required Rosehip Oil and Comfrey Root. The next two didn't need any of the empty ingredients, so they went to the bottom of the pile. The next order sheet was for two different salves, one that would require Nettle, Comfrey Root, and Yak Oil, while the other called for Fire Onion Powder, so it got placed second. She sifted through the rest of the stack and found six more orders calling for the missing ingredients; they were also placed near the top of the stack. The third order she left as an elixir they could design so Apollyon didn't become suspicious.

With everything staged, Shylah wrote a note for Apollyon and set it in the center of the elixir table in case he woke up looking for her.

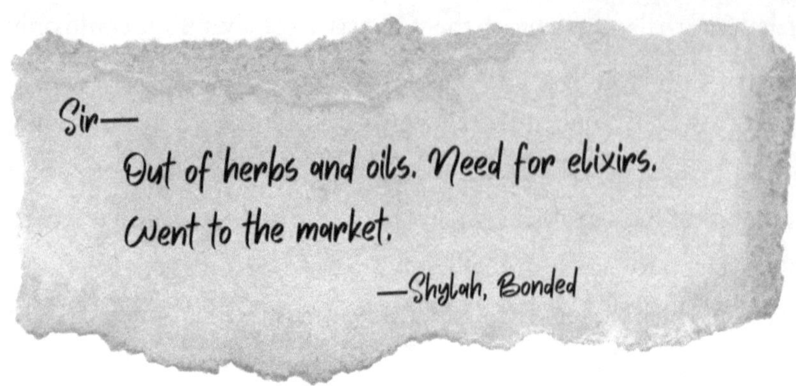

Shylah pulled out the drawer two below her key drawer and gripped her leather money pouch attached to the underside. It was the perfect hiding place. Apollyon never crouched, so she or Trulian always retrieved scrap items from the bottom drawers. Shylah shoved a handful of coins into her apron pocket and returned everything to its place before getting her morning tea and biscuit. By the time she finished eating, the sun had finished painting the sky, and the streets had begun to fill with people heading to the market.

Walking down the alley beside the workshop, she peered around the corner before entering the street. Stepping out behind a group of men walking by, she kept her eyes down and hands tucked into her apron. The yeasty smell of fresh bread mingled with fresh flowers, cinnamon-roasted berry nuts, and sweet puffed kernels grew stronger the closer she got to Pell Street. Licking her lips, she mentally ran through her shopping list. Besides the herbs and oils for the elixirs, she needed an alloy blanket, copper snips, a copper hand spade, and food in case the collection of the biting strobilus milk took longer than she wanted—*oh, and some willow bark for my head.*

Being prepared helped her shake the nerves of going to the Kyselina Desert alone, but it wasn't a guarantee. The acid rainstorms of the Kyselina Desert were among Dimmet's most unpredictable elements. They came up suddenly and could last for days. She had to be prepared and hopeful that if a storm came, it would last minutes rather than days.

The first artisans from the south market entrance, her entrance, were herbalists. Then she'd get some roasted berry nuts and two cardamom rolls on her way to the firesmith's booth before ending with the oilers. If she focused, she should be back before Apollyon woke, but first, she needed to rid herself of the boot-herbs.

She ducked into the last alley before the market and turned the first corner. Leaning one hand on the cool stone building, she loosened, pulled off her boot, and shook the herbs into the wind. The dried green and brown leaves mingled with the grime and shadows. Relief lightened her shoulders as she slid her foot back into the now-empty boot.

"You shouldn't be here alone."

Shylah tensed, pivoted, leaned her back against the stone, and continued tightening her boot.

"Especially as a Bonded."

Shylah stood, eyes searching for a face to match the voice. They landed on the figure of an older man only an inch taller than herself, with gray and amber eyes that seemed to swirl around the center. Her shoulders sagged, and some of the tension evaporated from her muscles. "I'm merely running errands," she said, stepping away from the wall.

The old man cut her off. "You should cover that," he said, pointing to her exposed wrist.

She quickly tugged her sleeve over the mark. "Thank you. But I really must finish my errands. My keeper is expecting my return." She threw in the last detail for good measure. If a would-be attacker thought her keeper was expecting her, he usually remained a *would-be*.

The old man grinned and bowed. "We Bonded must stick together," he said, tucking his long, graying hair behind his ear as he stood.

Her eyes found the mark on his neck, below his left ear, just before he captured her eyes again. The amber in his eyes whirled into the gray like debris tossed in a tornado. It was unnerving. She scurried past him, muttering another thank you, and quickly glanced over her shoulder. He waved and said, "Till we meet again," before ducking around another corner.

Goosebumps ran down her neck as she rejoined the throngs of people doing their morning tasks. No matter how many times she met another Bonded, she never felt completely comfortable or safe, but this was the first Bonded man she'd seen other than the husband of the couple who ferried them across the Astra Sea. Questions formed on the edges of her mind, but she shook them free. Entertaining questions about an old man, no matter how quickly he disappeared, would only put her mission in jeopardy. She had things to do and items to purchase.

Squeezing through the throngs of people, Shylah ignored the whistles and darted just beyond the reach of the bored vagabonds who came to the market to pass the time or solicit coins, willingly or not, from distracted shoppers. She had no time to be someone's entertainment. Pulling her sleeve over the feather shackle tattooed around her left wrist, she turned the corner and met a line of waiting buyers at the firesmith.

She leaned around the line and waved to Aidan, hurriedly exchanging coins for goods. Hoping he would motion her to the front, she waved, but he turned his back and retrieved a hammer for the next customer. Her shoulders sagged.

The line moved slowly, and her heart clenched tighter each time she saw Aidan grab an alloy blanket or copper spade from the back wall. She crossed her arms over her chest when three men sauntered up to the table. The red-haired one drew the firesmith's exclusive attention. *Of course.* If a man knew the right people, had the right profession, or had the right amount of money, he could circumvent any civilized custom he wanted. Even Aidan's attention drifted to them. Shylah rolled her eyes and tapped her foot once before looking away. Getting frustrated would only lead to poor decisions and longer errands. She couldn't afford any more distractions.

When she finally reached the table, small flames flickered in Aidan's pupils. "What can I get you?"

Shylah quickly nodded and said, "An alloy blanket, copper spade, and copper snips."

Aidan smiled and placed all three items on the counter, and she retrieved her coins.

A gloved hand covered the alloy blanket. "We'll take this, too."

CHAPTER FOUR

DURMAD

Durmad leaned forward as the tallest turret of Dimmet's castle peeked over the treetops; the large feathers carved from the black stone that covered the entire top half made it look like a shadowy figure materializing in the morning twilight. "Almost home, Atlas," he whispered, dragging a hand down the muscular neck of his horse and patting Atlas's shoulder before adjusting himself in the saddle.

Atlas huffed, shook his head, and slowed his pace.

"He's about as anxious as I am to get back to the capital," Liam said as his horse, Eclipse, fell in step beside Durmad.

"It's been two and a half years. Don't you want to see your family?" Durmad asked, running a hand through his messy black waves.

Liam chuckled. "Jorden, maybe."

"You're a strange lot," Abaddon said from Liam's other side. "I haven't seen a woman or smelled one in the last year of training." He closed his eyes, and drew in a lung-filling breath before licking his lips. "Let alone tasted one."

"Don't be too desperate," Liam said.

"Desperate animals get trapped quicker," Durmad added.

Abaddon smiled and took a few sniffs of the air. "I'll be the one tracking and trapping."

Liam shook his head. "You're a fool, truly."

"Hey. We can't all be the Queen's heir with every whim tended to by —"

Before Abaddon could finish, Liam shoved him so hard and so suddenly that the greasy man slid off his saddle. His right foot caught in his stirrup. As he struggled to free his ankle, Liam smacked the backside of Abaddon's horse.

"Hey," Abaddon yelled and coughed as the dragging of his body engulfed him in a cloud of dust.

Durmad snorted. "You know that's just going to egg him on. You're better off just laughing and letting him believe whatever he wants."

"Like you?" Liam asked.

Durmad shifted in his saddle again.

"You know she's going to expect an answer before the week is out. She wants us to start advanced training to take over the hunt."

Durmad turned toward Liam. "What is it we're supposed to be hunting anyway? And why can't she tell me that before I make my decision?"

"Only the commanders truly know, but it's supposed to be a better way of containing the pestilence." Liam glanced at Durmad. "I would have thought you'd be all for that with your parents and all."

Durmad dropped his eyes and clenched his jaw, no matter how much reassuring Liam gave him. Durmad hated being reminded of his parent's death. For the first few months of training, Liam assumed he hesitated to accept his position in the Green Willow Guard be-cause of his status as an orphan. Durmad let him. It was easier to let someone believe a lie or a half-truth than relive the horrifying scene or acknowledge the guilt that still ate away at his heart. Even now, when complete exhaustion prevented him from creating a barrier around his memories, he'd dream about being locked out of his family cottage, peering in through the window as his father rocked and cried over his mother's dead body cradled in his lap. He'd only been nine years old when the pestilence claimed his mother and then his father a few short days later. He remembered pounding on the door, crying on the ground outside, asking his father to let him in, and finally falling asleep in the mud of his tears. That's where his uncle had found him a week later, still balled up outside the door to the cottage with both his parents dead inside.

He'd come to terms with it as much as a child could, but when the King and his family died a few months later, and the King's distant daughter came with her two sons, the hunting began. The new Queen started recruiting for the Green Willow Guard, and on Durmad's eighteenth birthday, he'd agreed to join. But it was another year before he actually left for training. But in that year, so much had changed. The Green Willow Guard had brought back an entire boat filled with young girls ranging from seven to fourteen from the other kingdoms. Two of them were placed with his uncle: one as an apprentice and the other as a cook. He didn't know how a nine-year-old could be expected to cook, but he looked out for Trulian and helped behind his uncle's back. Then, training came, and he had to leave. He'd thought Trulian's older sister would be glad to have him gone. He had tormented her for the entire six months that they had been in his uncle's care, but somehow, she had looked upset, even angry, the day he left. Leaving the girls wasn't where his guilt came from, though.

In the first few weeks of training, he discovered why he had been recruited —his ability to control the body's cells. The guilt came once he knew how to control his ability and just what it could do. His idle moments were filled with "if onlys," and his dreams featured his father cradling his mother's body again. If only he'd been able to learn and control his ability sooner, he could have saved them both. Or, at least, that's what he kept telling himself.

"If it's the Bonding you're worried about," Liam's voice cut through the suffocating pressure of reflection, "you don't need to be. Don't listen to the rumors. She protects her Bonded as if they were her own children."

Durmad raised an eyebrow at Liam. "You don't want to be tied to her either, and you're her actual son."

Liam rolled his eyes. "That's something different, and you know it. Now you're just deflecting."

Durmad pulled Atlas to a stop. "Look. She might care for the Bonded and even protect them as if they were her children, but the fact remains, they aren't. She doesn't force you to do things. But she can compel a Bonded to do things, even if they wouldn't under their own power. I don't know that I want to be tied to her for the rest of her life, let alone controlled by her for the rest of mine."

Liam cocked his head to the side. "You know I wouldn't let her do that to you, right?"

"I don't know that you could stop it."

"Of course I can," Liam huffed. "My abilities far exceed that of my mother's."

"Do they now?" Durmad asked, kicking Atlas into a trot. "Is that why you still mumble a woman's name when you sleep and yet entertain no women during the day?"

Before Liam could respond, Atlas turned the bend in the road. Abaddon stood patting dust clouds from his pants as his horse lazily ate grass beside him.

"Whoa, Atlas," Durmad said, stopping beside Abaddon. "Nice ride?"

Abaddon slapped his leg one more time and mounted his horse. "Of course. My clothes were too clean anyway. Gotta set myself apart from the two of you somehow."

Liam stopped just behind Abaddon. "How do you figure that?"

Abaddon flicked the collar of Durmad's leather jacket. "Your leather's barely creased. At least I look like I fight my battles instead of sending others to fight for me."

Liam smirked. "Ah, but you don't have to fight when you have money and prestige. Only the peasants fight their own battles."

Abaddon's face reddened.

"Gentlemen," Durmad interjected, "I need a drink before seeing my uncle, not a fight."

"And before I enter my mother's presence again," Liam said.

Abaddon's face returned to its normal color as a grin spread across his cracked lips. "Then you can buy the first round."

"Not a chance in the stars," Liam said.

Durmad turned Atlas back into the road. "You did give him a dust bath. A drink is the least you could do."

"He said he was grateful. I helped him set himself apart."

Durmad rolled his eyes. "Come on. Let's get the horses to the stables and find a place to stay tonight."

"You aren't staying with your uncle tonight?" Liam asked.

Durmad raised an eyebrow. "Are you going to the castle?"

"No." Liam smiled. "I have to buy a man a drink," he said, smacking the backside of Abaddon's horse again.

Abaddon pulled back on the reigns. "I don't need help getting my horse moving."

"All right." Liam shot Durmad a side glance. "I was going to give you a head start. Last one to the stables pays for the room."

Durmad kicked Atlas into a full gallop a split second after Liam.

They blew past the guard and barreled through the streets before he could stop them.

"Make way," Durmad yelled in case the sound of pounding hooves went unnoticed, but luckily, the early hour meant less crowded streets. Most people were merchants heading to the market who pressed themselves against the nearest building. A few yelled and shook fists, but Liam only prodded his horse to go faster. Glancing over his shoulder, Durmad made sure Abaddon was close but still behind him. Liam needed to win, but that didn't mean Durmad had to lose.

CHAPTER FIVE

DURMAD

Durmad gave Atlas fresh hay. "Rest up, boy."

"I'll take good care of him, Sir," said the stable boy as he handed Durmad an apple.

"Thank you," Durmad said, holding the apple in an open palm for Atlas. "I'll be back tomorrow."

Atlas shook his head and took the apple before backing away from the stall door. A few moments later, Durmad joined Liam and Abaddon outside. The wind blew the cool morning air across his cheeks and around the tip of his nose. Scratching his four-day-old beard, he said, "So, Abaddon pays for the room, and Liam gets the drinks. I guess that leaves dinner to me."

Abaddon huffed. "You mean that leaves dinner to your uncle."

Durmad shrugged.

Liam smacked Durmad on the back. "To the market boys," he said, and they walked down Morena's main street toward the Pell Street market.

Finding out a week ago that they would return to Morena made the two years of training feel like not enough time away, but the closer they rode to the capital city, the more Durmad let himself imagine what life would be like if he stayed. The mixed feelings and looming decision made every side street and building feel familiar and foreign at the same time. He wasn't sure if he was coming home or simply passing through. If he was honest with himself, he wasn't sure which one he wanted.

As they reached the edge of the market, Abaddon said, "If I'm paying for the room, I get to pick the tavern."

"Fair enough," Liam said. "Where to, mighty commander?"

"The Even-tide Tavern just through the Pell Street market," Abaddon said with a smirk. "The drink is good and the beds warm." He clapped a hand on Durmad's back. "At least for the two of us."

"My bed is warm enough."

Liam faced Durmad. "So, you will return home then?"

Durmad shrugged. "Not sure. That will depend on my uncle, but I do not need help warming my bed."

"More warmth for me then," Abaddon said, stepping forward. "I'm parched."

Liam fell in step beside Abaddon, but Durmad walked a pace behind. The morning bustle now filling the streets made him feel more at home than he ever did during training, but it wasn't his family's land. *Two weeks*. He had two weeks to make his decision. Before this morning, he thought he knew the answer. He'd serve out the remaining years of his commitment and return home. Now that he was here, it didn't feel like home. After this morning's ride into town, it was obvious the decision Liam wanted him to make. Durmad shook his head. There was time to make the decision. Right now, sitting on a chair that didn't move with a drink sounded like heaven.

The three men stepped onto Pell Street, and peddlers immediately began vying for their attention and their coin. A gray-haired man cut across Durmad's path so quickly that Durmad jumped to the side to avoid knocking the old man over. He opened his mouth to yell after the man, but it froze in silent response when his eyes caught the streaks of red hair glowing in the morning sun as they wove through a flaxen braid. He knew he'd see her, but he thought it would be at the workshop and after at least one drink warmed his veins and dulled his nerves.

She waved at the firesmith from tiptoes but dropped her heels when he didn't wave back. Her skirt brushed the top of her boots as she returned her hand to her waist and turned to her side. Her hair was duller and less red than he remembered, but two years had turned his uncle's apprentice into, well, a woman. A short woman who still couldn't see over the shoulder of the average man, but a woman nonetheless. Suddenly aware his mouth was dry from remaining open so long, Durmad rubbed his chin.

"What's the hold-up?" Liam asked, stepping between Durmad and the back of the apprentice.

"Just avoiding old men."

Liam glanced over his shoulder, a smirk crossing his face as he turned back to Durmad. "Old men? You sure it isn't a certain skirt you're avoiding?"

"What skirt?" Abaddon asked, clapping Liam on the shoulder.

Durmad stepped around them. "There's no skirt," he said, lowering his voice while giving the firesmith's line a wide birth. *Distract them, but with what?* They had rooms and drinks figured out. *Dinner.* A plan materialized with each step toward the firesmith's table. "The firesmith made me think of dinner."

"That's an odd thought," Liam said, keeping pace behind Durmad.

"A new dagger for my uncle will soften the blow when he learns we'll have dinner with him tonight."

"Brilliant," Abaddon said. "I haven't had a home-cooked meal in over three years."

"Don't you mean two?" Durmad chuckled.

"Nope. Mah died about a year before I started training, and I was left to fend for myself while my father mourned. The Green Willow Guard gave me food, clothes, a place to sleep, and something to do instead of watching my sister try to poke and prod my father from his stupor."

Liam raised an eyebrow. "Now that explains everything."

Durmad kept his back to the line as his uncle's apprentice neared the front. *Would she recognize him?* A silent chuckle shook his shoulders as he retrieved his coin pouch from the inside pocket of his leather riding coat, but Liam pressed a hand to Durmad's chest.

"No need," Liam said and tipped his chin, pulled the glove from his right hand, revealing his signet ring, and motioned to the firesmith. The mountain of a man darted around his apprentice with the speed of a young gazelle and bowed slightly to Liam, making the two men equal in height.

"Sir, what can I grace the house of Dimmet with? My craft is at your disposal."

The firesmith's apprentice with his similar stature, nose, and jawline —most likely the massive man's son —scowled at Liam. Durmad made eye contact with the boy and shook his head. Whatever emotions fueled that scowl, jealousy or bitterness, were not worth it. Tipping his head back toward the line, Durmad hoped the boy understood. Even more, he hoped Liam would take long enough and the boy would move quickly enough that his uncle's apprentice would reach the table before their business was concluded.

Each time the firesmith produced a dagger for them to inspect, Durmad scrutinized it. As he tossed the kilt of the fifth dagger in his hand to measure the weight, her voice cut through the market's chatter. He squeezed the hilt, set it down on the table, and nodded his approval to Liam before turning toward his uncle's apprentice.

She faced forward, not looking to the side —all business. Durmad smirked. The firesmith's apprentice placed the three items she requested on the table: an alloy blanket, copper spade, and copper snips. *Curious*. He knew his uncle kept these items locked in a box, so there was no chance these were replacements. He pursed his lips to contain a smile and placed his hand on the alloy blanket. "We'll take this, too."

CHAPTER SIX

SHYLAH

nger flared in her chest. She took a deep breath and tried to
quench the fire inside, but there was no time. She could not
fail in her errands today. Too much was at stake. Trulian was at stake.
Exhaling, she barked, "Hey, I'm buying that," and pushed the hand off
her blanket.

"Get a different one."

A husky voice tickled the hair on the top of her head.

First the old man and now this? "I'd sooner face a wyvern. This is
mine." She slapped the coins on the counter and spun around. "You'll
have to..." The rest of her retort caught in her throat as her sapphire
eyes met Durmad's emerald ones. The round face of the boy who kept
her secret her first month in Dimmet was more angular with dark scruff
clinging to his jawline and upper lip. He wore his dark hair longer now,
reminding her of burnt twigs curled by the heat of flames. Two and
a half years of training with the Green Willow Guard had turned the
boy she had been weary of into a cocky man. The once loose tunic
pulled tight across his chest and shoulders. The darker-haired stranger

41

just behind him slapped Durmad's back, winking at Shylah, while the fire-haired one crossed his arms, looking bored.

Durmad grinned and nodded to the firesmith, who took her money and pushed the alloy blanket and other items toward Shylah. "You've changed," Durmad said, shifting his weight to a single foot.

"That tends to happen. Sir. Time didn't stop in your absence," Shylah said, smiling. Her voice dripped honey from each vowel.

Durmad's dark-haired companion smacked the bored one on the chest. "Bet you didn't know we'd see a lovers tiff today."

The red-haired man's stoic expression softened momentarily before he tilted his forehead toward Shylah, who crossed her arms in front of her chest.

"No. Just a Bonded who's tired of serving as every bored boy's entertainment." She glared at Durmad, letting any hint of sweetness evaporate from her. "I didn't need the absent nephew of my caretaker doing it, too." Burning pain ignited her binding. Clenching her jaw, she squeezed her left hand into a fist and scanned the crowd for Naamah. Fear bloomed in her chest. Where was she? "I don't have time for this nonsense. Go back to playing knight." The burning ache of her feather shackle became a vice grip of fire. Shylah's eyes locked with the amber and sapphire eyes of the stoic red-haired man as she cried out, and her knees buckled.

Durmad gripped Shylah before she hit the ground. "Liam," he said, snapping his head toward his stoic companion. "What happened to taking care of the Bonded?"

Panic threatened Shylah's throat. Liam was the name of Naamah's oldest son. He activated her binding. *What would he tell his mother? What if he knew why she needed the supplies?* Apollyon might be cruel, but Naamah made him look like an annoying fly buzzing around a corpse.

Liam glared down at her. "Unless a Bonded insults or threatens family."

Durmad helped her stand on her own again. "She wasn't threatening me. I'm not family," he said.

"Her lack of respect is a threat, and you're more family than anyone else in my life. I will always help you."

The pain faded, but her eyes remained locked on Liam. *Could he really be that upset that I didn't say, Sir? Of course he could; he was Naamah's son, after all. Why didn't I realize it earlier?* Shylah chastised herself.

"I didn't need your help," Durmad said, wiping sweat from her forehead. He lifted her chin, pulling her focus to his eyes. "Going on a trip?"

"What?" She glanced over Durmad's shoulder and quickly added, "Sir."

He motioned to Shylah's items, which were still sitting on the firesmith's table. She snatched the blanket, copper snips, and spade, dropping them into her apron pocket before he could claim them. Schooling her tone, she said, "No. Merely running errands on my Replenish Day, Sir." She stepped forward, but one of Durmad's companions stepped in her path.

"Does my uncle know you're here?" Durmad asked.

Shylah stepped to the side, and Durmad's dark-haired companion gripped her arm. "He asked you a question." She glared defiantly at his dark eyes and yanked her arm. His fingers gripped tighter, pinching her underarms, and she fought back a wince. "It's not that easy," he said, running his eyes over her from head to toe.

"Are you fighting his battles now, too?" The words escaped her lips before her brain could reel them in, and the dull ache returned to her wrist. Flaring her nostrils, she took a deep breath and glanced at Liam. He stared at his nails, feigning disinterest. *You're making it worse,* she told herself. *Stop.* She yanked her arm again, but the man gripped harder still.

"That's enough, Abaddon," Durmad said, placing a hand on the guard's chest, who sneered and released Shylah's arm.

Turning to Durmad, she asked, "May I continue my errands now, Sir? Or do you and your friends want to waste more of my time?"

"I only have one more way to waste time," Durmad said, mischief dancing on his lips.

Shylah's eyes darted to his lips and then back to his eyes. She longed for the annoying, scrawny boy from that first month. It was easier to maintain her disdain for him. Instead, he was a boy playing at being a soldier. A grin crossed his face. She crossed her arms and wrinkled her nose. "And what's that?"

"I want to introduce you to my friends, so you know their names at dinner tonight."

Shylah stiffened. *Dinner, they were coming to dinner? Liam was coming to dinner?* Instinctively, she rubbed her left wrist. Trulian would be near someone who could influence her Bond. For the past three years, Shylah had insulated her sister by taking every job Naamah requested, so there was no reason for her to visit. The closer the binders got to Trulian, the harder it would be to hide her true ability.

Durmad shoved the guard, who stopped her in the shoulder. "You've already met Abaddon, but this," he gripped the shoulder of the man standing to his right, "this is Liam. He's the best of us all."

Liam's expression stayed hard, and he tipped his head to Shylah.

Shylah tipped her head to each, but in her mind, she kicked each in the nethers. "Your uncle said nothing," she said.

"We only returned this morning. I haven't been home yet," Durmad said. "But it was fortuitous that we found you here. Now you can tell him and make sure all is prepared."

She schooled her facial expression and said, "Fortuitous indeed. Now, may I return to my errands? You have given me quite a few more to take care of."

"Of course." Durmad stepped back and mockingly bowed to her.

She stormed past him, intentionally bumping into his shoulder, but instead of him wavering, she bounced off him. One or all three snickered. She wasn't sure, but it didn't matter. It took all her strength and resolve to continue walking without faltering or looking back. The gods must despise her. Now, she'd have to get three more chickens for dinner, and spiking Apollyon's drink with Lull was out of the question now.

Why could nothing be simple?

CHAPTER SEVEN
DURMAD

Durmad stood and leaned back against the firesmith's table. It had only been two and a half years, but the frail fourteen-year-old girl he had spent six months tormenting with pinches and pranks, all while admiring her dogged care for her sister, wasn't so frail anymore. Chuckling, he pulled his glove tighter, remembering how she snapped at him and shoved his hand to the side. And those eyes—her frustration made them flash like sapphire gems.

Rubbing his chin, he watched the sun illuminate the strands of red glowing beneath the lighter hair like the embers of a fire waiting to ignite. His forehead wrinkled. The red isn't as bright as it should be, he thought as she faded into the crowd.

"What's that about?" Abaddon asked, shoving Durmad's shoulder.

"She works for my uncle."

Abaddon frowned. "We gathered that, but that's not what I mean."

Durmad raised an eyebrow. "Then what?"

"The flirting," Abaddon said, crossing his arms over his chest.

"I didn't—"

Liam placed his hand on Durmad's shoulder. "You did. You couldn't take your eyes off her."

"Don't be so asinine. She's like —" his thoughts fumbled for something less embarrassing than flirting, "a sister," Durmad said, shrugging off Liam's hand. "An annoying one at that."

"Your dagger, Sir," the firesmith said, handing the wrapped paper bundle to Liam.

Durmad snatched it.

Sister? Really? That's what your mind decided to throw into your mouth.

"Thank you," he said, tucking the dagger into his jacket pocket.

No way that won't come back to haunt me later. Why hadn't I just said friend or acquaintance?

Abaddon rubbed his lower lip, looking into the crowded market. "Then you won't mind me tasting that tonight. You know how much I like dessert."

And there it was. Durmad clenched his jaw, glaring at Abaddon.

"Unless," Abaddon raised his eyebrows and tilted his head, "you are besotted."

Liam grinned. "Even if he is besotted, it'd never work with a Bonded."

Snapping his glare from Abaddon to Liam on his right, Durmad said, "And why is that?"

"My mother."

Durmad sighed. Liam was right. He'd have to request a change to Shylah's Bonding if he wanted to do more than bed her, which meant Naamah would have to give up control of her. Naamah never gave up control of anything willingly. He'd have to trade something, and he didn't have much beyond himself. Then there was Trulian. Shylah would never change her Bonding if it meant leaving Trulian behind. He rubbed his forehead.

Liam sneered. "I can compel her to bed you. Get her out of your system."

"He won't know what to do, but I would," Abaddon said, stepping between Durmad and Liam. "The way that skirt fanned out from that tiny waist." He held his hands before him as if to grab an invisible Shylah by the waist and hold her in front of him. "I could—"

Durmad yanked Abaddon's shoulder, turning him around, and punched him in the face, knocking his companion flat on his back. "She may be a Bonded, but she is a valuable elixir designer, not your plaything." Durmad kicked his leg.

Liam pulled Durmad back. "Control yourself. The market is watching."

Durmad, chest heaving, scanned the crowd. Anyone within ten feet of them had stopped and stood staring at the three men. Even the firesmith gripped an axe and held it at the ready. Durmad held his hands in surrender to the firesmith before removing his glove, shaking his hand out, and running it through his hair. *Get it together*, he chastised himself. Everyone slowly returned to their tasks, but he could taste their unease. He had to settle their apprehension, or Naamah's reprimand would be swift and severe.

Sucking in a breath, he said, "No hard feelings," and reached his hand out. "You're still a bastard, though."

Abaddon wiped his nose, taking in the blood on his glove. "You sucker punched me," he said, taking Durmad's hand. "You only had to say she was yours. I'm not stupid enough to cross you."

"I did," Durmad said, dropping Abaddon's hand.

Liam chuckled. "Actually, you said she was your sister. Most men don't want to bed their sister."

"I don't want to bed her," he said, turning his back. "I need a drink."

"The Even-tide Tavern is just around the corner. Come on," Liam said, patting Durmad on the back. "First jug of Fire Onion Juice is on me."

"Can we drink it before you shower in it?" Abaddon said, trailing behind.

Without looking back, Liam swung his fist into Abaddon's gut. "Clean yourself up. We'll save you some Juice." Liam nudged Durmad with his elbow. "Maybe." The two smiled and picked up the pace, leaving Abaddon bent in half as the crowd slowly returned to their errands.

Durmad knew he'd have to show Liam and Abaddon he was back to normal. Creating a rift in their threesome right now would put him, Shylah, and Trulian at risk. If Liam or Abaddon suspected an attraction, or worse that it could sway his loyalty, they'd report it to Naamah. She didn't tolerate anything less than complete and total loyalty. He'd heard the stories during the first months of training — the ones about Naamah removing the object of distraction to ensure her most valuable subjects remained loyal. If it came down to it, he didn't know which would be more valuable to Naamah: him or Shylah. Rubbing the back of his neck, he followed Liam through the tavern door.

Liam walked to the table nearest the door and took the seat with the wall to his back, saying, "Jug of Fire Onion," while holding up three fingers to the hireling as he headed toward the table.

Minutes later, she set a jug and three mugs on the table. Durmad took a long swig and smiled. Fire Onion Juice always reminded him of when he tricked Shylah into drinking it.

His uncle had only been Shylah's caregiver for three weeks when sickness confined her to her room. His uncle's frustration had been the perfect motivator for her to believe anything he said. He'd told her it was an elixir Apollyon had made for her. She'd smelled it and squished her nose.

"If you'd rather be a bonded without a caregiver, I can take it back to my uncle."

She'd hardened her face and downed the entire bottle of Fire Onion Juice in one shot, followed by a solid minute of coughing.

"Thank you," she whispered.

He had suppressed a smirk. "I'll bring you another dose in ten minutes." Doubt had tugged at her eyes. "He said you'd need to be well enough to mix tomorrow, or he'd put you and Trulian on the street. We need to drown your illness in juice."

Ten minutes later, he'd brought another bottle full of Fire Onion Juice, and she'd downed it in a single shot again. The second time, the coughing was mild.

"Feeling better?"

She nodded and stood—or tried to. He caught her as her step wavered, and she looked up at him. "Your eyes are like emeralds. I like emeralds."

His eighteen-and-a-half-year-old self had kissed her forehead before saying, "And you're drunk." Even now, he could see her puzzled expression slowly shift to anger. She'd pushed herself back, swinging a fist that he easily dodged, sending her face-first onto her sister's bed. She hadn't trusted him again.

"What's that smirk about?" Abaddon asked, pulling Durmad from his memories.

"I was remembering your face the second before my fist hit it. You were so surprised." Durmad laughed and took another drink.

Abaddon sat, snatching his own mug from the table. "Surprise is the only way you can best me with fists."

By the time they finished the jug, all three were amiable. "Well," Durmad said, standing, "You go take care of your business. I'm going to check in with my uncle."

Liam motioned to the hireling. She brought over another jug. "My business can wait."

Abaddon grinned, and he poured himself another mug.

"I'll meet you back here before dinner tonight," Durmad said, walking out of the tavern. He'd have to prepare his uncle for guests but especially for Naamah's heir. He grinned, picking up his pace. And there was Shylah still to tease.

CHAPTER EIGHT

SHYLAH

With three hens draped over her shoulder, Shylah pushed through the workshop door to find Apollyon scowling at the stack of orders.

"Where've you been, Bonded? We're out of the ingredients we need," he said without looking up.

"Didn't you see my note?" she said, motioning to the paper lying untouched on the table where she left it that morning. "Getting the missing ingredients." She pulled the items from the front pocket of her apron, setting the bottles and pouches of herbs on the elixir table in front of him.

She had less than two minutes to leave the room before he put her to work. He'd know what she was planning if he discovered her other supplies in her apron. Without another word, she walked through the back archway to the kitchen.

"Hey," he yelled after her, "breakfast time is over."

She tossed the hens on the counter beside the sink. "We needed more hens for tonight," she hollered back and quickly ducked down

55

the stairs to her room on the lower level. Lifting the foot of the mattress, Shylah stashed her supplies and ran back up the stairs. She needed to get the water heating so she wouldn't be missed, and Trulian could pluck the hens. Scaling the final step, she pulled the stock pot from the lower shelf, placed it in the sink, and flipped the water on. She fell into the familiar opening allegro of her daily orchestration as Dimmet's rising Elixir Designer.

"Your job is to design these elixirs," he said, waving the orders as he walked through the kitchen arch. "Do not make meal decisions unless you want to take the one thing away from that sister of yours that makes her useful."

Shylah hung the pot of water and swung it over the fire. She hated it when he belittled Trulian, but no one could know what her ability truly was, not even if it would put him in his place. Instead, she stared at the water, willing it to boil as quickly as her temper.

He gripped her shoulder. "I said this is not your job," shoving the pile of orders into her hand. He yelled, "Trulian, get in here and prepare the hens. Your sister is hungry today." He looked down at Shylah, who stood six inches shorter than him, and sneered. "Now, get in there—"

A voice interrupted Apollyon, "She's only doing what you would ask her to about five minutes from now."

Apollyon raised his eyebrows and turned around, "Durmad."

"Uncle." The two embraced.

Shylah glared at the non-boiling water in the stock pot. *Why hadn't he taken longer?* She could have used at least two more hours without him there to adjust her plans for tonight. She straightened, plastered a smile on her face, and turned to face the men.

Apollyon held Durmad at arm's length and surveyed his nephew's stature. "The Guard has turned you into a man." He hit him on the shoulder, but Durmad barely registered the force. A smile lit Apollyon's face. "And a strong one at that. But you need not worry about a simple apprentice designer," he said with a wave of his hand. "Come. Tell me about your training."

"You will hear all about it at dinner when Sir Abaddon and Sir Liam join us."

Apollyon's step faltered. "Sir Liam —is coming here?"

Shylah turned back to the water and stared at it as if uninterested in their conversation. Her ears twitched at Apollyon's nervousness around Sir Liam. Not so confident after all, she thought, letting a genuine grin lighten her face. Only members of the royal family cracked Apollyon's mask.

"Yes; he and I have trained together these past years, and he is not ready to return home yet. We're staying at the Even-tide Tavern tonight. And I thought a nice home-cooked meal would be good. You don't mind entertaining Sir Liam, do you?"

Apollyon laughed uneasily. "Mind? Of course not. I only want to make sure that we present our best."

The conversation faded as the two walked out of the kitchen. Shylah relaxed a little. They wouldn't be spending the night. She'd only have to spike Apollyon's drink with Lull. Her tension returned as the first bubble broke the surface of the water. She still had to do it under the nose of three of the Green Willow Guard.

Trulian turned the top step and whispered, "Is Apollyon gone?"

Shylah nodded. "The water is just beginning to boil. The hens are on the counter. We will have three guests tonight, so make sure you take extra care." She crouched and looked into Trulian's eyes. "I must get ingredients tomorrow. Today must continue smoothly. Otherwise, I may not be granted leave, and you will not get your Quiescence."

Trillian grinned as she raised her eyebrows. "I will make sure you can leave."

Shylah kissed Trulian's forehead and left the kitchen, pausing just inside the workshop to glance over her shoulder.

Trulian grinned.

Shylah wasn't sure what reaction she expected from her sister, but a grin wasn't it. Especially when it came to something as important as having Quiescence to keep her hidden. Shylah turned her back on the kitchen. There would be time to ask later. Right now, she had a stack of elixirs to design before tomorrow.

Three hours later, the men returned to the elixir workshop.

Apollyon led the way, brandishing a brand-new dagger. "Look what my nephew got me at the market today. It's absolutely wonderful," he said, patting Durmad on the back. "I will add it to my treasures. But now, I must take a nap. One must be fully rested before entertaining Dimmet's heir." He turned down the main staircase to his room below.

Shylah continued mixing elixirs without glancing at Durmad. It wasn't until she stood on tiptoes to reach a jar of dried honeysuckle blossoms that she became acutely aware of his presence.

He leaned into her and reached a hand above hers. "Let me help."

Retrieving the jar, he held it in front of her chest. His warm breath tickled her ear.

"See? Much easier."

Shylah held her breath as her heartbeat thudded in her ears. He's still pushed against her back. She reached for the jar and pulled it away, saying, "Not funny." Shoving her elbow into his side, she turned and walked back to the table, glancing at him from the corner of her eye.

He leaned against the cabinet below the shelves and crossed his arms. "I know what you're planning," he said.

Her hand hesitated momentarily before spinning the jar open and adding four blossoms to the mortar. "What's that?" she goaded.

He couldn't know, could he?

If he did, she needed to be sure he wouldn't interfere. *Look as if there are no plans*, she told herself and added two pinches of nettle and a sprig of lavender to the mortar.

He stepped forward and placed both hands on the table beside the pestle.

She grabbed it, her fingers brushing his.

Leaning on his hands, he whispered, "You're going to the Kyselina Desert."

Shylah pounded the pestle into the mortar.

Typhon Toes!

She should have known he'd put it together after seeing what she bought from the firesmith. Gripping the pestle, she ground it into the ingredients until her knuckles were white. She hated his constant smugness. Part of her thought two years of training would have pounded that out of him.

"What does it matter to you? You have no say over my replenish day. That is one thing I have as a Bonded," she said as much to herself as she did to him.

He smiled and smacked the table before pushing himself back. "Now, you have two. You have a guide."

She froze, staring at the pulverized herbs in her mortar.

"Good. It's settled. We leave in the morning."

She slammed the pestle on the table and turned to face him. She scolded her expression to remain neutral, but her jaw clenched. "No. I do not need a guide. I have been many times these three years you have been gone. You were not missed on those trips and are absolutely not needed on this one."

"Durmad," Trulian trilled and wrapped her arms around his middle before he could respond.

He braced his hands on the table, pushing against the unexpected force before facing her.

"You're back," Trulian said, still gripping Durmad's stomach.

"For two weeks, yes. I have a few things to take care of before the next training camp," he said, glancing over his shoulder.

The second their gazes crossed, Shylah returned to crushing her herbs.

"But I had to come see my favorite redhead."

"Shy lost most of hers when you left."

At the mention of her name, Shylah looked up again. His emerald eyes flashed at her.

"Why is that do you suppose?" he asked of Trulian but smirked at Shylah.

Shylah slammed the pestle into the already pulverized herbs. "I grew up," she snapped.

"I see," he chuckled. "You're all grown up, too."

"Not if you ask Shy," Trulian said.

"She's just jealous," he said.

Reaching for the carrier oil, Shylah said, "I am not."

Trulian stuck her tongue out and pulled Durmad toward the kitchen. "The pot is too heavy for me to dump in the alley. Could you?" she asked in the half request, half demand only she could pull off with him.

"Of course," he said, letting her guide him.

Shylah was grateful that he saw Trulian as his little sister, too. In the first months they'd been there, he had always looked out for her and kept her insulated from Apollyon's taunting. She'd started trusting him—not really as family but as a type of friend. It's part of what had made his leaving so hard.

She shook her head.

"You're a Bonded, and he's part of the Green Willow Guard. They burned your parents alive. It would never work. Besides, he leaves again in two weeks," she chastised herself and continued working

CHAPTER NINE
DURMAD

"I knew you were coming back, and I'm glad," Trulian said, putting a tray of five dough discs in the icebox opposite the fireplace.

Durmad huffed a chuckle. "Of course, I will always come back for you, little one," he said, grabbing a blackberry from a bowl beneath the window.

"Hey, that's for the dessert. Don't eat them all, or your uncle will keep Shy too busy for replenish day."

Durmad popped the berry in his mouth, rolled it around on his tongue, and smashed it against his mouth's roof. The sweet, slightly tart juice coated the top of his tongue.

Blackberries had always been one of his favorites. As a child, fields of wild blackberries were edged by the most fragrant honeysuckle where his family fields ended and the forest began. It had been his mother's favorite place, so they spent nearly every spring morning collecting blackberry leaves and honeysuckle blossoms for tea that would last through the winter months. He hadn't been back to the fields since he came to live with his uncle when he was nine after his parents died of the same infection that brought Naamah back to Dimmet.

Durmad watched Trulian pour water over the plucked and gutted hens in the pot. He'd been eighteen and a half when the Green Willow Guard brought the sisters to the elixir shop. Shylah was a brazen and defiant fourteen-year-old who masked her fear with anger. But Trulian had only been nine. Maybe that was why he felt so connected to her. The vacant looks and screaming nightmares reminded him of his own tear-filled sleepless nights when he'd first arrived.

Trulian swung the pot back over the flames and returned to the produce on the counter. She placed her hands on the counter and mumbled something he couldn't hear. Then she bent down and opened the cabinet, taking out one basket and another before returning them all and repeating the process with another cabinet.

"Looking for something," Durmad said, leaning against the counter and snagging another few blackberries.

Still searching through the cabinets, Trulian said, "The marmalade. I need it for the crostata."

She turned back to Durmad and crossed her arms. "No more blackberries unless you are going to get me more." She uncrossed her arms and smiled in the way only she could. "And get me some marmalade."

He snatched a few more blackberries, popping them into his mouth. "Anything for you," he said, rumpling the top of her head, which now hit him just below his chest.

She frowned up at him.

"I need to make sure Liam and Abaddon are situated anyway," he said.

"I need to start the berries marinating in the next hour. So don't get distracted."

"You're growing up way too fast, little one."

She turned him around and gave his back a shove. "We all have to. Now, go get me blackberries and marmalade."

He raised his hands in surrender and stepped out the back door.

Once the berries and marmalade were collected, he found his training mates still drinking at the Even-tide Tavern. He sat in the same seat as before, "Have you even left?" he asked.

"Why leave when they have rooms available? I even got you your own," Abaddon said, shoving Durmad's shoulder. "In case you have a little visitor tonight."

Durmad knew better than to respond to the last comment and merely said, "Thank you," before looking over at Liam, who stared at a woman with wine-colored hair. "Did you talk to your mother?

Eyes still glued to the back of the woman's head, Liam said, "No, sent a messenger."

"That won't go over well," Durmad said, looking back at the woman. He'd never seen her before, and there didn't seem to be anything suspicious about her.

So why is Liam staring at her so intently?

"Not sure I care," Liam said, eyes still locked on the woman with wine-colored hair.

Abaddon raised his empty mug in the air. "That's a bold stance to take with the Queen."

"I agree," Durmad said, reaching out and lowering Abaddon's arms as he waved off the approaching wench. "I think you've had enough, my friend. Besides, my uncle will have his best wine for you at dinner."

Abaddon returned his mug to the table and crossed his arms over his chest like a pouting child who'd just been sent to bed without dessert.

Durmad followed Liam's gaze more directly now. "Do you know her?"

Liam shook his head and finished off his mug in a single breath. "She reminds me of someone."

"Your mystery woman, no doubt," Abaddon said, leaning forward. "Every time we enter a city, you find some woman to ogle. You're the heir of Dimmet. Just take the woman already."

Liam's nostrils flared, and his jaw clenched as he locked eyes with Durmad. "Did you talk to your uncle about Naamah's proposal?"

"I did."

"And?" Liam asked.

"I'm not sure I want to be a Knight Commander," Durmad said.

Abaddon leaned back in his chair. "I'd give my left nut to become a Knight Commander. What is there to think about?"

Durmad smirked. "Just the left one?"

Abaddon shrugged. "Eh, it's the smallest."

Liam shook his head and sighed. "What did he say about the Bonding?"

"I didn't tell him about that."

Abaddon sat up. "Bonding?"

Looking straight at Durmad, Liam answered, "That's the condition of becoming a Knight Commander."

Whistling, Abaddon raised his empty mug again. "I wouldn't become a Bonded. Not even for a knight commander post."

"That's because you'll never get a higher post," Liam snapped, returning his attention to Durmad. "Why would you choose your aged uncle over my mother as a caregiver?"

Durmad snickered. "The same reason you won't even talk to her." He stood. "I have to get this back to Tru-the cook for dinner. Uh. Be at the elixir shop in three hours," Durmad said, leaving the tavern.

With the morning's events, he'd almost forgotten about the Knight Commander post. His stomach tightened and even the blackberries no longer sounded appetizing. *Why did Liam have to bring it up?* He kicked a rock down the street.

"Hey, watch it," someone yelled down the street.

"Sorry," he mumbled without looking up.

The post of Knight Commander was a prestigious one, sure, but it would mean more training, campaigns, and travel; *all good things, right?*

Initially, the news excited him, but then came the catch, because Naamah did nothing without a catch. If he wanted the post, the purse, the prestige, the travel, and the ability to continue alongside Liam, he would have to commit himself willingly to Bonding with Naamah.

"But my uncle is my caregiver," he'd said.

"Caregiver, yes; guardian, no. You are still an orphan in need of a guardian," Naamah had cooed with a glint in her eye. "The throne is the only one who can offer you such a leap."

He'd opened his mouth to argue, but she was right. He was an orphan, and his uncle had never wanted to take total responsibility for him. He'd never been bonded to a guardian. He did want adventure, and his uncle wanted his share of the purse but was that worth his freedom?

Maybe it wouldn't be giving up all his freedom. His thoughts drifted to Shylah. Eventually, she would take over as Master Designer. After seeing how his uncle treated her earlier that day, that would be sooner rather than later. She'd gain her freedom and a consistent purse. He smiled as he turned the corner. One she wouldn't have to hide under drawers.

Even Trulian would be better off once Shylah received her own promotion. She'd be safer. Shylah would never turn her sister out on the street.

He kicked the dust from his boots on the back step. Naamah wanted an answer by the end of their visit home. Two weeks wasn't much time, but it was all he had.

CHAPTER TEN

DURMAD

The closer it got to dinner, the more agitated Durmad's uncle became. He fussed over the state of the workshop, the table, the kitchen, and even which wine would be considered the best. While Trulian finished cooking and the whole place filled with a warming scent of herbed chicken and sweet berries, Shylah was left to cater to his uncle's every whim and desire.

She scurried past him, nearly dropping her armload of dishes. "Here, let me help," he said, reaching for the smaller plates atop the stack.

"I'm fine. If you take anything, it will upset the balance," she snapped, twisting away from him.

He smiled at her stubbornness and retrieved six glass goblets from his uncle's office. Each glass sat at the top right corner, except for Liam's, which he placed on the left.

Apollyon burst into the room. "What? Why are there six plates and goblets? Take two back into my office. They can eat in the kitchen."

"Uncle, Sir Liam expects Shylah and Trulian to eat with us."

"But why?" he huffed. "They just take up space. They are no Master Designer." Apollyon puffed up his chest, standing taller.

"Not for long," Durmad mumbled.

"What did you say?" Apollyon squinted.

"Not the Master Designer, but as Naamha's firstborn and heir, their Bonding extends to him. He expects to assess the care of those under his protection." Durmad wasn't sure if Liam cared one way or the other. Liam had said that morning that the bonded were treated like children and cared for as such, but he wasn't sure exactly how far Liam would extend that care given how he controlled Shylah's bond mark in the market, but his uncle didn't need to know that. He only had a handful of days to see the sisters, and after their meeting in the market, he wanted to see Shylah.

Apollyon huffed. "Very well. I suppose they can stay then." He finished pouring wine into the men's goblets as the knock sounded at the elixir workshop door.

Shylah answered the door and ushered in Liam and Abaddon. He introduced them to his uncle, and they all sat, leaving two empty seats between Liam and Durmad.

Trulian brought a fresh loaf of bread and salad, followed by Shylah, who carried the savory chicken crostata. Trulian placed the bread in front of his uncle and offered him the salad.

Apollyon waved her off. "What am I, a rabbit?"

The sparkle in Trulian's crystal blue eyes dimmed, and Durmad was sure he saw a bit of the glow in her red hair fade. "I will take some salad, Tru-ulian," Durmad said, holding his plate for her. She tipped her forehead to him, smiled, and dished him some salad. As she walked behind him, Durmad locked eyes with Abaddon and Liam.

Both reached their plates out to her, and the bounce returned to her step.

"Some chicken pie for you, *Master Designer*," Shylah said with a mock bow before flinging a slice of Trulian's crostata onto Apollyon's plate so quickly that gravy splashed onto his chest. She stepped back, and Durmad read the shock of reality on her face. He'd almost forgotten how much he enjoyed seeing it.

"You spiteful little bonded," Apollyon said, snatching Shylah's wrist.

Shylah's shock quickly shifted to fear as she tried to pull her wrist from his grasp.

Durmad and Liam stood so quickly that their chairs clattered to the floor behind them. "Uncle," Durmad said, drawing Apollyon's attention to the rest of the room.

Apollyon released Shylah's wrist and fumbled with his napkin. "Just an accident, My Lord. No need to make more of it."

Despite the shakiness of his words, Durmad read the anger behind each rub of the napkin down his uncle's chest. Trulian righted Liam's chair while Durmad righted his own.

"Looks like dinner here will be more eventful than the tavern," Abaddon chuckled, holding his plate out to Shylah. "I'll take some of that chicken pie," he quickly pulled his plate back, "but without the gravy shower, please."

Durmad suppressed a giggle as Shylah smirked and offered a mock curtsey before gently setting a slice of the crostata on the plate. He knew the quick spin of her back to his uncle was her way of sticking out her tongue, and he waited for the mocking grimace she always used. Instead, she plastered a smile across her face and walked to Liam, who remained standing.

"My Lord, Sir, would you also like a shower-free slice of chicken pie?"

Liam still glared at Apollyon, jaw clenched, without acknowledging Shylah.

She dropped all pretense. "Sir Liam, would you like more than salad?"

Durmad cleared his throat. "Liam."

Liam's eyes shifted from Apollyon to Durmad, who motioned towards Shylah, still standing at his elbow. "Of course," Liam said, smiling as he sat in his chair. "It appears your designing goes beyond simple elixirs."

Shylah glanced over her shoulder at Trulian. "This meal is not my doing. I surely would have burned the crostata and served you fallen bread. My sister is the cook."

The flush of Shylah's cheeks did not escape Durmad's notice. He curled his toes inside his boots. *Was she attracted to Liam? Even after he manipulated her Bonding in the market? Or was it merely a side effect, the compelling Liam had mentioned?* "I'll take some as well," he said.

He quickly pulled out the chair beside him when she neared it. "You can dish it from your seat next to me." She gave him a quick smirk and sat in the chair. Leaning over her shoulder as he pushed her chair in, he whispered, "The gravy shower is up to you." She turned her head and watched him take his seat. He glanced over her head at Liam, whose side glances jumped between sisters. When he locked eyes with Abaddon across the table, the man smirked and raised an eyebrow. Durmad's face steadied as he heard Abaddon's voice cut through his thoughts.

Like a sister, huh?

Durmad rolled his eyes and avoided Abaddon's gaze. This was one of those times when he was glad Abaddon could only project his own thoughts into minds and not hear other people's.

Liam turned his face to look directly at Trulian. "Your eyes are quite extraordinary. I have never seen such a bright blue, but the shifting is quite remarkable. One minute, they are filled with the ocean, and the next, blue smoke." He reached out with his left hand.

Shylah tensed, gripping the edge of her plate. Durmad thought she'd break it any minute.

Trulian grinned. "They are hardly as interesting as yours. I've only seen one other person with one sapphire and one amber eye like you."

"Interesting. I was unaware you had met my brother."

Shylah sucked in breath beside Durmad. He didn't know when Trulian had ever left the workshop. What he did know was that Shylah was about to jump over her sister and strangle Liam. Bonding be damned.

Durmad stood, drawing everyone's attention. "Enough talk of eyes. Let's have a toast," he said, lifting his goblet. "To a restful leave, productive training, and a safe final year." Each man raised their wine. "May we all be like," he searched the room for something to finish his comparison, "the crostata." His smile wavered at the questioning looks. Really, the crostata, he thought. "Um, warm and buttery on the outside, but soft and tasty on the inside."

Liam cocked an eyebrow as his lips formed a tight, restrained smile.

Durmad plastered a larger smile across his face. *Sell it!*

Shylah lifted her water. "To crostatas."

Everyone else repeated the refrain.

Durmad drank his entire goblet of wine in a single breath before sitting back down. "Let's eat." He glanced at Shylah and mouthed, "Thank you." She shrugged, taking a bite of crostata.

The conversation for the rest of the meal consisted of Apollyon asking Liam a litany of questions ranging from training to sleeping to Dimmet's future military plans within Ethereal. At the same time, Abaddon drank several bottles of wine, and from the grimaces on Shylah's face, and the occasional glare she shot Abaddon's way, Durmad knew the wine was making him bold with his telesthetics.

Trulian was the first to finish and begin gathering dishes. "Dessert will be served around the fire."

Shylah shot up and moved to follow Trulian, but Apollyon cleared his throat. "Shylah. Light the fire, then help her."

She paused. "It's the middle of the summer —"

"If I want a fire," he stepped closer, positioning himself between Shylah and Liam as he half whispered, half spit, "You. Will. Light. One."

"But—"

"Fire!" Apollyon yelped, pointing over her head.

Shylah nodded and darted into the front room.

"Uncle, we don't need a fire," Durmad said, peering after her. He'd never seen Shylah openly contradict his uncle but much can happen in two and a half years. Maybe her stubbornness made her bolder, he thought.

"Nonsense. There is nothing better than dessert and some more wine," he winked at Abaddon, "beside the fire. It isn't every day we host the Great Naamah's heir."

Durmad glanced at Liam and mouthed, "Sorry" for his uncle's skewed sense of self and decorum as they walked into the workshop's front receiving room. It was quite a small room with a long bench on one wall and a tall-backed chair upholstered in green silk that his uncle usually sat in closest to the fire.

Shylah blew past them on her way into the dining room, almost knocking Durmad over. It was as if the receiving room was the last place she wanted to be in the entire world. He shrugged it off and leaned against the wall nearest the workshop while Liam and Abaddon sat on the bench.

"Oh no, Sir," his uncle said, ushering Liam to his feet. "That bench is beneath you. Here. Take my chair."

As Liam stood, the fire erupted into pops and sprays of embers. A shower of sparks hit the chair and ignited the silk fabric in a single breath. Time seemed to slow, and the air suddenly felt like a heavy viscous liquid. In the few seconds it took Durmad to register what happened, flames engulfed the entire chair. Water, followed closely by white powder, flew through the receiving room, leaving no man unscathed. When the dust settled, the chair sat smoldering. Beside him stood Shylah with an empty bucket and Trulian with an empty bowl.

"I must have missed a pinecone," Shylah said, quivering her chin and reaching to cover her wrist.

Trulian stepped forward. "The saleratus smothered the flame."

"My chair," wailed his uncle.

CHAPTER ELEVEN

SHYLAH

Shylah grabbed her satchel from beneath the foot of her mattress and kissed Trulian's forehead, grateful the Quiescence still lasted more than one night. She hadn't realized just how uncertain she was that it would until she woke up the third time to check that Trulian was still sleeping soundly and not traveling.

At least it helped me wake up earlier, she thought. Few elixirs offered a complete guarantee of lasting effectiveness —too many factors: the quality and age of ingredients, the internal chemistry of the person taking the elixir, the timing, the amount, her own ability to distill the completed elixir; the list of variables went on.

She had gotten better at predicting the effectiveness, adjusting dosages, and distilling her own ability to amplify its effects until two nights ago. Now, she wasn't too sure. Trulian's last dose of Quiescence hadn't been the full amount, and Shylah had been too depleted to distill it completely. She would have had more confidence if she'd been sleeping instead of playing in the damn moonbeams. Instead, she couldn't be sure of anything except that she had to get the ingredients to make a new batch soon.

Tiptoeing up the stairs, boots in hand, again, Shylah reached the kitchen with only a few faint creeks. As long as she left before anyone woke, Apollyon couldn't try to insist she had unfinished tasks from the week that had to be completed first. In the faint light of the kitchen, she slipped her feet into her boots and took inventory of her tools: the alloy blanket, copper snips, copper spade, and gloves. She ran her fingers over each item again.

No jar.

Ducking into the workshop, she retrieved two empty glass jars: the honeysuckle nectar and the biting strobilus milk. Without glass bottles, she'd never be able to get the harvested milk back to the workshop.

The one time she'd gone alone, she thought harvesting the whole root and squeezing the milk out later would be more efficient, so she put the root on a piece of fabric. Within minutes, the fabric disintegrated from the few drops that fell from a single cut. Leather was supposed to slow the process but didn't stop it. There was no way she wanted a hole burned into the bottom of her only leather satchel.

On her way back through the kitchen, she grabbed some scrap food to add to her market purchases in case the trip took longer than expected; no, longer than she hoped. The Kyselina Desert was the most unpredictable place in all of Dimmet, and it would be a long day —an even longer walk. She paused at the back door. The idea of digging through acid-soaked clay made her muscles ache and skin itch.

Taking a deep breath, she squared her shoulders and pulled her thin cloak from the hook. It wouldn't do much to protect her if it rained, but that's why she had the alloy blanket. She swung her cloak over her shoulders and stepped into the cool morning air. A shiver ran down her spine as she pulled her hood up and wrapped the cloak tighter around her body. The city still slept, but the shadows overpowered the meager morning light.

When she neared Morena's city gate, the muscles in her neck finally relaxed. The only person she saw all morning sat in his chair, leaning back against the gatehouse, snoring.

The clip-clop of hooves on stone echoed through the empty streets, keeping time with the clamor of armor. She tensed again and kicked the guard's foot. He snorted, yawned, and stretched before acknowledging her presence. "Business?"

"Herb collection beyond the walls." She pulled her hood lower, shifting her weight as the horse drew closer.

He scratched himself and stood. "Apprentice, huh?"

"She's an Elixir Designer." The horse stopped behind Shylah. "One of the best ones in all of Dimmet." The horse sighed, making her hood flutter around her face.

Durmad? What was he doing here?

The Durmad she knew slept in till noon like his uncle and demanded she bring him breakfast in bed. He never would have called her an Elixir Designer or praised her to a stranger. The conversation the day before popped into her mind. *A guide.*

No.

He wouldn't spend one of his few days back in Morena trapesing through the barren desert of Kyselina with her, would he?

Another horse shifted behind her.

Perfect. He wasn't alone. Did he bring Liam to help control me? Or Abaddon?

She shivered at the memory of all the lewd thoughts he'd forced into her head the night before. If it was, maybe the rain would melt that handsome face of his. She smiled at the thought but kept her eyes forward as the guard opened the gate.

She said, "Thank you," and slipped past him as soon as the gate opened just wide enough for her slender frame.

"Shylah," Durmad called through the gate.

Ignoring him, she quickened her steps. He might give up if she got far enough before his horse could fit through the gate. The strike of the hooves as they galloped after her sent her into a sprint. A few feet later, two alloy-clad horses blocked her path. She moved to get around them, but they matched her. Yanking her hood back, she glared at Durmad. He sat astride a chestnut courser covered in scales of alloy armor. A black courser, similarly clad in armor, stood riderless beside him. At least he was alone.

"I don't have time for this. Clear the path."

He smiled and leaned down. "That's why I'm going with you." He patted the armored neck of the black horse. "This one's for you."

"Thank you, Sir. I don't need a horse." She darted around them. "And I don't need you, either," she mumbled, continuing down the road.

He sauntered alongside her. "Shy. Let me help."

The use of her nickname rankled her nerves, and she stopped just inside the tree line. "Shylah," she said. Only her family ever called her Shy, and he was not family. "My name is Shylah."

"My apologies. I meant no offense."

"And yet you gave," she snapped and continued walking.

Durmad hopped off his horse and jogged to her side, spinning her to face him. "I'm trying to apologize. Why won't you let me?" He tipped his head to the side and flashed a coy half-smile.

"Apologize for what?" She yanked herself free of his grasp. "For letting your uncle treat us like chattel? Or your friend's leering and lewd comments—excuse me, his thoughts—last night? No, you wouldn't apologize for that." She crossed her arms over her chest. "Or for leaving Trulian protector-less to go play soldier?"

His half-smile disappeared, and a satisfied smile crossed her face. Her words had finally struck true. After years of imagining how she'd respond when she saw him again, the idea of wounding him even a fraction of what she had felt in his absence those first few months emboldened her.

"Only a fragile boy would run away to the Green Willow Guard instead of standing up to his uncle."

His shoulders sagged, and she stood straighter.

"I don't need your apology. I don't want it."

Durmad's hands formed fists at his sides. "At least accept my help."

She shook her head.

He ran a hand through his hair and sighed. "Look, it will take you at least two hours on foot to get to the Kyselina Desert. It's at least five miles from there. A horse will cut that time in half. Be angry with me, but don't let it blind you to reason."

She hated it. "Fine."

A subtle smile tugged at the corner of his lips.

"Well. I'm an Elixir Designer, not a rider. How do I get up on this thing?"

"Right." He stepped beside her. "Grip the saddle, put your right foot in the stirrup here, and swing your other leg over."

Shylah barely reached where he indicated on the saddle, and her knee was almost in her chest when she got her foot positioned in the stirrup. Her skirts fell away from her knee and toward her waist. She bounced a few times and tried to pull herself up, but her hand slipped off the saddle.

"Whoa," Durmad said, catching her around the waist. He set her down and knelt beside her. "Stand on my knee," he said, offering her his hand.

She brushed her skirts down and straightened her cloak before holding his hand in her left and trying again. This time, as she bounced, he gripped her waist and lifted her the rest of the way onto the horse.

Without a word, he climbed onto his horse.

The moment his back turned, Shylah pushed herself up in the stirrups and tried to pull her skirts free from beneath her. She draped them over the flat piece of hard leather pressed into her front. She wasn't a rider, but she knew enough to know a long ride with fabric unevenly bunched beneath her butt or shoved into her front would quickly become uncomfortable.

The coolness of the firm leather touched her skin, and goosebumps erupted on her stomach. He looked over his shoulder, and she immediately stopped fidgeting as a flush warmed her cheeks. Sitting tall in her saddle, she asked, "So how does this work?"

He grinned.

She hated that grin. It was the one he gave her when he knew he had the upper hand. She hated it when he had the upper hand.

"She'll follow mine and keep pace. That's why I chose her for you."

Shylah flared her nostrils; even her horse would follow him like a lost puppy.

She imagined herself shrugging, kicking the horse's flanks with her heels, and leaving him to follow her. Despite her longing to lead, her mind returned to her first attempt to mount the horse.

No; she had to follow for now.

Clenching her jaw, she nodded. "Right. Let's go then."

The fresh rays of morning sunlight bursting from between the trees reflected in his eyes, and they shone like a freshly cut and polished emerald. She looked at his lips instead.

Nope, no better.

She shifted her focus to the trees and adjusted her weight in the saddle. The only reason she allowed him to help was Trulian. It was a job and nothing more.

"Hold on," he said, and his horse leaped into a lope.

Shylah gripped the flat edge of the saddle's pommel as her horse jerked forward.

CHAPTER TWELVE

SHYLAH

The ride to the desert was shorter than walking, but Shylah's legs ached from rubbing back and forth against the saddle's leather. Breeches would have been much more sensible, but then again, she hadn't planned on riding a horse for an hour.

Then there was the bouncing. Her head ached. A few times, Durmad asked her how she was doing and if she needed to stop. She only smiled and said she was doing fine and didn't need to stop before slumping a bit in the saddle the second he faced forward again.

Stopping might have been a smart idea, but she didn't want this trip to drag out any longer than it needed to. There was no guarantee she'd be able to find a biting strobilus plant, let alone harvest its milk before an acid storm hit the desert. She'd only been to the desert twice in as many years. Usually, Apollyon took care of harvesting the difficult ingredients, which was the one thing he didn't ask her to do.

She wondered if that was because he wanted to keep some control of the process, since she had surpassed him in designing ability so quickly. He had only asked her to collect the biting strobilus because he had broken his leg the week before and couldn't ride or walk that far. The necessity of an elixir for Naamah herself had dictated that Shylah go without him. No one denied or delayed Naamah and her plans, not if they wanted to continue living relatively unscathed.

The eight weeks it had taken for Apollyon's leg to heal had been the longest of Shylah's life in Dimmet. Most of the time, she put her head down and got things done without much disruption, but Apollyon demanded that she not only make all the elixirs but also wait on him hand and foot. Even with Trulian's help, Shylah had barely slept. But her elixir-designing ability had grown faster than she thought possible.

The first day Apollyon returned to the workshop, he was so surprised at how smoothly everything ran in his absence and how happy customers were that he forced her to sit and take inventory all day. He did not appreciate competition or feeling beholden to anyone. The fact that his attitude and feeling had worn off on her left a bitter taste on the edges of her tongue.

The horses slowed, and Shylah focused on the landscape. The trees had shrunk to bushes at least 10 minutes ago, but now, there was nothing. There was no greenery of any kind and barely any sign of life aside from the occasional ribbon of dirt pushed by the body of a snake or a circular ridge marking the site of a predator buried and lying in wait. The air pressed on her shoulders, weighed down by the silence. No bird's song reached the desert, and no wind rustled the fabric of her skirts. Even the horse's steps were swallowed by the desert floor.

Durmad's horse stopped, and hers stepped beside him. "Where to now?" he asked.

She glanced at the tall cliffs of black rock that encircled the Kyselina Desert, with its sets of stone fingers reaching up to trap anything that dared to float into its grasp. One unlucky wyvern had fallen prey to the desert's acid storms, leaving only a rib cage and skull beneath their stone grip. She shuddered.

"The shadows," she said. "The biting strobilus clings to the shadows where the ground is softer and slightly less acidic."

"To the shadows then," he said as he trotted to the nearest rock finger. The closer they got, the more it hovered over them. Once in its shade, Durmad hopped off his horse and inspected the ground. "What am I looking for? There seems to only be sand."

Shylah shifted to dismount.

"Stay in the saddle. I will be your eyes. Just tell me what to look for."

She sighed. The idea of giving her legs a respite from the rubbing had given her new energy. But the heat and his insistence put her raw nerves on edge.

"You won't see green. It's the wrong season. If there's anything above ground, it will look like a dried twig, or you'll catch its thin shadow. You only need the roots, so look for faint impressions in the sand, like veins or leafless trees. If the impressions are curved, it's a snake, not the strobilus."

Durmad walked from one rock finger shadow to the next while beads of sweat ran down Shylah's legs. She knew the skin had been rubbed raw when the sweat reached a spot just above her knee. The sting of salt forced her to suck breath in through clenched teeth.

Durmad looked up at the sound. "What's wrong?"

"I'm not a rider, remember," she said, gripping a fistful of skirt near her waist.

Understanding passed over his face, and he turned toward the cliffs. "Liam told me about a cave..." his sentence trailed off.

A gust of wind rustled the end of Shylah's braid, and she glanced back at the entrance. A wall of sand as tall as the cliffs barreled toward them. "Durmad, the sand," she yelled, panic pinching her voice.

"Cover your face," he said, turning the horse's tail toward the approaching wall. He pulled up the hood of his cloak and leaned against the horse's alloy armor.

Shylah pulled her hood up and leaned forward. The sand glanced off her cloak and her horse's armor, but the skin between her boots and the hem of her skirt remained exposed. The sand peeled away the layers. Reflexively, she jerked her feet up, but her skirts, which usually reached the top of her foot, lay sprawled across the horse's girth and pulled up by the saddle. A whimper escaped her lips as she prayed for the storm's end. It came in a few minutes, but the sand had done its job.

Durmad shook the sand from his cloak.

She pushed herself up in the saddle. A sob escaped her lips as the skin across her calves pulled taut with the movement.

"What is it?" he asked, moving to her side.

"My legs," she whispered, telling herself to keep it together.

A hiss echoed through the air. "Let's find that cave." He scanned the far side of the cliffs.

Shylah squeezed her eyes closed. *Find the cave,* she pleaded in her mind. She knew what always followed the sand walls.

The rain.

"There," he said, swinging back up on his horse as the clouds closed in. He kicked his horse into a gallop.

The whinny and jump of her horse pushed a scream from Shylah's throat as pain shot up through her leg and into her core. She forced herself to breathe as she gripped the pommel through her skirts and glanced at the sky. It would be mere moments before the clouds made a complete mass.

They'd never make it before the rain. Durmad must have known, because their horses sped up. Lightning sparked between the nodes, and a deafening crack echoed through the walled-in desert. Then the rain.

There was no such thing as a gentle drizzle in the Kyselina Desert; nothing was gentle. Like the sand, a wall of acid rain pressed down on them.

Shylah screamed and jerked violently as the rain burned her exposed legs. She focused on the black stone wall they raced toward and saw the cave. It was still at least 100 yards away. The rain burned through her already raw skin.

The alloy blanket.

She released the pommel with one hand and gripped the flap of her satchel, but the next bounce sent her flying from the horse.

The acid rain pooled on the ground, splashing her cheek when she landed. She screamed again. She wanted to shrink into a ball, but that would be death. The acid would eat through her clothing and then her skin. She pushed herself to her feet and reached into her satchel. Fumbling as she stumbled forward, her fingers gripped the corner of the cool metal fabric; relief allowed her muscles to relax a breath until she felt the acid drip from her hood onto the tip of her nose. Yanking the blanket free, she flung it open and draped it over her as she crouched low.

Pain pulsed through her entire body. She still had over fifty yards before she reached the cave.

Am I still heading in the right direction?

The black stone walls, thick clouds, and heavy rain made everything so dark that she wasn't sure. Her chest tightened and her lungs refused to fill.

It doesn't matter. I have to move.

Staying still meant death. Breathing grew harder, and she gasped for air. The darkness thickened and expanded around the edges of her vision.

"No!" she screamed. She couldn't succumb to the pain of death. She took another step.

The black refused to listen. Her next step faltered, and she fell into the darkness.

CHAPTER THIRTEEN

SHYLAH

Shylah's head bounced off leather, and her eyes opened the moment before Durmad carried her into the cave's protection. He set her down against the cave wall and ran to the horses.

The cave was shallow, only about twenty feet deep, with walls of black stone. Hardness surrounded her. Even the thin layer of sand on the floor beneath her offered almost no cushion from the hard-packed earth beneath.

She leaned against the stone, letting its coolness seep through the blanket and what was left of her clothing. Her skin hummed with pain, and her nerves shot daggers with each shift of clothing. The tears running down her face diluted the acid, but the salt bit the exposed meat beneath.

"You have to stand."

She looked up, tears blurring her vision, and shook her head.

"You have to," he said, gripping her arm and yanking her up. "Use the wall if you need to, but you must remove your clothing."

She knew it was only a matter of time before the acid soaked through her top layer of clothing and was trapped against her skin. But her fingers wouldn't move as fast as her mind told them. She pushed off from the wall, dropped the alloy blanket, and fumbled with the clasp of her cloak.

He dropped the armload he retrieved from the horses and unclasped her cloak. "I'm sorry, but you have to move faster."

She nodded and dropped her hands. "I know," she whispered.

The cloak fell to the ground in seconds, and he began untying the front lacing of her overdress. Once loosened, she pulled it down her arms, letting it join the cloak around her feet. Stepping forward, she reached behind her back, but the tie of her skirt slid through her fingers as she turned her back to Durmad. He quickly untied the waist, and it, too, dropped to the ground. Taking a deep breath, she turned to face him.

He pursed his lips. "The tunic, too. The arms already have holes, and the bottom hem is soaked. We have to get the acid off your skin."

She nodded and pulled her arms out of the tunic sleeves, wincing in pain as the fabric rubbed against her arms.

Durmad gingerly gripped the fabric just below her waist, saying, "Let me help."

She hesitated, but the pain vanquished any resistance, and she lifted her arms above her head.

The humming of her skin turned to ice pricks as the cold air flowed over her bare skin. She squeezed her eyes shut.

Please let that be all. Please let the rest be unmarred.

She hoped her breast binding and underwear had been untouched by the acid. Focusing on deepening her breath, she waited in darkness for his instructions. She couldn't look into his eyes, not like this.

"Just the boots now."

Eyes still closed, she flinched at the pressure of his hands on her ankles as he untied her boots. He could have left her to die in the rain —he should have— but he didn't. He risked his own safety to come back to her.

Why?

The Durmad she knew, the one she remembered from two and a half years ago, would have left. He had left.

She opened her eyes and stepped out of one boot, then the other.

He stood quickly and locked eyes with hers. She fought the urge to turn away.

"I have to dilute anything still on you." He raised a waterskin.

She nodded and closed her eyes. The water poured down her head and over her shoulders. Her chest shook as she stifled a gasp.

He poured water down each arm before kneeling and gently lifting each foot until her knee bent. He poured water across each thigh and down each calf.

She drip-dried briefly while he retrieved a light blanket from his horse and draped it over her shoulders. When the edges brushed against her arms and legs, they tickled, then sent blades of pain cutting to the muscle.

"Sit. I'll start a fire," Durmad said, picking up her clothes and draping them over the back of her black courser.

She shifted, stifling a whimper as white pain flashed across her vision.

Closing her eyes, she took a shaky breath and leaned her head back; pain and exhaustion tugged on her mind.

Why did I come to Kyselina Desert? Why did I risk my life in the acid rains?

She knew it was important, but every time her thoughts got close to grasping the answer, her muscles twitched, or her nerves popped like cracking ice.

It wasn't long before the fire began warming her skin, making the shadows along the walls dance. The shifting light revealed delicate purple buds and tiny forked leaves like a tongue poking out from the corner created by the sand meeting the cave's black stone wall. She squinted and sat up.

Biting Strobilus.

Trulian's scream echoed through her mind, burning away the fog. She was here to harvest the milk from its roots and keep her sister safe. Shylah tried to stand, but the pain tore her own scream from her throat.

Durmad knelt beside her. "You mustn't move until I can heal you."

She squeezed her eyes tight. "I didn't bring any salve with me."

"That's not what I mean."

Shylah took a few deep breaths and exhaled each slowly. "What do you mean then? Or are you going to make me sit here in pain playing your guessing game?"

"It's just..." He sat back on his heels.

"Just what?" she asked, sighing.

"I have to touch you."

She opened her eyes and stared at him, but he looked down at his hands. There had to be more explanation than that. He'd already touched her, and nothing had been healed.

What was he not saying?

His timidity irked her. "Durmad." He continued looking between the fire and his hands. "Durmad. What are you not saying?"

He ran his hand through his hair, finally looking her in the eyes. "My ability. I'm a Vacuole Wielder. I can manipulate the cells in the body. From a distance, I can make them separate—that's easy, and that's why the Green Willow Guard recruited me—but to make them stitch themselves together…I have to touch the wound."

His last statement melted into her mind as she took inventory of her injuries. She had acid burns on her hands, arms, face, and legs. All her extremities, but nothing on her core. Her mind started to relax, and she stretched her legs out.

A shock of pain made her breath catch. She'd forgotten about where the armor and saddle had rubbed her inner thighs raw. The thought of him touching her there made panic rise in her chest at the same time as her body warmed.

"You. I. We can't," she said, struggling to communicate.

CHAPTER FOURTEEN

SHYLAH

He pursed his lips. "If you are going to be able to harvest what you need, I have to." He reached his hand out.

Shylah pulled back. The thought of being touched sent waves of tension through her entire body, nearly drowning out the pain screaming across her skin. Nearly.

"It won't hurt," Durmad said, touching the burn on her cheek.

At first, his touch was cold, and her neck tensed. Then the cold dissipated and was replaced by a warmth that pulled her toward him, and she pressed her cheek into his hand. She closed her eyes and let it pulse through her neck muscles. He pulled his hand away, and the warmth faded.

Opening her eyes, Shylah took in his soft grin.

"See, better, right?" he asked.

She nodded.

"I need to heal your legs next."

She stiffened.

He held his hands up. "Only if you're alright."

"Arms first," she whispered.

He lowered his hands. "Your legs have the worst wounds. If I don't heal your legs next, I may not have enough energy, but I can leave them for last if you feel more comfortable."

More comfortable, she thought. She'd be more comfortable if he didn't have to touch her at all. Glancing at her lower legs, she winced. The skin was pitted, blistered, and raw. The quick shower of water had diluted the acid but not removed the trauma from her skin. None of her salves could do more than take the pain away. She had to let him heal her legs. She had to let him touch her.

She took a deep breath, looked at the cave ceiling, and said, "All right."

She flinched at the initial touch of his hands, but squeezing her eyes closed, and forced herself to sit still. Every deliberately slow breath and flare of her nostrils sent chills down her back in spite of the warmth slowly climbing her legs as the healing seeped into her skin and muscles.

The image of Trulian's red hair blowing in the wind as they picked honeysuckle flowers swam across the back of her eyelids, helping solidify Shylah's resolve. It didn't matter what happened to her as long as she could protect Trulian, and this would make that possible.

As the healing progressed and the pain began to subside from her left leg, her neck relaxed until the warmth faded, and she opened her eyes.

He wiped the sweat from his forehead and sat back on his heels. "I need water, but the worst of your left leg is done." He pushed himself to his feet and wavered momentarily before slinking to the horses for another waterskin.

Shylah took the opportunity to inspect her leg. Everything was healed except for a dark spot on her lower calf. Not even a scar remained below the knee. "Durmad."

He wiped his mouth and chin with his forearm.

"Would food help?" she asked.

"Yes, but I didn't bring any."

Of course, he hadn't planned or prepared for the possibility of the acid rainstorm still scorching the ground beyond the cave. "I have food in my satchel."

He lifted the edge of her clothes, still draped over her horse, and retrieved the satchel. Stumbling slightly, he brought it to her. She reached her hand out but quickly let it fall; blisters now covered the meaty parts of her palm. "You'll have to. There are cardamom rolls and roasted berry nuts."

Pulling out a roll, he ate half of it in a single bite before taking another drink of water. "Here." He offered the rest to her, and she took a bite.

"Thank you."

He offered her another, but she shook her head.

"You need it more than me," she said.

He ate the rest and wiped his hand on his leather pants. "Let's get that other leg taken care of."

This time, she watched him touch her ankle. His skin glowed green where it touched hers. The glow intensified where the wounds were more severe until the green matched his eyes.

"Why did you come back for me?"

Durmad kept his focus on his hands and her leg. "I knew you were in trouble when your horse ran past me without you."

"That's not what I asked."

"I couldn't let anything happen to you." His hands stopped, but he still focused on her leg.

"Why? Your uncle can get another apprentice."

He shook his head. "But Trulian can't get another sister."

She let out a slow breath.

Of course, he would be thinking about Trulian. His concern warmed her heart.

But why don't I feel better? I'm glad he thought of Trulian, aren't I? No, he just cared for Trulian. That's all it was.

"Is that why you insisted on coming with?"

"No." This time, his emerald eyes darted to hers. "I mean," he focused back on her leg, "I knew you needed Eclipse. She mutes magic's effect."

Understanding cleared Shylah's mind. She knew the acid rain resulted from Naamah's excess and abuse of magic. The Queen could mimic and amplify the ability of others, and over the years, she had cajoled, elicited, and commanded the assistance of the most potent warlocks and wizards in Dimmet. Rumors had begun that her Green Willow Guards searched all of Ethereal for even more power, so she could break through the barrier of Pith once and for all. The excess magic she created or duplicated evaporated. Of course, magic never completely disappeared once it entered the world, so it accumulated in the clouds.

Shylah glanced around the rock walls and imagined how it must have been before Naamah had banished her magic here. Kyselina hadn't always been a desert, although Shylah had always known it as such. She had seen images of a vast lake with inlets and floating islands filled with beautiful birds. The massive fingers that seemed to pull things into the sand must have once reached for the sky full of life.

"You gave her to me to counter the rain?"

He nodded

"So, can yours do the same?"

"No, I don't need it, because I can heal myself even faster than others and with less effort. It's part of why I advanced so quickly through training." His hands reached her knee, and he stopped.

Shylah shoved an open palm in front of him. She needed more time before he healed her thighs.

He nodded and placed one hand on her palm while pressing the other firmly against the back of her hand. By the time his hands were up to her shoulder, his eyes and shoulders sagged. His dark waves clung to his forehead and temples.

"Have some roasted berry nuts and more water," she said. "I can wait, but it doesn't look like you can."

Without protest, he retrieved the berry nuts from the satchel and offered her some. She popped a few in her mouth and enjoyed their sweet, cinnamon crunch of the dry roasted berries. Once the first few were gone, she grabbed a few more and let them sit inside her cheek until the coating was gone, and all that remained was the rehydrated remnants of the fruit. She knew it would help keep her mouth moist so that she wouldn't need as much water —Durmad would need most of that.

He finished healing her other arm and sat back on his heels again. "I need to finish your legs now."

Shylah assumed he was trying to be polite, but she wished he would just finish so they could move on. Stopping to inform her felt like he was asking permission, like he cared what she thought or how she felt, which meant—she didn't want to think about what that meant. She took another deep breath and nodded.

He placed one hand on the outside of her thigh and the other on the inside, just above her knee.

The warmth seeped into her skin and muscles again. She closed her eyes, and her breathing became shallow; goosebumps sprouted from her skin despite the warmth sliding up her leg. The scent of spiced sweat filled her nostrils. Her muscles twitched.

Opening her eyes, she saw his emerald eyes inches away and staring into hers. She didn't know how long he'd been staring at her, but everything around them blurred. All she saw was the glistening green pools that seemed to spark and flash, drawing her in until a scream echoed through the cave.

CHAPTER FIFTEEN

DURMAD

Durmad's head snapped toward the entrance of the cave. Someone was in the rain, but Eclipse ran past them and into the storm before he could react further. Shylah's thin cloak still clung to the armor plates.

"My cloak," she said.

Durmad shot to his feet but froze.

Am I seeing things?

Trulian stood next to his horse. He rubbed his eyes. The healing must have taken more out of him than he realized. That was the only explanation. Squinting, he focused his eyes on the back of the cave. Trulian's glowing blue eyes and fiery red hair were unmistakable, even in the dim light.

She was there, but how?

"Why are you standing there," Shylah said, stepping before him. "Eclipse..." She started and ended her sentence.

Durmad stared over her head as she turned, facing the same direction as him. He furrowed his brow and whispered, "Trulian? How?"

Trulian waved and disappeared.

He looked between the empty space beside his horse and Shylah's face several times.

How could she get here so quickly? She couldn't.

His thoughts drifted to the shower of white powder last night. She had been ready like she knew this saleratus would be needed—the Lull, the nightmares. He turned Shylah to face him.

"You don't just want nightmares to go away."

Shylah's mouth dropped, but she quickly closed it and pulled out of his grasp. "Are you feeling alright? Maybe you depleted your ability healing me, and now," she touched his cheek, "you don't have enough to finish healing yourself. When I exhaust my distillate ability, I get debilitating headaches and hear the herbs talking. Maybe—"

"I did not hallucinate." He scowled. "Trulian is a peripatetic. Isn't she?"

Shylah snorted. "Ah, what? Of course not. Trulian has no—"

"I may not be more than a boy playing soldier to you, but I am not daft."

She stiffened and shook her head, pulling the blanket tighter. "I never said you were daft. I'm just concerned. There's no way Tru—"

"Stop. I know what I saw." He backed away a step. "You aren't out here for Lull."

"What do you mean? Of course—"

"I may not be an elixir designer, but I know that the only elixir that dampens a Peripatetic's ability is something my uncle calls quietiscent."

"Quiescence," Shylah corrected, immediately covering her mouth with her hand.

"See, I knew I was right. You aren't out here for Lull." He rubbed his chin and walked to the pile of clothing that had slid off Eclipse when she ran out. He inspected the skirt and tunic. The skirt had only a few minor burns, but it was the same one she had worn last night, so those could be explained away. The tunic, on the other hand, had so many holes in the arms that it was only a breath away from being lace. He touched an edge of the sleeve, and it disintegrated between his fingers. She'd need a different tunic.

He searched the space around Atlas. Trulian was nowhere to be found. Rounding the front of his horse, he slid his hand under the armor covering Atlas' forelock. "She was here, right, boy?" Atlas huffed in response and shifted his weight. "That's what I thought," Durmad said, turning toward Shylah. He looked her in the eyes, but she looked away.

She knows. Why hasn't she been honest with me? I'd never do anything to jeopardize Trulian or her safety.

"Here." Durmad flung Shylah's skirt at her. "Get dressed."

"Where's my tunic?"

"Burned." He tossed it into the fire. "Too many holes. You don't want my uncle to find it." He turned his back and walked to Atlas. "He'll know where you went."

"Does that mean you aren't going to tell him?"

He checked, or rather, pretended to check Atlas's armor, working his way to the saddlebags. In training, he would have supplies and clothing for emergencies. But this wasn't training, and he wasn't prepared for it. He'd wanted to ensure she didn't leave without him, and she almost had. He knew there was no replacement tunic, but taking the time to make sure would at least give him time to think.

"Durmad."

He glanced over his shoulder at her, hugging the blanket around her. Riding back into Morena with only a blanket for covering would raise too many questions.

"Durmad." Her voice was quieter now.

He tilted his head back to look at the cave's ceiling and drew in a deep breath. The scent of vanilla and green earth filled his nostrils. Her scent. She had to be right behind him.

"Will you help protect Tru?"

He exhaled slowly.

Why would she question me? His breathing quickened, and his fists clenched. *How many secrets have I kept of hers? And still, she doubts me?*

Heat thinned his blood.

"Durmad, answer me."

The weight of her hand on his back ignited every muscle. He spun around and glared down at her. She recoiled, but he gripped her shoulders. "You doubt me that much?"

"I... I..."

"I have kept every secret. Even the hiding places."

Shylah furrowed her brow.

"Yes. I know where you hide your elixirs and your money, but I have never told my uncle. I have never held it over your head. I have always protected Trulian. Protected you." Even now, he'd been thinking about ensuring she wasn't questioned when they returned to Morena and the workshop. His grip tightened.

She twisted, and he let her pull free of him. "I need my boots," she snapped and grabbed them from the ground.

He watched her storm back to the fire, boots in hand, trying to kick up dust clouds with her feet. He relaxed his shoulders and fists.

At another time, he would have laughed at her tantrum. Not now. He had every right to be angry.

He yanked off his jacket.

She'd lied to him for three years, and still, he was giving her the shirt off his back.

CHAPTER SIXTEEN

SHYLAH

Shylah swallowed the panic rising in her throat.

He knew about Trulian. Would he tell Apollyon? Or worse, Naamah? After all, he was a Green Willow Guard now. His duty was to Naamah, not Trulian, and definitely not to her. Sure, he had kept her secrets before, but that was small. This was not.

Shylah cursed herself, and a small pebble punched into her heel at the same moment. She bit her lower lip to keep from wincing. She would not show weakness. She couldn't.

Flopping down beside the fire, she shoved on her boots before rubbing her arms. She'd never seen him so intense, so angry. He had been the one person since she was forced to become a Bonded who had never directed his anger at her. *Until now.*

How does he know so many of my secrets? Why hadn't he said anything? What did all this mean? What am I supposed to do now? The question swam and splashed through her mind as she hugged her skirt to her chest.

"Here."

Shylah's whole body tensed, and she snapped her head up to see Durmad standing beside her, holding out a tunic.

"Where..." The rest of the sentence stuck in her throat as her eyes took in his bare chest. She knew training had strengthened him, but knowing that and seeing it were two very different things. Dark hair speckled his chest as if a shadow had kissed his skin. It thinned and narrowed, disappearing just above his navel only to reappear a whisper above his leather pants.

"I can't take your tunic," she said weakly, reaching for it, eyes still glued to his chest.

He let the tunic fall into her hand. "I still have my jacket. Besides, a man with no tunic is less noteworthy in Morena than a girl would be."

She thought of all the men in the market working without a tunic. Even the firesmith only wore a heavy leather apron, so his clothes didn't burn. Shylah conceded, letting the blanket drop as she stood and pulled the tunic over her head.

"Thank you," she said, tucking it into her skirt, but when she smiled at him, he had already returned to his horse.

Picking up the blanket, she uncovered her satchel and looked at the purple buds poking out from the sand at the base of the far wall. No matter how training had changed Durmad's build, there was biting strobilus milk to harvest. She quickly folded the blanket and walked over to him.

"I don't need this anymore. I found some biting strobilus," she said, handing the folded blanket to him. "If you're willing, I could use your help."

She didn't wait for a response and strode to the fork-leaved plant. *It didn't matter if he helped or not,* she told herself. But a treacherous part of her wanted to be close to him. Maybe he would keep this secret, too. Squatting beside the plants, she retrieved the glass bottle, copper snips, copper spade, and copper-infused gloves before taking a deep breath.

"How can I help?"

She screeched and fell backward.

Durmad caught her, and she felt the solid strength of his arms steadying her. Her muscles wanted to melt into his.

"I didn't mean to startle you," he said, shifting from his heels to his knees in the dirt. "Tell me what to do, and I'll do it."

She wanted to say, "Hold me again and never let me go," but that was only her distraction talking. All that mattered was the ingredients for the Quiescence for Trulian.

"Hold the bottle. It's less draining if I'm not trying to keep it from spilling while I harvest the milk."

He pulled the cork from the top of the bottle and held it out. "Ready."

She huffed. "Great. But you can relax a bit. I have to dig up the roots first," she said, smiling as she put on the gloves and began shoveling dirt from the base of the plants.

"Right," he said, sitting back on his heels. "Why all the special equipment anyway? Can't you use your ability to extract it like my uncle?"

Still focused on gently moving the dirt, she smiled. "That's not quite how it works with something like this—it's too dangerous, even for him."

Durmad huffed. "Uncle never does anything dangerous, but why would it be for you? You're stronger than he's ever been."

Shylah's cheeks flushed. *Just focus*, she told herself, glancing at Durmad. The intensity of his gaze made her mind go blank, and her hands paused.

His brow furrowed. "Is everything all right?"

"What?" She shook her head, turning back to uncover the roots of the biting strobilus. "Yeah, sorry. To pull a plant's essence free, a distillate must pull it through themselves more or less—the spirit of it anyway—and when they do that, trace elements of the plant are left in the distillate. The sap of the biting strobilus is just as acidic as the rain. The traces would be enough to kill your uncle—even for me, but my ability doesn't work like that."

"Huh," Durmad said, sliding his legs out to the side, "I thought it was all the same."

Shylah shook her head. "No, I don't extract the essence; I amplify it—make it more potent." She glanced over her shoulder. "That's why my elixirs are more requested than your uncle's now. If I apply my ability in just the right way, I can control the direction of the plant's essence, which is why holding the bottle helps. It frees up my concentration so that I can be more cautious."

"So you need the sap. Pulling it would be faster," he said, gripping a delicate bloom and pinching it off before she could protest.

She smacked the back of his hand.

"Not like that. The roots process the acid rain underground. They hold the highest concentration of the milk. Their roots grow from underground cavities that catch the acid rain, which means I know I'm close when I start to see wet dirt."

"Like that?" Durmad pointed to the bottom of her hole.

"Like that," she said, chuckling as the moist dirt transitioned into muddy clumps before liquid acid seeped into the hole. Focusing on her distillate ability, she blew on the dirt, trying to clear it away from the dry roots faster. Each speck of dirt came into sharp focus just before her vision muddied. A sharp pain etched across the top of her head, and she winced.

"What's wrong?"

CHAPTER SEVENTEEN

SHYLAH

"Nothing, only a headache," she said, ignoring her body's warning signs. She had to finish collecting the ingredients. She could sleep tonight.

Wiping her forehead, she returned to slowly chipping away at the dirt walls, getting closer and closer to the roots. At the first sign of the tuber roots, she set down the shovel and began using her fingers to work around the edges until she could gently pull up the plant.

"It looks like hairy potatoes," Durmad said, leaning forward.

His spiced sweat scent tickled her nose.

"Except these aren't hard. Each one is filled with a thick white liquid."

"That's why it's called milk," he said with the pleasure of a child who just learned how to skip.

"Mhm." She twisted toward him, and he peered more intensely at the roots. "Now I need the bottle."

"What?"

"The bottle," she said, motioning the entire plant toward the glass bottle resting in his lap.

"Oh, sorry." He held the bottle above his lap.

"Hold it over the dirt. If any misses, it will burn through your pants. And then where would we be?" The image of his pants being burned and even more of him being exposed pulled at the edges of her focus.

"Am I holding it wrong?" he asked.

"What? No, sorry." A flush warmed her cheeks. "I got distracted."

She cleared her throat, cut the bottom of the first root nodule with the copper snips, and positioned it over the mouth of the bottle. Gently squeezing the top, the milk dripped out in thick beads. Each bead took a few seconds to form, and then gravity pulled it from the root and into the bottle.

By the time she had squeezed the third one, the bottle was a quarter full, and what felt like an eternity had passed. She didn't remember it taking this long before. Then again, she'd held the bottle and panicked as she did it all herself. Time and movement slowed as if the air was a thick liquid instead of gas, but her heart still raced.

"How many plants will you need?"

"This one should be enough to fill the bottle."

His eyes were fixed on the roots and the liquid dripping into the bottle. Something about being able to share her knowledge with him, coupled with his genuine curiosity, excited her.

Since coming to Morena, Elixir Designing had become a task—a chore—something she must do whether she wanted to or not. The last time designing had excited her like this was the first time Shylah's mother taught her an elixir. But that was before the fire, before Morena, and before—Her eyes jumped to Durmad's face. His lips turned up slightly in a smile.

Maybe he would keep this secret, too, and maybe not just for Trulian. Do I want him to keep the secret for my sake? No.

She didn't care about why. Just that he kept it.

Right?

He hadn't even noticed she looked up until a drop of milk missed the bottle and landed on his hand. He sucked air through clenched teeth and yanked his hand back.

"Sorry." Shylah dropped the plant in the sand. Using a copper-gloved hand, she grasped his and wiped off the bead of milk. "Let me see." She inspected the side of his index finger where the liquid hit, but there was no sign.

"I can heal myself, remember?"

She pulled her hands back. "Right." Shaking her head and chastising herself yet again, she picked up the plant and continued milking it.

Once the bottle was full, she buried the remaining nodules in the dirt and filled the hole. "Done."

"Perfect timing. Looks like the rain stopped. I'll bury the fire while you gather your things."

She pulled a piece of scrap fabric from her satchel and wrapped it around the glass bottle before tucking it into an internal pocket that would rest against her body and keep the hard tools from bouncing on the glass. The last thing she needed was for the bottle to break and the whole trip to be a waste.

Resting a hand on the satchel, Shylah glanced up. Durmad headed back to the horse.

One horse. How would they get Eclipse back?

"Will Eclipse come back on her own, or do you need to go find her?" Shylah asked.

"I don't need to find her. She knows her way back to the stables," Durmad said, spreading the blanket over the saddle.

Shylah pulled his shoulder back till he faced her. "The stables? How are we going to get back? I still need to find some honeysuckle."

He grinned and patted the saddle. "We still have Atlas."

"Are you going to walk alongside the whole way?" she asked.

He chuckled and ran his hand through his dark waves. "Why would I do that when we have a horse as strong as Atlas?"

Atlas reared up and whinnied in agreement.

"Do you mean?" Shylah looked at the blanket draped over the horse's saddle and remembered the feeling of raw skin on the inside of her legs. She wasn't excited to have that feeling again.

Durmad grabbed her by the waist.

She put a hand on his wrist, stopping him.

"Wait. How do I keep, I mean, protect my legs?"

He spun her so her back faced him. "That's what the blanket is for. Now, up you go." He lifted, and Shylah lifted her left leg over Atlas's saddle.

She tried to tuck her skirts beneath her this time.

Durmad placed his hand on her thigh, sending a shiver up her back. "Besides, I can always heal you again," he said, swinging himself onto Atlas.

A warm sensation crept up her legs as she remembered his touch on her bare skin. "Stop."

"Stop what?" Durmad's thighs straddled her hips.

"I..." she hadn't meant to say that out loud. "I need to get honeysuckle nectar still." Glad he couldn't see her face, which she was sure was as bright red as the flames of the fire had been, she rolled her eyes at herself. "I need to fill an entire bottle, so we'll have to go to two different places."

"No, we don't. I know a place."

"Are you sure? We have to make sure we get an entire bottle; otherwise, I can't make the Quiescence."

He wrapped his arm around her and scooted forward until his legs were half under and half squeezing her in place. "Hold on to the front of the saddle. Do you feel secure?"

Shylah didn't know what else to do, so she nodded. She definitely didn't feel like she would fall off, but she didn't know how *secure* she felt.

He clicked his tongue and gently tugged Atlas's reins to the right. The first jump startled her a bit, and she leaned forward.

"Lean back. Let yourself move with me instead of opposite me. It will feel like we are one rider for Atlas."

Shylah took a deep breath and leaned back into his chest. It was as solid as it had looked when he handed her his tunic. Images of his muscular physique flashed in her mind.

He brought his arms closer, hugging her into himself while holding Atlas by the reins.

"Ready?"

She nodded, and they jumped into a gallop.

Every muscle tensed, and it took several yards before she reminded herself to relax and move with him. Durmad's thighs flexed around and beneath her in rhythm with Atlas.

After a few tries, she found the same rhythm, and instead of bouncing off his hardened chest, she moved with it—with him. She closed her eyes, sank into the cadence, and let the wind in her face carry her thoughts away.

CHAPTER EIGHTEEN

DURMAD

Stray hairs from her braid danced with the wind and tickled his chin. The faster they rode, the more Shylah leaned into his chest, and the slower Durmad wanted to go. But he knew there was no time to waste. If he was going to be able to help protect Trulian, Shylah had to trust him —or at least not doubt his protection. He was sure she'd understand if she only knew how similar they were. At least, he hoped. The only person who knew most of the details wanted to use that information to secure his loyalty.

His similarity with her was about more than just the details, though. It ran deeper. That's how he knew it would take more than words to convince her to trust him. She'd come up with reasons not to believe him, and he couldn't blame her. In his immaturity and misguided youth, he'd given her plenty of reasons to doubt his sincerity. No, words weren't enough; he had to show her to prove his worthiness.

Helping her collect the honeysuckle in one location should help. At least, he hoped it would, and he hoped the bushes still grew prolifically. In truth, he hadn't been back to his childhood home since he left twelve and a half years ago at the age of nine. It sat on the opposite side of Morena from the Kyselina Desert, and half the day had already passed. By the time the dilapidated cottage with its crumbling paddock fences came into view, the sun had reached beyond its peak, and twelve years had not been kind to the small home that had been in desperate need of repair before his father's death. He'd half expected someone to have moved in and continued working the land, but then again, everyone feared the infection. It had wiped out nearly half of all Dimmet, including the king and his entire household. The devastation and vacant throne had brought Naamah back from her life abroad. Her quest to purge Dimmet of the infection ignited her use of magic. Her own ability to amplify and mimic the abilities of those around her increased with the addition of magic, and even after the infection was stopped, she continued.

Atlas slowed, and Shylah sat forward. "Where are we?"

"My home," he said, sliding off Atlas's back and tying him to a piece of the collapsing fence. "How are your legs?" he asked, reaching up to help her down. Instead of an answer, she looked at the homestead behind him with a furrowed brow. "It used to be my home," he added.

She placed her hands on his shoulders. "Why did you leave?"

"The infection." He lifted her from Atlas.

"Infection?"

He left his hands on her waist and smiled inwardly that she left hers on his shoulders. Baby steps were baby steps, even with distraction. "Naamah purged it from the kingdom, so it never traveled the seas to Castigation's coast. It killed almost half the kingdom, including the king, several years before you and Trulian came." He felt Shylah tense at her sister's name, and she pulled her arms into her chest.

Turning away from her, he said, "This was where my parents died." He heard the grass rustle behind him but focused on the cottage. His mind transformed reality into memory. The collapsing roof strengthened, with a row of sparrows singing from its peak. The sun reflected off the blade of his father's scythe at the peak of each swing as he cut the tall grass in the far field. His mother's humming filled his ears as he watched a six or seven-year-old specter of himself bound in front of her toward the wild blackberry fields.

"The honeysuckle is this way," he said, turning to follow the familiar path. Shylah's hand gently gripped his arm. He stopped, but he couldn't turn. Salt threatened to do more than sting his eyes if he looked at her. It was one thing to win her over and another to allow salty tears to erode the exterior he had strategically reinforced over the years. Seeing the weeping and weak nine-year-old who couldn't save his parents would not build her confidence in him.

"But, you're not bonded."

"No. My uncle took me in almost a year before Naamah returned to rule in her father's place. That's when Bonding became a practice, so those of us who were orphaned and living with family were given a choice, or rather, our family was. My uncle chose not to take responsibility for me with such a commitment. He thought I was a weak and useless boy." He kept his eyes away, directed in front of him, but nearly broke when she squeezed his arm.

She whispered, "Like Trulian."

He nodded.

"So, you're an orphan."

A tear broke free from the corner of his eye. He pulled away from her touch and continued walking forward. "Just beyond the tree line is a field lined with more honeysuckle than you can imagine. There should be plenty for the Quiescence."

Running his hand over his eyes quickly and through his hair, he quickened his steps and only slowed when he heard Shylah jogging through the tall grass to catch him. He waited for her to say something, to ask another question, but she didn't. They walked in step and silence.

A field of blackberry brambles met them only a step beyond the trees. Even they had begun to encroach on the cottage.

Shylah exhaled quickly and walked a few steps ahead of him. "So, this is why you like blackberries so much."

He grinned at the back of her head. She turned to face him with arms crossed. Clearing his throat, he nodded. "Yes. My mother would come to collect leaves for tea, and I would collect berries in my cheeks," he said, puffing out his cheeks like small balloons.

She giggled, and her smile spread so wide that even her eyes twinkled. "I bet you did." She turned back to the field. "Trulian would love it here, too. She loves blackberries almost as much as you."

"She does?" He feigned surprise.

"Almost."

"Next Replenish Day, we'll bring her. But you came for honey-suckle. So, let's get you honeysuckle."

Honeysuckle vines filled with bright pink and white blooms climbed the trees on the forest's edge behind the blackberry field. The familiar scent triggered his muscle memory. He pulled the delicate hairs from the center of a flower and placed a drop of sweet nectar on his tongue. He gripped another set of hairs and, turning, offered it to Shylah, who stood staring at him.

He chuckled. "What?" He held out the honeysuckle nectar to her. "It's good."

"I can tell." Her grin grew. "I've never seen you like this."

"Well, you barely know me, so I'm not surprised you haven't seen me eating nectar from a flower." He dropped the nectar onto his tongue and retrieved another.

"That's not what I meant."

"What then?"

"I've never seen you happy."

He stiffened. His life hadn't been terrible, but she was right. He'd never felt at home or balanced with his uncle. It was hard to feel happiness when everything kept him off kilter. "It's hard to feel happy if you don't feel safe," he said, facing her.

She flipped open her satchel. "That I understand; now, stop wasting all the nectar. We have to fill this bottle."

Durmad defiantly sucked one more drop of nectar as she held up an empty clear glass bottle. She squished her nose up and tilted her head as she pushed past him. "And I've never seen you like this," he said.

"What? Determined? Focused? Tenacious?"

Durmad chuckled. "No, you're always those."

The sun flooded her sapphire eyes and kissed the top of her head when she frowned at him over her shoulder. Turning back to the honeysuckle vine, reaching for a bloom, she said, "Then what?"

He quickly closed the space between them, standing close enough that the earthy vanilla scent of her hair overwhelmed his senses, and said, "Enchanting."

She laughed and spun around inches from him. "Enchanting. That's—"

Smiling down at her bewildered look, he watched the wind blow swaths of loose hair across her forehead. His fingers itched to brush them behind her ear, giving him a clear view of her. "That's what?"

She said nothing, and for a moment, they stood staring —listening —breathing. Then she pursed her lips and squinted. "You're being cruel," she said, slapping him on the chest.

Durmad covered her hand, held it on his bare chest, and gazed into her eyes. She held his gaze for a breath before looking down. *How did I not see her playfulness before?* He brushed the hair from her forehead, tucking it behind her ear. He admired how she protected her sister with such ferocity. He lifted her chin until their eyes met again. Glancing at her lips, he smiled.

Her fingers flexed against his chest, and he pulled her hand away but didn't let it go. With his free hand, he traced the center vein of her feather Bonding mark, drawing a circle where it connected with itself again under her wrist. Lifting it to his lips, he quickly glanced at her. Her head tilted toward him, but her eyes were closed. He kissed the place he'd circled, lingering on her skin, feeling the warmth of her pulse against his lower lip.

He placed her hand over his heart and caressed her cheek. "I will never be cruel to you," he said.

CHAPTER NINETEEN

SHYLAH

Shylah's wrist still tingled where he kissed her feather shackle.

Too close. She was too close—he was too close.

The scent of spiced sweat mixed with the fragrant honeysuckle completely overwhelmed her senses.

Honeysuckle. I need to finish collecting honeysuckle.

She pushed off his chest and held the empty glass bottle between them. "If you've finished mocking me, filling this bottle will take at least an hour."

His eyes narrowed a moment before the neutral expression he wore the day he left took control of his face. She rolled her eyes and turned back to the honeysuckle. She should have known it was all to entertain himself. He may not see it as cruel, but she did. He would return to training in thirteen days, and she would return to being Trulian's sole protector.

After thirty silent minutes of painstakingly adding drips of nectar to the bottle, she stood up and stretched her shoulders. The more tedious a task, the more she tended to hunch over it as if making herself even smaller would make it easier—it usually didn't. She held the bottle up.

"Almost done," Durmad said.

She gripped the bottle tighter and gasped as a shudder shook her shoulders.

He gripped her upper arms, "Careful. Wouldn't want to spill all our work, or you'll have to spend more time ignoring me."

"We have a job to do," she said, freeing herself from his grip. "Or rather, I have a job to do. You're just along for the ride." She yanked free a honeysuckle bloom and ran it along the bottle's rim before tossing it at her feet.

"If I hadn't come, you would have died in that acid storm."

She spun to face him. "If it weren't for your interference, I would have only been halfway there when the storm hit, which means I would have missed it altogether."

"But you would still be collecting the biting strobilus milk, and you would have taken twice as long to get the nectar. Admit it. You needed me."

She clenched her teeth and fisted her hand around the bottle as her whole body went rigid. "Need you? I don't need you. I haven't needed you since the day I arrived. All you've ever done is torment me, put me on edge, complicate my plans, and put Trulian in danger."

He flared his nostrils and stepped toward her.

She stepped back.

He held up his hands. "You don't mean that."

She crossed her arms over her chest. "I absolutely do."

"You can't." He shook his head. His shoulders sagged, and he leaned against a tree a few feet away.

"And why not?" A smirk pulled at her mouth. She was winning. He was shrinking. Instead of her always being the one to shrink and acquiesce, he was the one giving up. He turned away, putting the tree between them, and she followed. "Oh, the big bad Green Willow Guard can't take the truth from a mere bonded? It will take more than a kiss on my wrist to sway my opinion."

"Stop!" he said, facing her so quickly and with such ferocity that she snapped her mouth closed and stood still. "You have no idea what you're talking about. I was an immature kid when we first met. I had no idea what to do or how to process what was happening."

She pulled her neck into her shoulders. Process what was happening? What was he talking about? she thought.

"They recruited me to be a weapon. I had no idea my presence mattered to you so much that not saying goodbye would cause this grudge and mistrust to fester for so long."

"You aren't making any sense." She turned back to the honeysuckle. "We still need more nectar," she said, moving to a fresh bush and further into the forest. The sun barely peeked above the trees now, thickening the shadows. She glanced at the bottle again and rubbed her forehead. At this rate, she'd be lucky to get more than a few hours of sleep.

"Shylah, you're not listening."

She sighed and reached for a fresh honeysuckle bloom. A flash of movement beyond the tree nearest the bush caught her eye, and the rest of Durmad's words faded into the background. She abandoned the bloom, stepped around the bush, and squinted into the deepening shadows. A branch snapped to the left —she stiffened and snapped her head in that direction. Something or someone was in the woods. Keeping her eyes focused in the direction of the snap, she waved her hand blindly behind her until she finally swatted Durmad's arm. "Something's in the woods."

"Shylah," Durmad sighed. "Animals are all over these woods. It was probably a squirrel or rabbit."

She peered into the shadows, darker now that the afternoon was fading into evening. "It looked bigger."

"It will be fine. Here, give me the bottle, and I'll finish harvesting nectar. You can go back to Atlas if you're scared."

She whirled on him. "I'm not scared. I'm just—" Another twig snapped, but something shoved her forward before she could turn back. "Hey!" she said.

The toe of her boot caught beneath a tree root, and she tried to alter her forward momentum. She flung her hands out in preparation for a fall, and the nearly full bottle of nectar flew out of her grasp. Her eyes clamped shut as her body braced for its inevitable meeting with the ground, but it never came. Instead, her body collided with a mass only slightly softer than the ground before a shock of pain radiated up her knee.

"Are you okay?" Durmad asked as he eased her into a sitting position beside him. He stated, inspecting her hands and arms.

"I think so." He inspected her ankles and pressed on her legs through her skirts. "Durmad, it's—" She gasped when he pressed on her knee.

"You're hurt."

Shylah pushed his hand off. "I'm fine."

"You're not. Let me heal you."

Shylah gripped his wrist. "I'm fine. I can handle a bruise." Flinging his wrist away, she brushed her hands off on each other and froze. Her hands were empty. She sucked in her breath. "The nectar! Where?"

Shoving him aside, she flipped to her hands and knees, suppressing a wince as a hidden root pressed through her skirt into the lower edge of her kneecap. "It can't break. I don't have another bottle. There's no time," she said under her breath.

Durmad pulled her to her feet and held the nectar in front of her face. She exhaled. "Thank you," she whispered, wrapping her hand around the bottle and pulling it to her chest.

"Please," he said, shrinking the distance between them to inches, "let me help you." He tucked her loose hair behind her ear again.

She glanced at his face. Her breath caught, and squeezing the bottle tighter, she stared at his chest. "You pushed me," she said.

"Don't be a fool."

She clenched her jaw, glaring at him. "Fool? I was pushed, and you're the only other person here. Do you think I'm lying?"

He rested a hand on each of her upper arms and, in a steady voice, said, "No. A lot's happened to you today. I only meant you were confused."

"Then say that, but don't call me a fool," she said, not releasing him from her glare. He grinned and hugged her to him. "What are you?" She squirmed in his grip for a second, but the strength of his embrace squashed her desire to get free, and tears began to pool in her eyes. The weight of his arms engulfing her reminded her of her father's bear hugs, of his joy, of his protection, of him. *It had been nearly three years; why am I thinking of my father now?*

Her cheek rested against his bare skin as he caressed the back of her head, whispering, "I'm sorry. I have been around soldiers so much, I forgot." He chuckled. "Well, that beautiful girls aren't soldiers, thankfully."

The nectar pulsed in her hand. The last time she felt the pulsing of plant essence, she walked away from her burning home. Her heart steadily gained speed and so did the pulsing nectar. She needed to calm down. Focusing on his chest's gentle rise and fall and the steady rhythm of his heartbeat, she tried to sync her own. Her grip on the bottle, still gripped to her chest, loosened. He pulled back, letting the cool air seep into her cheek in the absence of his skin.

"Let me finish collecting the nectar," he said, wrapping her hand in his. "You need to rest." She nodded and dropped her hand. "It won't take me long."

Shylah watched him collect nectar from a few blooms before her consciousness pulled itself from the brain fog caused by her distillate ability, and she sat right where she stood. It was the main drawback of her distillate ability; exhaustion made her lose herself in the essence of the flora nearest her.

Back home in Baylon, the swaying of the trees had rocked her mind to sleep like a baby in its mother's arms. A living plant's essence always brushed against the edges of her mind, but there were no living trees in a lower-level bedroom in the middle of a large city like Morena to calm her nerves and set her mind at ease. The swaying grass that nearly reached her shoulders gave her the sensation of floating.

It had been too long since she rested without the aid of Lull, and the exhaustion of the day pulled on her. She laid back, closed her eyes, losing herself in the essence of the flora surrounding her, and fell asleep.

CHAPTER TWENTY

DURMAD

Durmad added another drop of honeysuckle nectar to the bottle and glanced over his shoulder.

Shylah stood dazed.

She truly was exhausted. A part of him knew that lashing out at him was a symptom of distillate exhaustion; he'd seen it in both his uncle and mother, not to mention several of the soldiers he trained with. Some versions of the distillate ability were the most common. Even Liam fell under it, though he was the strongest Durmad had ever experienced and one of the few who terrified him in battle.

Regardless, he still messed up. *Why did you say she was being foolish?* That would definitely not win her trust, but he saw glimpses of her through the battlements she had erected. Her lightheartedness seeped out ever so slightly when she let herself be in the moment. He smiled, remembering the warmth of her wrist against his lips, and plucked another bloom. She had lingered with him at that moment. He'd felt her relax despite the pain back in the cave, but each time, she quickly sealed the cracks in her walls. Those few moments gave him hints of who she could be, and all he needed was the hint of a possibility.

He took a deep breath and let the last drop of honeysuckle nectar drip into the bottle. It had taken him nearly an hour to do what would have taken Shylah about ten minutes. With her distillate ability, she could concentrate the liquid and control it, ensuring every last drop made it into the bottle, but she needed rest, and he needed time to think. There was a piece of himself she didn't know. The piece he guarded so closely he tried not to think about it. He knew her guarded secret and that he would keep it. She probably saw it as something he could manipulate her with, which, given what the majority of their interactions had been when he was an immature boy, it made sense. But he wasn't interested in controlling or manipulating her, and the only way to truly show that he could be trusted was to trust her. Sharing his own guarded secret seemed the best way to foster that mutual trust, or so he hoped. There was time to deal with the fallout if she used the information against him, but he only had a few days to earn her trust.

He huffed, corking the bottle as he turned. A lifetime wouldn't be enough if he kept falling into his old ways of antagonizing her. "That's the last of it. We can head ba—" He looked out at an empty field.

"Shylah?" he asked, stepping away from the honeysuckle. *Where was she? Did I tell her to go back to Atlas?* He filtered through what he could remember from their conversation. *No. Maybe she'd decided that on her own. She must have.* In the fading light, he could just make out the cottage on the other side of the field, but no one stood beside Atlas or leaned on the fence.

His chest tightened, and he scanned the edge of the trees. Maybe her clumsiness had really been more. She thought he pushed her —he didn't, but maybe someone else did. "Shylah," he yelled a little louder, and he spun. Atlas. He could search faster on horseback.

Calling her name, he strode toward the cottage and nearly tripped when his foot kicked something hard—a boot. Shylah's boot. He dropped to his knees beside her and lifted her to sitting. Her head rocked to the side. "Shylah." She didn't move. Sitting back on his heels, he wrapped an arm around her back and quickly tucked the bottle of nectar into the satchel, still lying across her stomach, before tucking his arm beneath her knees and standing.

As he carried her back to Atlas, he took inventory of her cells. He sensed the swelling in her knee, but when he reached her head, he felt the widening gap between her skull and brain. A consequence of using a distillate ability too frequently without comfrey treatments. It was why his mother had grown it in the cottage's front garden. Shylah must have made too many elixirs too quickly, and then, using her ability to focus her efforts on the efficient collection today, nearly drained her mental essence. If he didn't do something fast, she'd —*nope, I can't think about that, I won't*. He broke into a run. As a vacuole wielder, he could manipulate cells but couldn't create them from nothing, and she was nearly out of base cells. He had to get the comfrey oils on her face and neck.

Atlas whinnied as they passed, and Durmad laid Shylah in the overgrown garden just beyond the fence. *Where was the comfrey? Think. There. Below the old kitchen window.* He yanked off ten leaves the size of his forearm and ran back to Atlas, pulled a small bowl from his saddle bag before yanking the last waterskin free. Kneeling beside Shylah, he ripped the leaves into the smallest pieces he could manage. He wished he'd thought to put a knife or dagger in his saddlebags, but he hadn't planned on making a poultice in the middle of an overgrown garden.

Once all the leaves lay torn in the bowl, he rubbed his forehead, trying to recall the poultice his mother used to make once a week and what the distillates used during training. *I have to pulverize the leaves before adding the water, but how? A rock would do it.* He fumbled through the weeds and grasses around them, but his fingers only found soil, roots, small pebbles, and clay. *The spade.* He retrieved the spade from Shylah's satchel and used the end of the handle to pulverize the leaves before adding the water and pulverizing everything more. Then he flipped it in his hand and dug about a fist full of clay, mixing it into the bowl until it made a paste.

He pulled up the edge of Shylah's top skirt, whispering a silent apology, and he ripped a six-inch wide strip from around the bottom hem of her underskirt. Sitting beside her, he pulled her head into his lap and smeared the poultice across her forehead before tearing the strip of skirt in half and tying it around her forehead, tucking the rest around her neck and just beneath her ears before gently tying the other strip about her neck. He thought a few of her red streaks brightened, but the fading light made it hard to tell for sure. With poultice still on his hands, he cupped both her cheeks in his hands and prayed he'd done enough.

CHAPTER TWENTY-ONE

SHYLAH

The scent of grass, damp earth, and spice tickled Shylah's nose as she stretched her legs and rolled to her side. A hand brushed her cheek, and she held her breath. *Was someone in her room?* Cool leather pressed her ear against her head. *Not her room.* She sat straight up and instantly pressed her palm into the ground to steady herself as her vision blurred and spun.

"Careful. Take it slow," said a calm male voice.

Touching her forehead, she felt the moist wrap. *Am I hurt? Why can't I remember?* Her eyes focused on the shadow of a figure sitting beside her. *Am I dreaming?* She felt the shadow, but instead of her hand brushing through the shadow of a dream, it stopped against the solid mass of bare skin. Her fingers flexed as the shadow's inhale pushed back against her hand —Durmad. The events slowly came back. She'd designed the most elixirs in a single day she had ever done and then sped up the nectar collection process after being injured by the acid rain.

"How did you know what—"

"To do?" he asked, finishing her question and untying the wrap around her forehead. "My mother mainly. She was a strong distillate. People came from miles around for her elixirs and remedies." He wiped the poultice from her forehead and glanced toward the house. "I think her influence is still here after all these years."

His fingers brushed her chin as he unwrapped her neck. Her skin tingled at the slightest of touches.

"I can't believe I remembered," he said, smiling as he ripped a clean end from her neck wrap and doused it with water. "I suppose I have seen the stronger distillates treat the lesser ones in training, too." He paused a moment as the sunset reflected in his eyes. "I'm just glad I realized in time, and it was enough." He wiped the remains of the poultice from her neck.

She covered his hand with hers. "Thank you," she said, smiling. "You've been saving me a lot today. I guess I did need a guide."

He smiled and continued cleaning the poultice off her skin. Part of her wanted to take the cloth and do it herself. Letting someone else clean her up felt out of control and childlike, but on the other hand, it reminded her of her mother's compassion and the desire to feel that again was winning out.

"That's the last bit. How are you feeling?" he asked standing.

"A little better, I think." She took the hand he offered. Her knees wobbled, and he pulled her tight to his chest.

"You sure?"

She nodded. "Just a little wobbly is all. I'll be fine." It took all her willpower to push off his chest and walk back across the garden to the fence. She couldn't explain it, but the feel of his arms around her and the solidness of his chest made her muscles relax and her worries fade.

He gently lifted her onto Atlas and swung himself into place behind her. They sat facing his childhood home, his arms on either side gripping the reins as if they would leave at any moment. The setting sun cast the gray stones of the cottage in tones of orange and purple. It felt like he was saying goodbye to the place as the sun said goodbye to the day.

The longer they sat, the more her nose itched, but any movement felt like it would break the spell. His chest pushed her forward, and he took a deep breath and exhaled slowly as the last ray of color disappeared into the shadows.

"Thank you for bringing me," she said.

"My pleasure. Lean into me. If you have any discomfort, we can stop," he said, turning Atlas away from the house. "Ready?" She nodded, and he kicked Atlas into a full gallop.

This time, Shylah met his rhythm faster. Her muscles relaxed, eyes closed, letting him guide their cadence. It wasn't until their pace slowed that she opened her eyes. The gates of Morena stood closed before them.

"It's kind of late for a ride, don't you think?" the guard said, walking along Atlas's flank. "That's a lot of armor."

"Yes. Is something wrong, Goshen?" Durmad asked.

The guard stiffened at the sound of his name and peered at them. His eyes widened. "Sir Durmad! My apologies."

Durmad clicked his tongue, and Atlas jumped forward.

The guard bowed and said something else, but Shylah didn't hear it over the echoing clop of Atlas's hooves as they trotted through the empty streets. Her original plans had her returning well before dark, before dinner even, but the storm in the Kyselina Desert, then the impromptu stop at Durmad's cottage, had added almost half a day.

She still had a long night of designing ahead of her before she could finally rest. Yawning, she tilted her head back slightly, and Durmad's chin bounced off it. His hand shot to his chin, and he leaned away from her. Cold air filled the space, sending a chill down her spine. The space remained until they stopped behind the workshop.

Durmad dismounted and slowly helped her down, but instead of stepping aside, he brushed hair behind her ear, resting the palm of his hand along her jaw. "I'm glad you're okay. When you didn't wake up, it...it scared me."

She leaned into it and dropped her gaze. The memory of the warmth she felt when he healed her in the cave surfaced. It would still be at least two hours before she could rest, but her cheek tingled with the magnetic pull of his palm. *Is he manipulating my cells and pulling them to him? No. Vacuoles couldn't do that, could they?*

Before a complete question could form on her tongue, he lifted her chin and dropped his lips to hers. The instant their lips touched, Shylah's breath caught, and her muscles tensed. His fingers buried themselves in the hair behind her ear. The tingling spread from her cheek to her lips, the back of her head, and down her neck.

She should pull away. She was bonded. He was an orphan. But her body told her brain it didn't matter, and she melted into the kiss. His hand wrapped around her lower back, pulling her closer until only her toes touched the ground. Shylah's hand rested on his bare chest, and her fingers tingled as they flexed against his muscle. The image of him standing half naked, offering her his tunic, lit the back of her eyelids. The tingling spread as the picture faded to Eclipse running past her. *Trulian.*

A shiver ran through her body, and she pulled away. The cool night air filled the space between them. She didn't want to feel the cool air;

she wanted to feel his warmth. She wanted to wrap her arms around his neck and pull his lips back down to hers—she shook the desire from her mind. "I have to go."

Durmad released her and stepped back. "I need to get Atlas back to the stables," he said, patting the saddle. "And you have some Quiescence to design."

"Right." She stiffened and walked past him, but he beat her to the knob. She signed, saying, "I have a long night. Thank you for your help today."

"I won't take much more of your time," he said, backing away slightly.

She turned and glanced up, expecting to meet his eyes, but they focused on the door just above her head.

"I." He shifted his weight. "It wasn't." He ran his hand through his hair and glanced back at Atlas.

"I really need to check on Trulian," she said, laying her hand on the doorknob. His gentle touch on her shoulder kept her from turning it. The moonlight reflected in his eyes when she faced him again. *Nope.* She pulled her eyes down, and they stopped at his lips. Her own lips warmed as they remembered the earlier sensation. Biting her lip, she dropped her eyes further. *That wasn't any better. Is there nowhere I can look where my body won't betray my logic?* Lifting her eyes slightly, she focused on the wrinkle in the left shoulder of his jacket. "It's late. I still have a lot to finish tonight."

"I wanted to apologize. So much has been forced on you in the last few years. I should've asked." He ducked his head till their eyes locked.

Shylah squeezed her eyes closed. She couldn't look into them, or she wouldn't be able to do anything, including thinking clearly. "Asked what?" She heard him shuffle his feet in the dirt but kept her eyes tightly closed.

"Everything. You didn't want me to go in the first place. I pushed. There is a honeysuckle closer to the city walls, but I dragged you to my family's decrepit cottage. I only wanted you to understand—to know my history."

Silence overwhelmed the space between them. He had shared a hidden part of himself with her, but all she had ever shared was her venom for Naamah, Dimmet, and the Green Willow Guard. She wanted to respond, but everything sounded trite and insincere in her head. She peered through a squinted eye. He was still close enough to touch. *Should I hug him? Reassure him that I appreciated his openness and his help—do I?* Her body shivered. *No.* Touching him would silence her mind —her reason, and she couldn't relinquish control again; she wouldn't.

He stepped closer.

Her eyes sprang open, and she stepped back, still holding the doorknob.

"I should have asked to kiss you," he whispered.

She turned the knob and nearly fell backward into the kitchen. "It's alright. It was nice, but I...I have to design the elixir. You need to get Atlas back to the stables and ensure Eclipse made it back safe. Goodnight," she said, closing the door on his bewildered face.

Leaning against the door, she slid to the floor. "It's alright? It was nice? What was that?" she whispered aloud. "His chin must have broken something in your head." She tapped her head against the door. "You daft girl." She sat on the kitchen floor a few minutes longer, wondering if he was still outside the door, evaluating what he said and how, while she debated whether she had heard Atlas clip-clop away.

But in the end, it didn't matter. She still had work to do. Standing, she caught movement out of the corner of her eye and froze. Searching the shadows, she slowed her movement and reached for the counter. There was a small pot of herbs just below the window. Her eyes, still peering into the darkness, stopped when her fingers grasped the pot. Stifling a scream, she hurled the herb pot at the eyes in the corner and ran into the workshop.

CHAPTER TWENTY-TWO

DURMAD

The door closed, and the air around him grew heavier. It was like trying to breathe submerged in sand; he couldn't. He'd opened up to her, and she'd accepted it. He rubbed his mouth and chin. Then he'd kissed her.

He breathed into the palm of his hand. *Was it my breath that made her pull away, or was my kissing that bad?* He shook his head. *No, just my stupidity.*

He'd screwed it all up. Again. It was the day after the Fire Onion Juice all over, only worse. This time, he'd wanted her to understand, to accept his apology.

He replayed the day in his mind. He'd told her the one thing only a few people knew about him. *Maybe she didn't understand, or maybe she did. Did I misinterpret the whole situation? No. I couldn't have. She'd hesitated. She'd searched for words.* The image of her with eyes closed and head tilted toward him took shape in his mind. *She'd relaxed. Hadn't she?*

He felt her phantom fingers flex against his chest again. *Was she being playful, or does she really think I'm cruel?* His shoulders sagged. *Did I only see what I wanted to see in her responses?*

He had to fix it.

Placing his hand on the knob, he turned it slightly and stopped. *Or had she had time to process the fact that I am still an unbonded orphan?* His throat dried, and he released the knob.

He had every right to go into his uncle's home and down to his own bedroom, but she'd closed the door without even peering back at him. There was no misinterpreting that action. She didn't want to be near him.

Setting his jaw, he turned to Atlas. "Then we will leave her alone."

When Atlas stopped at the stable's entrance, Durmad distractedly slid from the saddle. He licked his lips. *She kissed me back, initiated the second kiss. So, then, why the sudden cold shoulder?*

He leaned against Atlas. "What did I do?" Atlas only shook his head and huffed. "Let's get this armor off. Come on," he said, leading Atlas into the stable.

"Eclipse." The black horse stood just outside his stall, still clad in armor. He ran a hand over the armor covering Eclipse's flanks. *No cloak.* His hand stopped—a gap. "How did you lose a scale? These are not easy to separate."

Eclipse snorted and stomped a hoof before backing away.

Durmad held up his hands in surrender, saying, "No more questions. Ethereal knows I have too many unanswered ones already."

Once the armor from both horses had been removed and returned to the armory, Durmad tossed hay into the bottom of each horse's stall, topped off their water, and rubbed their foreheads.

Lingering on Eclipse, he asked, "Where did you run off to?" Eclipse tipped his head down and grabbed a mouthful of hay from the stall floor. "You put me in a difficult spot. She had to ride with me."

Eclipse tossed his head up, shaking his mane.

"You did. Poor Atlas had to carry us both." Durmad chuckled, leaning over the stall gate.

Atlas nuzzled Durmad's arm and nickered.

"Sorry, boy. No carrots tonight. I'll bring you some in the morning."

Eclipse huffed and kicked the back of his stall.

"What? Now you're angry with me? You're the one who left." Durmad pushed himself back from the stall gate. "And you took her cloak with you."

Eclipse dropped his head for more hay.

Durmad frowned. "You could've brought it back, by the way. Now she has no cloak." His frown shifted. He would get her a new cloak at the market in the morning. His grin grew to a smile: some flowers and roasted berry nuts. Gifts always warmed the coldest of shoulders.

The image of his blanket wrapped around Shylah's shoulders beside the fire sent prickles along his scalp. Despite all her determination and stubbornness, she'd been helpless at that moment. She'd needed him. His fingertips tingled at the memory of her skin beneath them. *I can compel her*, Liam's offer echoed in his ears.

He shook his head and walked out of the stables.

No. He wanted to protect her, not take advantage of her.

Kissing her is how I protect her? "Well, no," he whispered.

"Who are you talking to?"

Durmad spun, gripping for a sword that wasn't there and quickly raising his fists.

"Woah. Stand down," the boy said, stepping into the moonlight.

The moonlight highlighted the hint of green in the boy's lightning-blue waves, reminding Durmad of seaweed floating in the Astra Sea off the coast of Dimmet. He relaxed. "Jorden. You know better than to sneak up on me." He crossed his arms, peering at the thirteen-year-old boy. "What are you doing out here in the dead of night?"

Liam's younger brother smirked at Durmad. "I could ask you the same thing," he said, tossing an apple in the air before taking a bite.

"I was returning Atlas and Eclipse to their stalls," Durmad said, shifting his weight. "Your turn."

"Not sure I owe you an explanation. This is castle grounds, but I like to give the horses apples at night."

Durmad raised his eyebrows. "And?" He sensed Jorden was only disclosing safe information. Durmad knew Jorden's ability was connected to animals. Liam had told him as much, but he wasn't sure precisely what Jorden's ability was or why he'd be so fascinated with horses.

Jorden grinned. "I like to talk to them. Which reminds me, who were you talking to?"

"Talk to them?"

"Yeah. Animals listen." He swallowed another bite of apple and said, "They have lots of opinions and secrets to tell."

Durmad raised a hand. "Hang on. They talk to you?"

Jorden laughed, shooting bits of apple at Durmad's palm. "Do they talk to me? What do you think?"

Furrowing his brow, Durmad wiped his palm down his pants. "I don't know, that's why I asked?"

Jorden smirked. "Nice try."

"Nice try at what?"

"Changing the subject." Jorden glanced around. "Who were you talking to?"

Now you're changing the subject, Durmad thought. "Just myself."

"Do you habitually walk around in the dead of night, talking to yourself?"

"No," Durmad said through gritted teeth. "Do you?"

Jorden shrugged and stepped past him. "I'm not the one trespassing." He glanced over his shoulder. "I'm surprised my mother permitted you to ride Liam's horse. She gave him Eclipse for his sixteenth birthday. They've formed a bond. Liam is rather particular about who rides Eclipse, but you should know that after training with him for so long." Jorden turned his back, adding, "She was furious when Liam let me ride him that first week. For your sake, I hope you have not interfered with their bond."

Durmad registered the veiled threat and bowed. "I have taken enough of your time." Standing, he looked at Jorden and said, "Do you want me to tell Liam anything for you?"

Jorden visibly tensed, nearly dropping his half-eaten apple, and shook his head.

See, I can deliver veiled threats, too, Durmad thought. "If that's all, Liam is waiting for me at the Tavern." Durmad knew Liam would be sleeping or in the warmth of his mystery woman's bed if she were here in Morena, but Jorden didn't need to know that.

The boy waved an arm and disappeared into the stable.

Durmad snickered. Barely thirteen, and Jorden could already spin his words. He supposed it was a skill Jorden and Liam had picked up early in life; after all, Naamah was their mother. Jorden had said the horses had opinions and secrets. *Could Jorden talk to them?*

Durmad's chest tightened.

Could they talk to Jorden?

He spun to face the stable. Eclipse and Atlas definitely had secrets, and Durmad had just singled them out as targets. He stepped toward the stable and stopped. If he went barreling back in there, he'd raise suspicions, but if Eclipse and Atlas told Jorden about him sneaking them out this morning, Naamah might not give him a choice to be bonded. But, if he apologized and pledged to support Jorden and he accepted it, Shylah would be safe. *This is how I can protect her,* he thought and marched back into the stable.

CHAPTER TWENTY-THREE

SHYLAH

Shylah plastered herself against the wall between the fireplace and the herb cabinet. The chair that would have given her more cover had been removed, and she felt exposed.

The sound of footsteps pressed her even farther against the wall. Her heart raced. She tried to slow her breathing, but the more she tried, the more light-headed she became.

A whisper cut through the silence, "Shylah, you almost hit me."

Trulian. Her sister peered from the shadows. Shylah exhaled, prying herself from the wall.

"Tru. You scared me," she said, walking to the elixir table.

"I figured that out when the herb pot broke on the wall beside me," Trulian giggled.

Shylah darted around the workshop table and gripped her sister by the shoulders. Turning her side to side, she asked, "Are you okay? Did it hit you? You can't sneak up on someone like that."

Trulian placed a hand on each of Shylah's wrists. "I'm fine."

"Apollyon," Shylah whispered, glancing over Trulian's head to the darkness behind her.

Trulian covered her mouth, suppressing a giggle. "He'll be asleep for a while."

Shylah stepped back. "What?"

She giggled again. "I gave him some of your Lull with his nightly glass of wine."

"Well then," Shylah said, leaning down about three inches to Trulian's level. "I've taught you well." Stepping around her sister, Shylah lifted the satchel over her head and set it on the table. "Time to make some Quiescence."

Trulian retrieved the mortar and pestle while Shylah gathered the rest of the ingredients before unwrapping the honeysuckle nectar and biting strobilus milk.

"Is that why you were in the cave?"

Shylah stiffened. She'd forgotten about Trulian's appearance and disappearance earlier. "Yes, but how?"

"Why was Durmad? Umm." Trulian kicked her foot and leaned on the edge of the workshop table. "Touching you?"

Warmth flushed Shylah's cheeks, and she was glad for the dark room. "I got stuck in the acid rain. He healed me." A shiver ran down her spine as she remembered the warmth of his touch traveling over her skin. Snapping herself back to the present, she spun on her sister. "How were you there?" She leaned down, squinting at her sister's face. "And why did you spook one of our horses?"

Trulian shrugged. "She needed it."

"Who needed it? What are you talking about?"

"One of our bonded guardians. She got stuck in the rain, too, but no one was there to help her." Trulian grinned. "So I did."

Shylah's chest tightened and her breath caught. *Was Naamah in the desert?* "How did you know she was there?"

"I dreamed it two weeks ago." Trulian, dripping her gaze to the ground, kicked at the floor and swayed back and forth. "When I dreamed about the chair catching fire, and," she giggled and bounced on her toes, "the kiss."

"What do you mean you dreamed the kiss? What kiss?"

"You and Durmad by the blackberries." Trulian reached across the table and picked up the bottle of clear liquid. "I knew it was all going to happen, so I helped."

Shylah leaned on the edge of the table and rubbed her forehead. "What do you mean? We didn't kiss by the blackberry bushes, we," she stopped short. "How did you help?" The giggling stopped, and her sister froze. "Tru? What did you do?"

"I pushed you into his arms," Trulain said, beaming. "But, first, I had to dump out most of the Quiescence, so you would have to go to the market and."

"See Durmad," Shylah finished and massaged her temples. "But I gave you Quiescence, so how did you travel to the cave and the blackberry field?"

Trulian stood tall and pushed her shoulders back. "I've been practicing."

"Practicing?" Shylah's eyes widened. Practicing meant Trulian had traveled more than she realized. *Who else knew she'd traveled?* "Who showed you how to?"

"A nice old man with stormy gray and amber eyes. He said I needed to practice so I could teach my bonded guardian how to do it."

Shylah gripped Trulian's shoulders. "You must never teach Naamah how to travel. Do you understand me? She cannot know you can travel." Trulian squirmed beneath her grasp.

"Shy, you're hurting me."

She gripped tighter. "No one can know you're a peripatetic. Promise me you will stop practicing." Squirming, Trulian pried at Shylah's fingers. Shylah jerked her sister. "Look at me."

Trulian froze.

"Promise me."

"I promise."

Shylah released her grip slightly. "Promise what?"

Trulian exhaled. "Not to teach Naamah how to travel."

"Good," Shylah said, rubbing Trulian's upper arms and shoulders. "And the practicing?"

Trulian stepped back. "I'll be careful."

"That's not good enough, Tru. If you practice, Naamah will sense it. You have to stop, or she will know and force you to teach her."

Trulian smiled, walked back into the kitchen, and picked up the broken pot of herbs. "That's silly. She won't know I am a peripatetic until it's too late."

"Too late?" Shylah rubbed her forehead. "What are you talking about?"

Trulian skipped back to her sister and wrapped her arms around Shylah's chest. "It will all make sense, but I promise I won't leave you. You're all I have, too, ya know."

"I'm sorry. I just can't lose you, too," her voice pinched. "If she knew. If she knew you could travel." Wiping away a tear, she sighed and wrapped Trulian in a bear hug. Her chin rested on top of Trulain's head. "We have to stick together."

Trulian squeezed Shylah. "I'm sorry."

Shylah leaned back. Brushing strands of red hair from Trulian's forehead, she kissed it. "I know. Go to bed."

"I want to help."

"Thank you, but you need rest, and I work faster on my own." She glanced at the workshop window between the fireplace and the front door. The moon shone through the glass panes as if morning was already arriving. "I need to finish quickly so I can get some rest, too."

Trulian sweetened her tone, grinning. "So you can have your own dreams."

The warm flush washed over Shylah's cheeks again. "No. I'm nearly depleted. Give me those herbs," she said, cupping the pottery bits and herbs Trulian had picked up, "and get to bed." She spun her sister toward the kitchen and playfully patted her backside.

A few steps away, Trulian turned back. "It's okay, you know."

"I know. It will all be okay. Now get to bed."

"No. I mean Durmad. It's okay if you like him."

Shylah opened her mouth, but no sound came out.

"He's nice. You deserve nice."

Shylah pointed her finger toward the kitchen. "Bed."

"All right," Trulian said, skipping back into the kitchen.

Shylah listened for her sister's footsteps on the back stairs before collapsing onto the table. *Nice? Durmad? He was – what was he? He was an orphan. He was still a Green Willow Guard. He was still a tool of Naamah. And he was still a threat.*

She had to protect her sister even more now that he knew she had abilities, and some old man had been teaching her to practice. Maybe he could teach Trulian to control it, to stop it. Then she wouldn't need to make Quiescence anymore. She wouldn't have to worry. *No.*

Shylah had no idea who this man was or what he wanted with her sister. Trulian's words echoed in her mind, "so I can teach my bonded guardian how to do it." *Why would anyone want to give Naamah more power?*

Shylah started chopping, grinding, and mixing the ingredients. She wasn't going to let Naamah get her hands on Trulian. Quiescence was the answer. She reached for the bottle of white, biting strobilus milk and stopped. If it hadn't been for Durmad, she would have died in the acid rain. As annoyed as she'd been when he showed up with horses, she might still be out collecting honeysuckle if she had gone on foot.

"Shylah, you dolt," she whispered, gripping the bottle. He'd not only saved her, healed her, and opened up to her, but he'd also helped her get the ingredients she needed. And how had she thanked him? Shutting a door on him. She pursed her lips and added five drops of biting strobilus milk to the mixture.

She uncorked the honeysuckle nectar, and the sweet, peppery scent filled her nostrils. And that kiss. *Why had she kissed him?* He'd pulled away. She should have left it at that, but no, she couldn't even control her own mouth. Chuckling, she whispered, "Now I have another way my mouth has gotten me in trouble." Shaking her head, she added seven drops of honeysuckle nectar and heated the elixir to a rolling boil over the flame of a candle before pouring it into a clean bottle to cool.

Cleaning up, she glanced at the locked cabinet and back at the two bottles filled with their valuable liquids. She'd paid for the materials, used her time, and nearly died collecting them. *Why should I put them in Apollyon's cabinet?* Quickly, she wrapped them back in fabric. She'd have to make the hiding spot in her bed leg bigger, but these were her ingredients.

CHAPTER TWENTY-FOUR

SHYLAH

S hylah woke drained from the day and night before. It hadn't helped that she had had too few hours of sleep, so Lull wasn't an option. Her dreams had been a mix of fires, kisses, and screams.

It was going to be a long day of filling elixir orders. Most of the morning, she designed in silence. The silence heightened her exhaustion, letting the dreams and the fractured memories from the day before fight for her attention. As long as she stayed focused on the elixirs and ingredients, the dreams faded into the recesses of her mind.

It wasn't until nearly lunch that Apollyon joined her in the workshop. "The handle of my harvesting knife broke off," he said, tossing it on the table. "I need you to go have the firesmith fix it."

She nodded, picking up the blade and handle scales. Tucking them away in her apron pocket, she returned to the mortar and pestle in front of her.

Apollyon slammed his hand on the table, spilling her herbs and toppling bottles. "Now."

"But I'm in the middle of designing."

"I am perfectly capable of finishing the elixirs. You should have taken care of the knife yesterday instead of gallivanting all over Dimmet. You are an apprentice. That means you learn from me. And you learn from me by following my directions. Now, go."

Shylah brushed her hands against the front of her apron.

"The moment my nephew returns, you forget yourself," he mumbled to himself.

"This has nothing to do with—"

Apollyon pointed at the front door without looking up from the table and said, "Go."

Shylah nodded and darted into the street. At least she could take a break and see a friend.

The warm sun hit her face, and she fought the urge to walk with closed eyes. She used to take what her sister called blind walks through the forest around Baylon, but the plants and trees would gently direct her to clear paths there. In Morena, there were few plants along the street.

When she found herself trying to blind walk in the first month they'd been here, Durmad had used it as an opportunity to corner her in an alley. He'd yanked her braid and run off, leaving her to wander around the streets of an unfamiliar town. Apollyon had been furious with her for being gone so long, while Durmad smiled at her from behind his uncle.

She'd expected Durmad to come by the workshop this morning to see his uncle or Trulian. Then again, he slept in almost as much as his uncle, at least he did before Willow Guard training. She wasn't sure now, but he was probably still sleeping in whatever tavern they could find a room.

A horse whinnied behind her, prodding a smile from her until she stepped aside and saw it was the carpenter.

Why did I hope it was Durmad?

She turned the corner, and the rooftops no longer blocked the sun. It warmed her cheeks, and for a moment, she was transported to the cave and the warming sensation of Durmad's touch.

What are you doing? she chastised herself. *It's Durmad. He's leaving soon. He's a Green Willow Guard.*

The feel of his lips on hers sent a fresh wave of goosebumps down her neck.

Stop it.

She'd have to make herself an obliterate elixir. These memories, these thoughts had to go. She couldn't continue to be distracted. Somehow, she hadn't noticed Trulian's ability getting stronger or that someone had been training her. This was not the time to be a prattle-eyed little girl.

She turned another corner, and the firesmith forge lay a hundred yards ahead. As she drew closer, she searched the shadows for Aidan, but something silver moved to her right, catching her attention. Squinting, she sifted through the throngs of people.

What was it?

A few doors down the road, she saw a wave of gray hair disappear into an alley between two buildings—the old man.

Glancing to her left at the forge beyond, she weighed the options. Apollyon wouldn't know if it took her a little longer. He hadn't done any of his own errands since she'd arrived, so he didn't have any idea how long it should take her. She sprinted down the street and ducked into the same alley.

The old man leaned against the wall. "That was longer than I expected."

"Are you following me?" she asked.

"Wouldn't I need to be behind you then?"

"Well. I guess. But you. The street," she said, pointing behind her.

"If I didn't know any better, I'd say you were following me."

"Following you? Why would I follow you? I don't even know you."

He pushed himself off the wall. "Precisely. Did you have a question then?"

Do I have a question?

She wasn't even sure why she followed him into the alley, but she had followed him. "Well, I guess I want to know how you became a Bonded."

The old man nodded, "Ah, yes. But that's a story for another time. Another, perhaps?"

She searched the air above her and the space before her as if the answer lay somewhere in the vapor, just out of reach.

Her mind came back to Durmad.

Typhon Toes! I need that elixir.

The old man stood taller. "Ah, there it is."

She looked over her shoulder and spun in a quick circle. "There what is?"

"The question," said the old man, smirking.

"The, but I didn't have a question. My thoughts just wandered."

"To what?"

"To a distraction," she said as a flush colored her cheeks.

"Ah," said the old man, raising his eyebrows. "Distractions are only distractions if they do not bring about your purpose."

Shylah stared at the old man.

What was he saying?

She glanced over her shoulder. She should have left, but something kept her in the strange conversation, and before she knew it, she asked, "Is Durmad not a distraction?"

The old man smiled. "If you are not careful, he can be. Right now, he is not."

"By the stars!" she said, flinging her arms in the air. "What is that supposed to mean?"

"Only that your short-term purpose may change if you choose incorrectly."

"If I choose incorrectly? How do I know if I am choosing correctly or not?" She crossed her arms, shifting her weight to the other foot. This old man was crazy. He had to be. None of this made any sense. "That's a lot of pressure, and you still haven't answered my question."

His grin brightened.

"You're enjoying this, aren't you?"

He held up his thumb and forefinger. "Just a little bit."

"This is pointless. I have errands to run," she said, spinning back the way she'd come and nearly ran right into him. "What the?" She looked over her shoulder and back again.

How'd he moved so quickly and without a sound?

It was like when he disappeared before.

"You must make the correct choice. All of Ethereal depends on it."

"All of Ethereal?" she rolled her eyes and snorted. "Ethereal chose wrong. I'm just a," she looked over her shoulder and whispered, "Bonded."

But when she faced him again, he was gone. She glanced around, nearly colliding with a horse first and then a woman carrying a small child as she walked back into the crowded street. The old man was a distraction for sure, and right now, she needed to see Aidan about fixing a knife handle.

As she neared the forge, Aidan stepped out of the shadows, and a flash of silver caught her eye again as he waved to her.

She waved back and whispered, "Get it together, Shylah. You're just paranoid."

CHAPTER TWENTY-FIVE

DURMAD

Durmad gripped the small bouquet of wildflowers in one hand and tossed an apple with the other. Seeing Atlas always gave him clarity and focus. He needed it today.

He couldn't shake the feeling of healing Shylah or kissing her from his cells. When he closed his eyes, she was there. Her silhouette peered from the corners when he stared at the ceiling in his tavern room. When he watched the orange and pink sunrise from the tavern roof that morning, the clouds had become the braids laying down her back.

He shook his head. Even now, he thought he saw her in the crowd of people. Her apparition dodged an arguing family, and his body hummed like every cell pulled toward her.

Not an apparition. She was here. Perfect.

He could give her the flowers and roasted berry nuts without the risk of his uncle seeing and asking questions.

He waded through the crowd; she waved at someone just before he reached her. His step faltered as she jogged forward and away from him. Ducking into the shadows of the buildings across the street, he watched her race up to the firesmith apprentice and throw her arm over his shoulder.

A lump formed in Durmad's throat.

They smiled and laughed as she reached into her apron pocket and presented him with one of Apollyon's broken knives—only an errand. He swallowed and his the tension in his neck and jaw relaxed. He turned to leave when the apprentice bowed, kissed Shylah's hand, and spun her into the recesses of the forge.

Durmad's stomach tightened, and the humming turned to pinpricks across his skin. He was such a boulder brain. He'd assumed her hesitation had been something he'd done or that he'd been gone for so long that she didn't know him anymore. Maybe she'd never really known him. He had been gone for almost three years.

When he left, she'd been fourteen or fifteen. He wasn't entirely sure, but she'd felt like a child to his nineteen. So, he'd left without a thought.

There was nothing childlike about her now. She'd grown up. Time didn't stand still in his absence, she had suitors—of course, she would. Even Abaddon had noticed her in the market.

Durmad smiled to himself, remembering the market. She'd walked through the crowds and artisans oblivious to their looks, not caring what anyone thought of her, and it had made her even more compelling. He'd been tied in knots since she shoved his hand off the alloy blanket.

Still staring at the darker depths of the forge for the slightest movement, his thoughts drifted to Naamah's proposition. He only had a few days left to decide, and what once felt simple, or at least as much as anything involving Naamah could be, felt muddy now.

In a two days, Shylah had turned the ground to mud beneath his feet. It took all his strength to rip his feet from the sucking mud just to move forward, let alone decide to climb out of the muck till things dried out or dive into the water. Naamah offered to wash the mud off completely. But part of him liked the mud if Shylah was there.

His thoughts floated back to his family cottage. The land was still his. Maybe he could serve the rest of his term with the Green Willow Guard and return to it. He chuckled. It was funny how a single person could change his whole outlook.

When he'd left for training, he'd never considered returning. Life with his uncle hadn't been pleasant. There were moments he still wanted to forget and couldn't.

His family cottage had offered him warmer memories of his childhood before Morena—before his uncle. But it was such a long time ago that the memories were faint and cold now. He'd tried everything he could to forget about how his parents had been ripped from him.

Now, the cottage gave him a glimmer of hope. Shylah gave him hope.

He glanced back at the dark depths of the forge, and his pace slowed as doubt clouded his thoughts. Unless it wasn't just errands.

He needed a new sword, so it only made sense to commission one to be ready for his departure in a week and a half. Darting across the street, he jogged within fifteen feet of the open barn doors before he slowed, adopting a more casual pace.

The Master Firesmith dunked hot tongs in a bucket of water that instantly bubbled and hissed. Durmad raised the flowers but thought better of it and quickly switched to waving his apple hand. The hulk of a man he had purchased his uncle's dagger from two days ago, nodded.

Before Durmad finished closing the distance, a giggling bundle of skirts collided with him.

"Oh, excuse me. I didn't—" Shylah backed up a step. "You. What are you doing here?"

Durmad smiled. "Shopping." He held up the bouquet of wildflowers tied with a sapphire ribbon and said, "These are for you."

Shylah raised an eyebrow. "Why?"

He pushed them closer to her until she accepted them. "An apology for, well, yesterday. And here." He retrieved the roasted berry nuts from his pocket and handed them to her.

She smelled the flowers. "Thank you. You didn't need to—"

"Yes, I did. It's the least I could do."

"The least you could do for what?" the firesmith apprentice said, bumping his shoulder into the back of Shylah's.

Durmad nearly squeezed the apple into sauce.

Shylah nudged back. "Nothing."

"Aidan, get back to the forges," barked the Master Firesmith.

"Yes, Sir." Aidan grasped Shylah's hand, bowed, and said, "Till we meet again." Then, he kissed her hand.

Durmad gritted his teeth and gave the apple a few more finger-sized bruises.

Shylah kicked the air behind Aidan as he playfully covered his backside and disappeared into the forge again. She faced Durmad. "How did you know I would be here?"

"I didn't."

"You sure you weren't following me again?"

He smiled and held up the apple. "Nope. Just stopping by to commission a new sword on my way to see Atlas. I had planned to bring the gifts to you at the workshop when I came to dinner tonight."

"Does your uncle know you are coming for dinner? I don't think he told Trulian to make extra."

"He doesn't know yet. You could—"

"No," she said, walking away. "I am not telling your uncle for you. That's your job."

He gripped her hand, spinning her back to face him. Her hair spun in the sun, but the red streaks seemed to swallow the light instead of reflecting it.

He frowned. "You're still depleted. You didn't rest last night, did you?"

She pulled her head back. "How did you?"

Wrapping his hand under her braid, he gently draped it over the front of her shoulder. "Your hair."

"My hair?" she asked, furrowing her brow. "You noticed my hair?"

"Of course, I am quite observant," he said, tapping the tip of her nose.

Her confused smile sent his skin humming again. He cleared his throat. "You need to take it easy today."

She shrugged and huffed. "Like your uncle will ever let that happen."

He tipped her chin up until their eyes met. "Shylah, you almost died yesterday. You need to take this seriously. Take your time getting back."

She stared up at him and bit her lower lip.

He shifted forward, but dropped his hand.

What are you doing?

He looked at her forehead. He did not need this distraction—not when Naamah would expect an answer.

His body flinched forward as a hand slammed into his back. "What can I do for you, son?" asked the Master Firesmith.

Durmad dropped his hand, saying, "I'll see you at dinner tonight." He faced the Master Firesmith. "I need a new arming sword."

The man, who stood three inches taller than Durmad with arms the size of Durmad's leg, rubbed his chin. "What's your timeline?"

"It's quick in case the Queen sends us back sooner," Durmad said, glancing over his shoulder. Shylah meandered through the crowd, smelling the wildflowers. Smiling, he said, "Ten days," and followed the smith into the forge.

CHAPTER TWENTY-SIX

SHYLAH

By the time Shylah returned to the workshop, Apollyon had finished all the elixirs he deemed worthy of his attention and retired to his office, leaving the entire workshop in disarray. Setting the flowers on the elixir table, she picked up the stack of elixir orders.

Six.

She sighed and finished off the rest of the roasted berry nuts. There weren't many orders, but even the thought of making one elixir drained her energy. Pulling her braid from her back, she examined the streaks of red. They were dull and faded, but Durmad had noticed.

She smiled, and he was coming to dinner. If she didn't get some rest, he would scold her again.

Flinging her braid behind her, she took the flowers into the kitchen. The kitchen was empty.

Where was Trulian?

Shylah'd expected to see her scurrying around prepping food.

Shrugging, she grabbed the vase from the shelf. As the water trickled into the vase, she glanced out the window. The reflection of Apollyon's charred chair in the other room pulled a snort from her nose. She would never forget the sound of Apollyon wailing about his precious chair.

Motion in the shadows of the back alley tore attention from the chair. Trulian turned back to face someone—a man with silver hair.

Shylah shoved the flowers into the vase and flung the back door open. "Trulian!"

The man disappeared, and Trulian waved.

"Who was that?"

"Who?" Trulian parroted as she turned back toward the kitchen door.

Shylah sighed and walked past her to look down the alley, but no one was there. "You know who. The man you were just talking to."

Trulian opened the kitchen door. "That was just a friend I share our leftovers with."

"You do what?" Shylah asked, following her sister into the kitchen. "You should not be talking to strange men in alleys."

Trulian's voice shook, "But Shy, it's so lonely just cooking and running errands."

"I care more about keeping you safe," she said, peering out the window. "Your loneliness will fade. Besides, Durmad is coming for dinner."

Her sister squealed and flung her entire body into a hug that nearly knocked the air out of Shylah's lungs.

Shylah smiled before forcibly separating herself from Trulian. "I have elixirs to finish before he arrives, and you need to prepare food."

Trulian spun and skipped through the kitchen doorway as she said, "I know just what to make for dessert. His favorite: blackberry buckle."

Shaking her head and sighing, Shylah hung her satchel on a hook and replaced it with her leather apron. The next four hours were filled with pulverizing, mixing, steaming, infusing, and distilling the remaining six elixirs. When she finished, she sent Trulian to deliver them and cleaned the workshop.

"You've made a right mess of this place," Durmad said, walking through the front door.

Shylah frowned. "This is your uncle's doing, thanks to your advice to take my time returning."

"If you were able to rest, I will gladly take the blame."

"Then give him all the blame instead," Shylah said, sweeping dried herb bits from the table and into her hand.

Durmad stepped beside her. "You didn't rest?"

She shook her head and wiped the cold sweat from her forehead. Part of her hoped dinner went quickly, so she could take his advice. Of course, she'd never tell him he was right. "No. I had elixirs and this mess to clean up," she said, pinching bottlenecks between her fingers like glass claws. It would be easier to take a bottle at a time, but then she'd have to explain last night to him. Faster was better.

The Yak oil slipped from between her thumb and forefinger. She tried to catch it, but the other bottles prevented her from doing more than deflecting it to the floor. As the bottom broke and the oil spread, she grunted, "Perfect." When she got this depleted, she got careless.

Durmad pulled the stool over. "Sit. I will clean up." He took the bottles from her hands. "Trulian, bring me a cup of hot water."

"She's out making deliveries," Shylah said, bending over to clean the spilled oil.

He put the bottles away. "Shylah, I will take care of that as soon as I get you some tea." He stepped away but pointed at her. "Rest."

Shylah nodded and closed her eyes. It was all she could do to stay upright. She heard Durmad rummaging in the kitchen but couldn't be sure how long he had been gone.

"Here," Durmad said.

She opened her eyes as he handed her a mug of steaming water. He pulled a small pouch from his waist and dropped a few pinches of dried tea into the water. The delicate honey scent mingled with the earthiness of the tea and spicy notes from dried blackberries. Inhaling deeply, she felt her lungs opening, and warmth traveled across her scalp, starting at the base of her neck. It felt like a warm hand caressing her skull.

"My mother drank this tea every day to help revitalize her ability. It's why there were so many honeysuckle and berry bushes near the cottage." He put a hand beneath the mug and slowly raised it to her lips. "Sip it slowly. And rest."

She nodded and took a sip. The warmth that crawled across her skull traveled down her throat as the liquid coated the inside. The tea had a dry, almost bitter flavor tinged with a faint tartness of blackberry that pulled at the back edges of her tongue before the delicate sweetness of honey and vanilla awakened every taste bud.

Shylah had finished half the tea when Trulian returned, nearly knocking Durmad over with the force of her hug. "Durmad!"

"Whoa, Tru. Careful, or you'll crush that note," he said, pulling back.

"Oh. I almost forgot. The castle guard gave me this for Apollyon when I delivered his wife's elixir."

Shylah slid off the stool, set her mug on the table, and reached a hand toward Trulian. "I'll take it to him so you can finish cooking."

Durmad placed a hand on each of her shoulders. She pushed back, but her energy was still low, and it was more of a lean than a push.

"Finish your tea. I'll take it to him."

"Fine. But only because he's your uncle, and I've done enough for him today," Shylah said, sitting back down as Trulian bounded into the kitchen.

Apollyon came barreling out of his office and down the main hall toward his stairs a moment later. Durmad leaned on the doorway between the office and workshop, arms crossed, and smirked.

Shylah raised an eyebrow. "What do you know?"

He shrugged. "Not much. Just that Liam and the Queen have invited my uncle to join them in the castle for dinner tonight."

Shylah smiled. "So, Liam wants another dose, huh?"

"Sounds like it."

Narrowing her eyes, Shylah asked, "You didn't have anything to do with this *invitation*, did you?"

"What, Trulian? You need my help," Durmad said, pushing off the doorjamb.

"She doesn't need your help. You're avoiding the question."

Durmad stood in front of her and leaned in, placing a hand on the table to either side of her. "That may be, but you can't stop me."

She pushed against his chest, which only served to pull a smile from him. He didn't budge. She wished she had the energy to shove him back or storm past him, but she didn't, and he knew it. "Fine. Go help her with some imaginary task."

He beamed. "I will. And you finish that tea and rest."

"Yes, Sir," she said, tapping her fist over her heart and bowing her head.

"Funny," he said, tweaking her cheek before he left the room.

The highlight of dinner was the blackberry buckle dessert. It was the one dish the three completely finished. Shylah would have licked the dish clean if Durmad hadn't done it first. It was like the few relaxed nights they'd spent just before Durmad had left for training.

Trulian stretched her arms wide, accompanied by an exaggerated yawn. "I'm tired. Don't stay up too late," she said and bounded down the back stairs before either could protest.

Durmad jumped up. "I won't stay long. You need rest, too, but you should drink another cup of tea."

Before Shylah could protest, he'd already filled her mug with hot water from the kettle on the hearth and retrieved the same pouch. He handed her the mug and leaned against the counter.

Shylah inhaled the steam again and closed her eyes. "Thank you. It really is helping," she said and took a sip. The warming sensation crawled over her scalp and down her throat again.

"It's the least I could do."

"The least? It's more than you need to. You don't owe me any-thing," she said, sipping the tea.

He sighed. "I owe you a lot. An apology for the immature torments of a self-centered boy, a goodbye since I left without one last time, a thank you for not holding it against me, and an apology for how my uncle has treated you in my absence. Tea is the least I can offer."

Shylah took another sip of tea. She didn't know how to react. She had held it against him when he'd first returned and not just one part—all of it. It had taken her nearly a year to get over him leaving them without a goodbye, a note, or a buffer between them and Apol-lyon. *How can I apologize for all of that?*

Without another thought, she blurted, "Trulian pushed me."

He furrowed his brow and tipped his head to the side.

"By the honeysuckle. She's the one who pushed me, not you," she added, taking another sip of tea.

Durmad crossed his arms over his chest. "Huh. So she can travel?"

Shylah nodded.

"But why would she push you?"

Shylah choked on her tea and coughed. She hadn't thought he'd wonder why.

He closed the distance and took the cup from her hand. "Are you alright?"

Still coughing, she nodded and, between coughs, said, "I'm —just —tired."

He rubbed her back with one hand and placed the other on her throat. Her airway immediately cleared, and the excess moisture that had entered her lungs evaporated. "You should rest. We can talk more later," he said, kissing her on the forehead before he left.

As the door closed, Shylah exhaled. She hadn't realized she'd been holding her breath. This was definitely a night for the sound, dreamless sleep of Lull. She couldn't trust her dreams tonight.

CHAPTER TWENTY-SEVEN

SHYLAH

The following day, Shylah mixed nearly fifteen elixirs before Apollyon joined her in the workshop with his cup of spiked tea and crusty bread.

"I see you are finally making up for yesterday's little side quest," Apollyon said, ripping more than biting off a mouthful of bread.

Shylah focused on the yak oil steeping in front of her. "That was your side quest. I was perfectly happy designing elixirs here. I am more than an errand girl, you know."

He harrumphed, sending bits of saliva-kissed bread all over the table.

Quickly covering the oil with a hovering hand, she glared at him. "This oil is nearly done, and I am sure you do not want to prolong Naamah's request." She tilted her head and added, "Sir," with as much contempt as she could get away with.

"Naamah? When did she send a request?" He scuttled over to the list of orders and rifled through them.

Smiling, she pulled the order containing Naamah's seal from her apron pocket. "I have it here."

He snatched it from her grasp.

"Her messenger brought it by an hour ago." Shylah shrugged, gingerly dipping the tip of her pinky into the steeping liquid. "You were still getting your beauty sleep."

You could use more, she thought, smelling the oil for potency and touching it to the tip of her tongue for consistency.

"Besides," she paused, relishing the silence and only continuing when she was sure he'd reached the edict at the bottom, "Naamah requested I design it, not you." Facing him with the sweetest smile she could manage, letting her tone drip with mock admiration, she added, "Sir."

His face shifted three shades of red, darker than his usual ruddy skin color. "Fine. Continue," he said, holding the order out for her. When her fingers neared the parchment, he let it fall to the table. "I'll be in my office since your incompetence at fire building burned my chair." He sighed, taking in the charred fabric speckled with white dust. "After you design Naamah's order, take care of that chair," he said, throwing open his office door.

"I don't think I will have time to move the—"

He slammed his hand against the open door. "Trulain can deliver the elixir. You can move the chair before finishing the rest of the designs."

Shylah's insides smiled at his frustration. She dropped her tone, heightened her pitch, and said, "You must not have read to the end. Naamah requested I deliver it. Something about a discussion of future plans."

His back stiffened. "Have Trulian take care of the chair then," he said, slamming the door behind him.

A giggle escaped Shylah's lips as she returned to her work, reveling in Apollyon's frustration and disdain for her growing abilities. Soon, she would not only surpass him but render his efforts obsolete. As the new Master Designer, she could protect Trulian completely. No one else would be able to threaten her at the expense of her sister.

She strained the oil.

No one except Naamah.

Her heart sank in her chest as the weight of Naamah's threat hit her. If she were the Master Designer, there would be only one layer of protection between Naamah and Trulian: Shylah. No matter how frustrated she got with Apollyon, at least he provided an additional buffer; as feeble a layer as it might be, it was still a layer.

She extracted the juice of a fire onion. The sticky liquid reminded her of the cave and seeing Trulian there. Shylah sighed and glanced at the office door.

Maybe I shouldn't be so quick to surpass Apollyon. If I am the Master Designer, what would Apollyon do?

Not that she cared about what happened to him, but, for better or worse, her fate was connected to Durmad's. He knew her secrets.

What if he reveals them to get back at me for his uncle losing his job?

Shylah glanced at the kitchen archway. She couldn't let that happen. Stirring the fire onion juice into the oil, Shylah took a deep breath. It wouldn't happen. After she delivered the elixir to Naamah, she'd make Durmad promise not to say anything about Trulain; this time, it'd be in the blood.

Forty-five minutes later, Shylah poured the completed elixir into a bottle and sealed the cork with wax. "Tru," she called to the kitchen.

Trulain's blue eyes peeked from beneath loose red tendrils as she entered the workshop.

"I'm delivering an elixir," she said, removing her apron and laying it across the table. "I need you to take care of the chair."

Trulain dusted her hands on her fabric kitchen smock. "What shall I do with it?"

Draping her satchel over her shoulder and chest, Shylah evaluated the chair. "We might be able to clean it," she said mostly to herself as she placed the elixir safely inside a smaller pocket. "Set it out back. If I can restore it, maybe he won't take it out of our pay."

"Right." Trulian gripped the back, tipped it on two legs, and dragged it toward the kitchen.

"Here. I can help." The two carried the chair to the back alley.

"I will be back for dinner," Shylah said, turning toward the street.

Trulian latched her arms around Shylah and said, "It will all work out." She quickly squeezed Shylah. "See you at dinner." Before Shylah could respond, Trulian bounded back into the kitchen and closed the door behind her.

"Okay, Shy. In and out," she whispered to herself as she snaked her way through the alleys toward Castle Lane. At the last turn, she paused and coached herself, "If you tarry too long, she will suspect you're hiding something." She clutched the satchel strap where it crossed her chest. "You can do this," she said a little above a whisper as if giving it voice would give her strength.

Shylah sucked in a deep breath and stepped onto Castle Lane, about a hundred yards from the royal courtyard. She swallowed hard.

The castle was a wonder of dark stone with high towers at each of the four corners and a fifth that sat central to the rest. It was said that each tower stood for each kingdom in Ethereal. The one to the North had bricks of unpolished gems around the lower edge of the turret, pointing toward the gem-rich kingdom of Agrandize. The tower to the South had the enchanted vines of the Tear Lace plant with its blue vines and leaves of gray and green. It flowed over the turret's roof like the water of the Cerulean Causeway in the kingdom of Castigation. Atop the East tower sat perched gargoyles, wyverns, and griffins with wings spread as if to take flight, but each faced the open sea where the Kingdom of Coruscation floated. The constant shifting and changing of the islands made it the perfect place for all the winged creatures of Ethereal to nest. The West tower lay barren except for a single, polished white stone at its turret peak. As the plainest of them all, it signaled the hidden kingdom of Pith. The tallest central tower and turret for the Kingdom of Dimmet itself cast the Pithian tower in shadow almost completely blocking it from the view of Morena citizens—unless they stood behind the castle or outside the walls.

Shylah always stopped beneath the Pith tower when she walked beyond the capital's walls. It was her dream to take Trulian to the one kingdom she knew Naamah could not go. The one place strong enough to resist the Queen's power and pull.

Pith's ability to resist the Queen was why she had begun sending the Green Willow Guard into Ethereal so frequently. She didn't need the resources of the other kingdoms—that was a ruse. But each kingdom possessed a hidden doorway to Pith. Shylah was sure the doorway was Naamah's real goal.

Shylah took another deep breath. The ebony stone of the central Dimmet turret cast its shadow within inches of her boots as if pointing to her, calling her out.

Deceiving Naamah when she was stashed away behind the moss-flecked stones of the castle was one thing; standing face-to-face with her was another. For a breath, she considered turning back and having Trulian deliver the elixir instead, but that would put her sister smack in the den of Dimmet's most dangerous lion. She couldn't do that.

Shylah flexed her jaw, and stepped into the shadow of the turret.

CHAPTER TWENTY-EIGHT

DURMAD

Durmad paced the hallway outside the throne room, pulling at his gloves. It had only been a few hours since Liam had woken him up with the Queens summons. They'd only been back two days. He still had over a week to give her his answer. *Why did she summon me now?*

He wiped sweat from his brow and readjusted his helm. *Did Jorden tell her about taking the horses out?* His pledge to support Jorden that night in the stables should have prevented that. He stopped. Unless he did it wrong, or a higher pledge of Jorden's would supersede his, like that of a son to his mother.

"Idiot," Durmad hissed at himself. *Why hadn't I thought of that before pledging?* It wasn't the same as a Bonding, but breaking a pledge could mean exile. He tucked his helm beneath the other arm and continued pacing.

He turned and took in the painting of Naamah and her sons. Naamah sat on the throne, a long black braid that gradually transitioned to a light azure draped over her left shoulder. Liam stood solid and tall behind her right shoulder while Jorden sat lower and near her left knee; the azure tip of her braid matched the azure tips of Jorden's waves. Liam's deep red hair transitioned to white at the tips like a white flame. If it weren't for the top of Jorden's hair, Durmad would have thought the two brothers unrelated, but the top inch or so of Jorden's hair was the deep red of Liam's and transitioned to the azure blue of Naamah's. It reminded Durmad of water dowsing a flame.

His eyes drifted back to Naamah's angular face and pursed lips between her sons and thought of Shylah. *Did Naamah know about Trulian?* His chest clenched, and his mouth went dry. *Would she demand his uncle turn over Trulian?* That would crush Shylah.

"Sir, Durmad," the guard called from the throne room door, "she will see you now."

Durmad nodded, took a deep breath, and strode into the large room. He stepped firmly on the black marble floor. *Be confident*, he told himself and schooled his face. *Don't betray your thoughts*. It took him thirty seconds to reach the base of the steps leading to the throne. He dropped to a knee and bowed his head, staring at the black floor with its veins of gold and red. The edge of the red carpet with its gold accents stopped before the last step, taunting any visitor to kneel on the cold stone floor as he waited to be acknowledged by the Queen.

As a new trainee, Duramd had tried to kneel with his knee suspended to avoid the pain of bone on stone, but Naamah had waited until his muscles shook, and he collapsed in a heap at her feet. She addressed him and the other trainees only when he had given up his fight, "Strength comes from discomfort and pain." She stood before him and continued, "But never forget that only I can restore your comfort. Stand." The trainees had all stood, but she hadn't moved. "It is my word, my command, that presses you or elevates you." Their eyes had locked. "Not your abilities." It had felt like she knew he could mute pain and was warning him not to do so in her presence. He'd never used his ability near her unless she specifically requested it during her training field visits.

Now, he knew to lean into the pain in his knee until she said his name. The edge of her dress fluttered at the top of his view, but his head remained bowed, eyes fixed on the mirrored surface of the polished black floor.

"Sir, Durmad, rise."

He did and fought the urge to rub his knee. The pain reminded him that he was not in control. "My Queen," he said and bowed his head.

Naamah remained in front of him, unmoving. Even her deep blue dress with long flowing sleeves hung frozen—not even Naamah's breath coaxed the fabric to move. Her solid control of the very air around her had unnerved him that first day. It was like she could turn everything around her into a ridged, uncomfortable stone. By the fourth or fifth time he'd been in her presence, his mind and body had normalized the sensation—until now. Now, he had something to hide; someone to protect.

She turned her back to him. "I see you have not made a decision."

"No, my Queen. I am still unsure."

She sat on the throne, and the light from the stained-glass windows on either side illuminated the black feather pattern of her dress.

His mind drifted to Shylah's Bonding mark, and he forced it out. He had to stay focused on the task at hand, or his thoughts could betray him. He did not want the Queen to have anything to use as leverage with him, and if his thoughts meandered to Shylah, he knew her sister would not be far behind.

She tilted her head. "I see."

His muscles tensed.

"Liam was right. Your heart is divided."

"My heart is committed to the service of Dimmet and the throne."

"Is it?" she said more than asked. "Then it should be easy to demonstrate your commitment through Bonding." She straightened the fabric draped over her legs. "It is not a one-way commitment, you know."

"I know, my Queen."

She smiled and leaned into the throne back. "The throne will always provide for you, unlike your uncle." Her face squished as if a skunk had been provoked and sprayed the entire throne room. "You will be second only to Liam in my Green Willow Guard, and your family will be my family."

Durmad bowed his head. "You are a gracious Queen. I still have time to decide, do I not?"

"You do."

The throne room door opened, and footsteps echoed across the stone. Durmad straightened and kept his eyes on the throne.

"Ah, Designer. You have my elixir, I presume."

Durmad's muscles tensed. *Designer? Surely, my uncle wouldn't come here. No. She said Designer, not Master Designer.* His mouth went dry, and he couldn't swallow. *Shylah.*

He let his eyes relax, focusing on the throne, and concentrated on his periphery. Shylah bowed beside him, angling her face in his direction at the valley of her bow. She stiffened and shot upright. The tension seeped from her muscles, and he knew she'd recognized him. He bit the inside of his front lip. *What was the Queen playing at?*

"Yes, my Queen. I can return after you finish," she said before spitting out, "with your Green Willow Guard."

He didn't have to see her to see the disdain on her face. He could hear it in what she said as much as what she didn't.

"Nonsense. You may give it to my guard, and I will send him with payment."

Durmad faced Shylah, who shot daggers at him with a smug grin. "Thank you, miss," he said, holding an open hand.

Her smile retreated from her eyes, and she placed the bottle in his hand with such force that he almost dropped it. Then, without a word, she spun and walked the length of the hall. Despite her efforts, he heard the doubt and anger beneath every determined step.

Naamah waved him up. "Take this payment to your uncle." She placed a bag of coins in his hand. "But this," she produced a silver box the height and width of four fingers with a lid encrusted with feathers carved from black motion wrapped around blackberries made of black and purple sapphires. The vines and leaves, too, were crafted from motion, but the thorns were small shards of black opal. "Fill it for her," Naamah said with a nod over his shoulder and toward the throne room doors.

He furrowed his brow, looking from the box to Naamah. "With what, my Queen?" He didn't have enough coins to fill the box. Naamah must have known that. After all, she was the one who established pay levels. *What could I put in the box?*

Naamah grinned. "Oh, Durmad, you disappoint me." She spun the feather ring on her index finger. "Is she not the one tugging at your loyalties?"

Durmad opened his mouth to speak, but his words evaporated. *Did she hear my thoughts? Or did she know some other way?* "I."

Naamah chuckled. "Your lack of answer says it all. Remember, loyalty without a commitment is like a feather without a bird," she removed the ring from her finger and held it before her face. "A strong gust blows it to the farthest reaches of the world." She slid it back on her finger. "But if it's connected to the bird, it can conquer the wind, defying the forces that would pull it down." She stood and stepped to within inches of Durmad. "You were made to conquer the wind, to soar. Not to be manipulated and controlled by the wind."

She placed a hand on each of his shoulders, sending a shiver through his body no matter how he tried to control it. "I need your help to ensure the infection that took your parents does not spread to all Ethereal."

Durmad's fingers tensed around the box at the thought of anyone else watching their parents' bodies destroy themselves from the inside. The blood tears falling from his mother's eyes still haunted his nights.

Naamah's expression hardened. "Pith has remained complacent, letting us suffer when their headwaters would have cured your parents. My ability to contain the infection is waning."

Durmad's eyes widened. "Contain? But you cured it."

"I wish that were true. Only the headwaters can cure it, and Pith hoards it for themselves."

The corners of the box pressed through the thick leather of his gloves as he clenched his fists. *How could anyone knowingly doom anyone to the death my parents experienced, let alone an entire kingdoms?* His nostrils flared, and his breath became shallow.

"I share your anger." She turned her back and ascended the steps to the throne again. "I am trusting you with this information as a show of good faith. Liam is the only other person who knows the truth about the infection." She motioned to the throne room doors. "Now go, fill the box, weigh your choices. I expect your answer in two days' time."

He tucked the box away in his satchel. "Thank you, my Queen," he said, bowing before turning on his heels and exiting the hall as quickly as decorum allowed. Once the doors closed behind him, he abandoned decorum and ran through the castle halls. Servants and guards shot warning looks at him, but he didn't care. He had to catch Shylah.

Running down the front steps, he saw her near the stables. "Shylah," he yelled, taking the steps three at a time.

CHAPTER TWENTY-NINE

SHYLAH

She didn't have to look back to see who had called her name. Quickening her pace, she darted around the corner of the stable. The last thing she wanted to think about was why Durmad was standing before Naamah, let alone why he was wearing his guard armor. Of course, that was all she could think about. She needed to get back to the workshop. Designing always distracted her, and she needed to be distracted. She spun left, but Durmad blocked her exit into the side alley.

"Shylah," he said, chest heaving. "We need to talk."

She stepped around him. "I need to get back to work. I have a lot of elixirs to design."

Again, he blocked her path. "It's important, and the only elixir that mattered to my uncle was the one you just delivered."

"I need to get back to Trulian." She stepped, but this time, he countered. She darted to the other side, but he was faster. "Durmad," she said, crossing her arms over her chest. "Let me pass."

"After we talk."

She shifted her weight to her back foot. "Fine. Talk."

He shifted slightly, letting an old woman pass, and glanced over her head. "Not here. The tavern."

"What?"

He grasped her wrist. "No one will question us in the tavern." He glanced behind her again.

"Who are you?" She turned to follow his gaze, but he started walking down the alley. "Durmad."

He didn't respond or look back. Part of her wanted to yank her hand free, but her skin prickled with the anticipation of his touch despite his glove. Durmad was right. Apollyon would ask her if Naamah had another order, but he wouldn't question how long she was gone. She could at least hear him out.

They ducked into the Even-tide Tavern, and Durmad guided her to an empty table near the back stairs. She sat in the chair he pulled out for her. She expected him to sit across the table, but he dragged another chair around until they were within a breath of each other.

"I was called on guard business. Naamah needed to ask me a question about my training."

"Training?"

Before Durmad could answer, the bar wench sidled over and leaned her hips toward him. "Can I get you a drink, handsome?"

Shylah curled her toes in her boots, pressing her fingers into the tabletop. The wench's flirting posture and tone made Shylah's skin crawl.

Durmad waved her off without looking at her, saying, "Fire Onion Juice."

The wench straightened, frowning as she rolled her eyes. "Right away, Sir."

Shylah pressed her lips together, pinching back the smile. "I don't think I trust you with Fire Onion Juice," she whispered.

He backed away. "What?"

Blast. Did I just try to flirt with him?

She should have known she'd be no good at it. "Fire Onion Juice."

He looked at her with a blank expression.

She sighed. "When you told me it was medicine."

His eyebrows raised. "Oh." He chuckled, a smile briefly softening his expression before he leaned in closer and returned to a serious tone. "Naamah wants my assistance with a delicate matter. It had nothing to do with you or Trulian."

She stiffened at her sister's name.

The wench returned with two mugs of Fire Onion Juice. Shylah watched as the woman smiled and set one down in front of Durmad before glaring at Shylah and dropping the second on the table. The mug nearly tipped over, but Durmad held it upright.

"I'm sorry, Sir. Let me help," the woman said, pulling a rag from between her breasts.

Durmad immediately raised a hand. "I'm fine. Leave us before you spill on more than my gloves."

The woman spun around and stormed back to the bar. Shylah's chest warmed; she didn't fight the smile this time. As soon as the woman reached the bar and glared back at their table, Shylah let the smile stretch even wider, giving the woman a wave before gripping the mug with both hands and drinking off a third of the pungent liquid in a single breath.

Durmad removed his gloves and shook the Fire Onion Juice to the floor. When Shylah returned the mug to the table, Durmad covered her hands with his. Electricity shot through her, pulling her attention back to him.

"Shy, did Trulian say anything last night?"

She froze, not sure she could trust him. Pulling the mug and her hands from his grasp, she drank another third of Fire Onion Juice. The cooling sensation shifted to a slight burn with the second gulp before hitting her stomach like a flaming stone.

After setting the mug down, she wiped her mouth with the back of her sleeve and met his eyes. His emerald gaze fixed on her, she responded without thinking: "Yes."

Her eyes landed on his green-plumed helm beside his gloves.

No.

She couldn't tell him about Trulian. He was one of them—loyal to Naamah—no matter what he said. Their eyes locked again. At that moment, she saw the tenderness she'd seen at his family cottage. She quickly finished off her mug. If she was going to tell him what Trulian said, she had to stop overthinking.

When she set down the empty mug, Durmad smiled. "Developed a taste for Fire Onion Juice, have you?"

"No. It's still awful."

"Liquid courage then," he said, his smile dissipating. "You can trust me."

She leaned forward, making the breath space between them even smaller. "Can I? Can I really, Durmad?" Her eyes darted to the green feather at his elbow. "The Green Willow Guard took my parents. They burned them alive. Did your training include that history?"

He recoiled. "Uncle said wyverns destroyed Baylon, and the guard rescued as many as they could."

Shylah studied his face. He looked genuinely surprised.

But how could he be?

"Did you not wonder how the Green Willow Guard was able to respond so quickly or why it was only Baylon and not the whole countryside? We were not more than a morning ride from Typhon." She felt the flames of the Fire Onion Juice rise in her chest. "Or why it was only young girls that were saved? No boys? No adults?"

"Why didn't you say anything?"

"Who would I have told? You?" Shylah grabbed her mug and drained the final few drops.

"Yes, me. Or uncle."

Shylah couldn't control her laughter. "Your uncle wouldn't have cared. He doesn't care now." She reached for Durmad's mug, but he pulled it back, spilling some on the table. "And you. You were too busy torturing me and doting on Trulian."

Durmad leaned in closer. "I didn't torture you. Tease, maybe, but torture? You're being dramatic."

Shylah slammed her fists on the table. Her empty mug bounced, tipped, and fell to the floor, but she didn't care. "I had just heard my parents burn alive, been taken to a strange country I didn't know by the very people who burned them, only to be thrust into the care of a cold-hearted man and his calloused teenage nephew." By the end, she was yelling.

She hadn't intended to tell him all that but felt a lightness she hadn't expected. At least until the silence hit her, she saw the faces turning toward her. Her chest tightened, and she held her breath as her eyes darted from one confused face to another.

Durmad picked up her mug and held it toward the wench at the bar, who quickly retrieved it. As she neared the bar again, the patrons returned to their conversations, and Shylah finally released her breath.

"I didn't..." Durmad ran his hand through his hair.

Shylah flattened her hands on the table, wishing she could crush it into a pile of splinters. "I wasn't even fifteen."

Durmad covered her hands with his. "Shy, I'm sorry.

The warmth of his hands on hers spread up her arms and across the front of her chest. Her heartbeat and breathing slowed, and the burning of the Fire Onion Juice began to subside. She thought about freeing her hands, but the calm pushed out her fight. Her shoulders sagged. For a long moment, she stared at the backs of his hands that completely covered hers. In spite of his warming touch, his calloused and worn hands felt heavy and rough on hers, even more than she remembered in the cave. Of course, then she had been so self-conscious and nervous that she'd kept her eyes closed for most of his healing. She hadn't noticed the pinkish-white scar running from the base of his left middle finger to an inch past his wrist like a worm rising to the surface of wet sand.

She freed her left hand and ran her fingertips over his scar. "How did you get it?"

His hand tensed. "Training."

She looked up at him, leaving her fingertips on his scar. She said nothing –only looked into his eyes.

He pulled his gaze from hers and shifted it to her hand on his. With a sigh, he said, "It was a test. To see if I truly could manipulate the cells of the body."

She furrowed her brow. "A test?"

He pulled his hands back and drank his whole mug of his Fire Onion Juice. Shylah pulled her hands back to the edge of the table.

He must need his own courage to answer that question.

Empty, he raised his mug and tipped his head toward the bar before setting it on the table's edge.

Shylah smiled at the small line of foam above his upper lip.

"What?"

"You drank so fast, you left some behind," she said, pointing to her own lip.

He wiped his mouth as the same woman who retrieved Shylah's fallen mug arrived with two freshly poured mugs in exchange for Durmad's empty one. He took another drink before setting it in front of him and slowly turning it in his hands.

Shylah took a drink from hers but kept her eyes on him.

He rubbed his mouth with one hand and said, "After six months of training, the commander called me and Liam to his tent." Durmad took another drink. "He put a Cartwheel plant between us and told Liam to kill me with it."

CHAPTER THIRTY

SHYLAH

Shylah sucked in a breath.

"Liam is a Cultivator, like you. While you are an Augmentive-Cultivator or as you call it a Distillate, and you amplify natural qualities, he is an Impel-Cultivator."

"Wait. He can manipulate them?"

Durmad nodded and took another drink. "He made the thorns grow to the size of knives in seconds, and each oozed poison." He made eye contact with her. "Shy, I've never been so scared."

She didn't know how to respond. Durmad, the trained knight who saved her life by running into acid rain, was scared. What's more, he admitted his fear to her, *but why?*

"He sent a thorn at my shoulder. My training kicked in, and I mostly dodged it, but not completely. It cut through my gloves and the back of my hand." He made a fist with his left hand, sending a flash of white through his scar. "He would have sent more thorns if the commander hadn't stopped Liam. The commander wanted to test the strength of my ability. It took me a week to completely heal the wound because so much poison had entered it." He flexed his hand, spreading his fingers wide. "That's why there will always be a scar. The longer it takes for me to heal the wound, the more permanent the scar."

Shylah took another drink. "Why are you so close to Liam if he tried to kill you like that?"

"He was the one who told me I needed to touch the wound with my other hand until I trained my ability. Liam was only doing what he was commanded."

"He could have killed you."

"But he didn't. He stayed by my side until it was completely healed and helped me hone my ability afterward. He even helped me experiment with throwing it like he did the thorn. And I mastered it." Durmad grinned and leaned in again. "Don't you see? That's why you can trust me. I can protect you and Trulian. I can make a person's insides bleed."

Shylah's mouth dropped. Knowing he could kill someone so easily didn't make her feel safer. It was the opposite. She fought the urge to bolt out of the tavern, take Trulian, throw consequences to the wind, and swim across the Astra Sea back to Castigation. "But Naamah isn't just anyone."

"No, but I can't help if I don't know what's going on."

She took another drink. Her body felt as if every fiber was floating. Licking her lips, she focused on his scar. "I could kiss it."

"What?"

Shylah's focus snapped to Durmad's face. Had she really said that out loud? "What?"

"You said something, but I couldn't hear you. I think you said something about a kiss."

Her brain whirled, groping for anything to explain away what she said. "Trulian knows about our kiss."

His eyes widened as his smile grew. "Talking about it already, are you?" he said, fishing off his drink.

"What? No. She dreamed it."

His smile faded. "Dreamed it?" He leaned back, and his eyes searched the ceiling.

Every muscle twitch and face tilt told Shylah he was trying to piece together all the information. Maybe he wouldn't figure it out, or he'd be forced to return to training before he could, she thought.

He leaned in closer and whispered, "She's a Peripatetic."

Shylah nodded and finished off her drink.

"But it's more than just dreams. She was actually there in the cave, wasn't she?" he said, still in a whisper.

Shylah glanced around the tavern. No one looked their way or seemed to be paying attention to them. She took a deep breath and told him what Trulian had said the night Shylah thought she was an intruder, including the strange man who had trained her to overcome the Quiescence. When she finished, she scanned the tavern again. No one paid them any heed. She focused on Durmad again, who sat in stunned silence.

"She must be an Evocative then. She not only dreams of the future, but she can travel to it." He scooted his chair forward and leaned closer. His lips brushed her ear, sending chills down her neck as he whispered, "And impact, maybe even change it."

He sat back. Without his breath, her ear twitched, and goosebumps cascaded down her shoulders. "But what about the man? The bonded? I've only ever seen one other bonded man, and he was the one who watched over us and the others."

"Others? I didn't realize. I mean, I only met you and Tru."

"There were about fifteen of us, but I don't know what happened to the others. They divided us up at the man's house."

"Did you know the others?"

"Trulian knew more than I did. Most of the girls were closer to her age. I only knew Althea and Josephine, because we had lessons together." Shylah pictured all the girls huddled in the man's kitchen. They had all huddled together, crying into hands and shoulders. Tears pooled in her eyes; this was why she avoided looking back into this room – into that night. It was why she used the Lull herself, but now, seeing every bent head and huddled mass of clothes, she realized what they all had in common besides the awful fire. She placed a hand on Durmad's arm and said, "We all had red hair."

"What?"

"All of us. We all had red hair, slightly different shades, of course, but it was all red. I don't know why I didn't realize it sooner."

"I do." Durmad huffed. "You were young, had just lost your parents, and the only home you'd ever known. Your mind was trying to process and cope, not analyze your surroundings. It happens to us in battle training, too. You focus on the big threats and react. It isn't until you have years of battle experience that your brain starts to see the small threats."

She nodded. Knowing Durmad didn't fault her and that he understood emboldened her. "So what do we do about this man? We can't let Tru train Naamah in her Peripatetic skills. Right?"

Durmad stood, grabbing his gloves, he put them inside his helm and tucked it under his arm. "Let's get you back to the workshop."

Dazed by the sudden shift in topic, Shylah followed him into the back alley until he spun around, and she nearly ran into his chest just past the tavern's back door.

"Keep designing elixirs like nothing has happened." He looked over his shoulder as two women walked around the corner. Shifting, he blocked her from view and added, "Keep everything normal."

He cupped her face in his hands, and she held her breath. "I'll ask around about this bonded man. That way, if I am caught, you will still be insulated. I can make up a story about seeing him in the market or something." He brushed a hair from her forehead.

"Durmad."

Shylah knew that voice; it still echoed in her mind from dinner, but Durmad dropped his lips to hers before she could react to Abaddon's presence. Shylah's breath caught, and her muscles tensed. His hand slid from her cheek to the hair behind her ear. Her skin warmed and tingled in response. She should pull away. She was a Bonded.

He cradled the nape of her neck with one hand resting the other on her hip as his helm bounced at her feet. She closed her eyes. His warm breath gently tickled her skin while his tongue caressed her lips. Her muscles relaxed, and the Fire Onion Juice drowned out her mind. But her body told her brain it didn't matter, and she pushed herself up on tiptoe, returning his kiss.

Abaddon said something, and Durmad's body pressed hers into the wall just before he pulled back, glancing at the tavern's back door.

Her lips quaked at his absence, and her body shivered.

He turned to her and whispered, "I will protect you and Trulian. Trust me."

She nodded slightly and wrapped both arms around his neck, pulling his lips back to hers.

Her hands slid down his chest. The image of him standing tuni-cless in the cave flashed through her mind. She wanted to feel every muscle. His muscles flexed beneath her touch. Her body remembered the warmth of his hands as they healed her burns—as they touched her. She wanted to touch him. Her lips parted, and he slid his tongue between her lips. Light exploded across the back of her eyelids.

Drawing in a breath, his spiced scent was like the perfect elixir. He pulled her closer, deepening the kiss. She wanted him to carry her away, away from Dimmet, away from Apollyon, away from Naamah.

Naamah. Trulian.

Her brain pushed out the Fire Onion Juice and seized control of her body. Shylah pulled away.

What are you doing?

She was here to protect Trulian. She wiped her mouth with one hand, and the other smoothed her skirt. She looked at his emerald eyes. Mistake. They peered at her from beneath a questioning brow. She knew the question, and there was no way she was answering it. She wasn't even sure she knew the answer, not entirely anyway. "I. Trulian. I need."

He grinned and kissed her forehead. "I'll see you tomorrow." He retrieved his helm from her feet and headed back toward the tavern.

Shylah finally exhaled when he disappeared through the door. The slightest grin tinted her face. She'd missed his heart all those years ago, but now she saw every pinch, prank, and touch differently. She floated all the way home. For so long, she'd been Trulian's sole protector. The weight of the truth, of lying, of hiding had taken its toll, but now she had someone to share that weight.

CHAPTER THIRTY-ONE

DURMAD

His body buzzed all the way back to his room. She'd trusted him. She'd told him about Trulian, and what's more, Trulian was an Evo-Peripatetic. The possibilities collided in his mind. She might be able to tell him how to get back into Pith or how to cure the infection. She could help make sure that Jorden didn't share their secret.

Entering his room, he tossed his satchel on his pillow, removed his helm, and placed it on the small table beside his bed with his gloves. He flopped onto his bed and rolled onto his back. Finally, she trusted him.

"You look happy," Liam said, following Durmad into the room. Durmad tensed.

"I take it the meeting with my mother went well."

Durmad sat up. He'd been so consumed with his own thoughts that he hadn't seen Liam standing in the hallway. Durmad's boots hit the wood floor.

"Or was it that kiss?"

"What kiss?" Durmad said as he searched his memory for how Liam would know he kissed Shylah. His searching stopped at Jorden. Durmad felt the Fire Onion Juice bubble in his stomach.

Liam chuckled. "You really need to do a better job checking shadows in alleys. I didn't think you'd forget all your training so quickly."

"The alley? You mean, just now? Did Abaddon say something?"

"Of course, just now. Unless…" Liam leaned onto his knees and raised an eyebrow. "There is another kiss you haven't told me about."

"What? No. Of course not. I mean." Durmad cleared his throat and walked to the small chest of drawers near the window. He needed to put his back to Liam. Liam could always read his face, and he couldn't give away that he was hiding something. "I haven't had time to do more."

"Sure you have. Typhon knows Abaddon has."

Durmad removed his bracers and set them on the dresser before moving to the pauldrons over his shoulders. "I'm not Abaddon."

Change the subject.

He glanced over his shoulder. "What are you doing lurking in alleys anyway?"

Liam snorted. "You're changing the subject."

Durmad ignored him and started removing the greaves from his shins.

"Does she know about the Bonding?" Liam asked.

Bonding. That's right. This is my chance.

"I've never seen a Bonded man. Would I be the first? Or are there others?"

"Most are Willow Guards and a few remain close to my mother. I think a few even live here in Morena. My father was Bonded to my mother as she was to him. But since –the only men I know of are married to someone who was already Bonded to my mother, or like you, receive promotions in her Willow Guard."

Durmad leaned the greaves against the side of the drawers. "So what? The ones who stay behind and marry, do they have to be Bonded to Naamah in order to marry? Or does she choose that, too?"

Liam shrugged. "Not sure. Like I said, there aren't many."

"Are there any guards who are married?" he asked.

Liam leaned forward on his knees. "Not that I know of. Why?"

Typhon Toes, too much.

"Just trying to understand what I am walking into. It seems strange that there are so few married Bonded. Doesn't it?"

"Not really. Since my father's betrayal, she's been anti-anyone and anything that could distract her from her goals. The Bonding secures loyalty, or it's supposed to anyway. I guess it didn't do that with my father."

"Why didn't you tell me this before?"

"When would it have mattered?"

Durmad unbuckled his leather chest piece. Surely, Liam wasn't that forgetful. "When you said you could compel Shylah to bed me."

Liam chuckled again.

Durmad hated the nonchalant way Liam approached life, especially that chuckle. His fingers itched to punch something. Instead, he scowled as he turned his back to Liam and removed his remaining armor. He had to keep his cool if he was going to get answers for Shylah—for himself.

"I thought you just needed to get her out of your system. You know, try the forbidden fruit and refocus on your training." Liam crossed the room in five strides. "I had no idea she meant anything to you. Had I, I would have led with that part." Liam set a hand on Durmad's shoulder. "Regardless, I need you as my second, so I may have an idea."

Durmad had to find the man training Trulian first. He backed away and sat on the edge of his bed. "Where can I find one of these bonded men? I'd like to talk to him before I make my final decision."

Liam half sat, half leaning on the edge of the drawers. "I'm pretty sure one of them lives in the castle. At least he did before we left for training."

"Has he been bonded long?" Durmad asked. He had to find the old man Shylah described. He was most likely the one training Trulian.

"I think he was bonded about two years before we went to training. Why?"

Curses. Not long enough.

"Time usually equates to wisdom. I just figured someone who'd been bonded for a while would give stronger guidance."

Maybe age wasn't the key. Shylah said the man's feather was behind his ear.

"Where would the mark go if I decide to, which I haven't yet?"

"I'm not sure. Each one is in a different location. Always the same feather, but not always in the same spot. Why?"

"No reason. I wasn't sure if the markings were the same for men. I thought maybe we didn't notice the Bonded men as much because it might be somewhere like his chest, back, armpit," he kept his eyes glued on Liam as he added, "or maybe behind his ear."

Liam stiffened and narrowed his eyes. "Why would you ask that?"

There was something significant about behind the ear. Who was the old man to Liam?

Durmad's heart raced. "You know, since we don't see that many, I thought it might be that the mark is in a less conspicuous place." He kept his eyes on Liam, gauging whether he was still walking the line of curiosity or if he jumped clear off into suspicion.

"No. My mother's marks don't go behind the ear. Not anymore." Liam strode to the door. "I have a meeting with my brother." He walked halfway through the doorway before turning back. "If Shylah is more than forbidden fruit, you should tell her what you've been offered. I'm staying at the castle tonight. See you tomorrow." Then Liam shut the door.

Durmad listened until his footsteps faded. Then he counted to one hundred before finally sighing. Bonded men could be married to a Bonded. Naamah hadn't said he needed to be married to anyone.

Would she force me to marry? Would it even be allowed since I'm a Willow Guard? And what about her husband's betrayal?

She'd been the single Queen her entire rule in Dimmet. It made sense that she had been married—she had two sons.

But what was the betrayal, and where was he now? Liam had said not anymore. *So, what changed? Why didn't the Queen's Bonding mark go behind the ear?*

His mind was drowning in more questions when he'd hoped to gain answers for Shylah—for himself.

Flopping back flat on his bed, his head landed on the satchel. Pain flashed white across his vision, and the back of his head throbbed—the box.

He quickly pulled out the box Naamah had given him.

Fill it. What can I fill it with?

It had to show Shylah he was grateful for her trust and reinforce that she could trust him. Liam's last words rang in his ears. Durmad would tell Shylah what he'd found out about bonded men and Naamah's request of him. Maybe, as a Bonded man, he could still care for and protect Shylah. It might even make it easier. She had opened up to him; he would open up to her.

He opened the box.

But what should I put inside?

It had to mean something. He chuckled. Fire Onion Juice wouldn't fit in such a small box. It was too small, even for a Fire Onion.

Biting Strobilus blooms? No.

That would take too long to retrieve, and there was no guarantee that the plants they harvested milk from would still be in the cave.

He jumped up, grabbed his satchel, and ran out the door. He knew exactly what to put in the box.

CHAPTER THIRTY-TWO

SHYLAH

Shylah woke the next morning with an excitement she hadn't felt since she was a child, conspiring with her childhood friend, Kieran. They'd plot pranks aided by his Aerify ability. He would become one with the air and breath, making it possible to float around Baylon unseen. The two of them had done everything together.

Since the day she arrived on the shores of Dimmet, she'd imagined him in the breeze. She spoke into the wind, sharing her heart, fears, and secrets. But no matter how much she wished or imagined, he, too, had fed the flames of Baylon.

But now, with Durmad, she felt breath on her skin again. For the first time, she didn't carry the burden of Trulian's secret alone.

Who would have thought Durmad would be my co-conspirator?

She smiled at the thought as she dressed. He'd be able to question people without suspicion, or at least less suspicion than if she did. Grabbing her apron from its hook and her boots from the foot of her bed, she pictured Kieran floating on the breeze again. Kieran would approve of her conspiring. She took a breath so deep that she felt it travel to her fingertips and toes. Kieran would approve of Durmad.

Carrying her boots, she walked to the kitchen steps, imagining what she would do or say when Durmad appeared again. Maybe he was already there, waiting for her. The anticipation jump-started her feet. She took the stairs two at a time, her skirts hiked and flying around her knees.

The kitchen was empty. Still in stocking feet and gripping her skirts, she bounced into the workshop. It was empty. Her shoulders fell as her skirts dropped to her ankles. She leaned against the elixir table and slid on her boots.

He could arrive now, she thought and snapped her head back to the kitchen. Disappointment weighed on her smile. Or it could be dinner time before he reappeared. He had only said *tomorrow,* not when.

What if he asked too many questions to the wrong person? What if he was caught and wasn't going to come?

Her smile flattened.

What if he changed his mind? No.

She couldn't think about it. She needed a distraction: Designing. It always gave her focus and made the time pass quickly. She picked up the top elixir order. It was a salve for joint pain and gout. She retrieved the yak oil, devil's claw, stinging nettle, blood cherries, and beeswax and set all the ingredients on the bottom shelf.

Before Shylah could grab the pestle and mortar, Trulain popped her head into the workshop. "Morning, Shy. Want a biscuit and blackberry jam?"

Shylah smiled at her sister, but she wasn't really seeing Trulian. Her mind was in the blackberry field again with Durmad. They were picking fresh berries and feeding each other.

"Shy. Shy?"

"Huh?" Shylah shook her head. "What did you say?"

Trulian grinned. "Do you want me to make you breakfast?"

Shylah shook her head. "No. I don't think I can eat anything right now." The butterflies were already filling her stomach. There was no room for anything else. "Maybe after I design a few elixirs."

"Okay," Trulian said, tying her apron.

Shylah gripped the mortar, but before she could move more than lifting it, a knock sounded on the door. She set it back down as the smile bloomed across her face. Her heart pumped blood to her cheeks twice as fast as normal, and she walked to the door.

Opening it, she said, "Durmad, you don't have to knock at your own door. You can just..." Her voice disappeared like breath on the wind as her eyes landed on six armor-clad Green Willow Guards. She searched for Durmad's emerald eyes but only saw pools of darkness staring back at her. "You're not Durmad."

"No. We need the Master Designer."

The first guard pushed in through the front door, shoving Shylah aside and almost knocking her over.

"I'll get Sir Apollyon," Trulian said, disappearing into the kitchen.

The Green Willow Guard, who'd shoved Shylah aside, removed his helmet. Abaddon. He walked past the fireplace. "I see you removed the chair."

Shylah rolled her eyes. "Yes. No need for a tattered chair to remain. We discard tattered things all the time." She crossed her arms over her chest, waiting for him to look her way before she frowned.

He chuckled without looking in her direction and continued his jaunt around the workshop, fingering herbs and oils. His hand moved toward the stinging nettle.

"Don't touch that. It will sting you."

He faced her, a smile cracking his façade. "You do care." He sighed, and the smile quickly turned to a frown. "But you address me as an equal." He stepped toward her.

Shylah's chest tightened. She stepped back several steps until the solid mass of another guard arrested her backward progress.

"Little bird, I am not your equal."

She should have let him grab the stinging nettle. Maybe it would have stung some of the cocky creep out of him. It was probably the only way he'd learn not to touch things that weren't his if that was even possible with someone like Abaddon.

"My apologies, Sir." She sidestepped him. "Can I get you some tea, Sir?" She barely got past the elixir table when he grabbed her arm, spinning her to face him.

"You're fast," she gasped. His frown shifted to a leer, and she immediately regretted letting her thoughts take form.

"That's why they call me Caracal on the battlefield."

Battlefield, what battlefield?

All he'd done was train. She imagined him running at the first sign of resistance and fought the urge to laugh in his face.

"I already had my morning tea, little bird." He licked his lips. "But I was called to duty before I had time to eat."

She pulled and twisted her arm, but his grip only tightened. "I will get you a biscuit, Sir."

"I prefer pheasant for breakfast. You know what pheasant is, don't you?" He leaned forward and inhaled deeply near her temple.

She glanced at the other guards over his shoulder. None of them moved. The one who dared to look her way stood grinning. She clenched her jaw.

What did I expect from men trained to do someone else's bidding?

"Mmmm. You smell like earth. I could fall asleep to that."

Her mouth went dry. She searched for something to fight with, but nothing was on the elixir table. She hadn't started designing yet. The fireplace was too far away, and the table stood between them and the herb shelves. She only had one option—stall.

"Yes. I know what pheasants are. They are beautiful creatures but difficult to hunt. You must be a skilled hunter if you can catch them and still maintain your training, Sir."

He straightened, puffing out his chest. His grip loosened slightly but not enough. He needed to relax more, and false flattery was working.

She softened her tone, "I bet you even cook it yourself to ensure no one destroys the tender meat, Sir."

Glancing past him, she asked, "Has he ever made this breakfast pheasant for you, his brothers in arms?"

He smirked. "They aren't ranked high enough for that."

"Oh." She thought about Liam's reaction at dinner. "You must have made it for Liam, then, Sir. I'm sure he enjoys a breakfast pheasant and would hate the meat being destroyed just as much as you, Sir."

That hit the mark, and he loosened his grip more.

Apollyon came barreling into the workshop from the hallway near his office.

Shylah took advantage of the distraction, ripping her arm free, and darted to the opposite side of the elixir table. Squaring, she kept it as a barrier between her and Abaddon.

Apollyon bowed to Abaddon and the other guards. "How can I be of service to Naamah's Green Willow Guard?"

"We have come for the girl."

Shylah tensed. They said girl, not designer. She edged toward the kitchen.

"Surely, Naamah would not deprive me of my apprentice. What do you need her for?"

"Not your apprentice."

Shylah's heart stopped. They were here for Trulian.

Apollyon, furrowing his brow, said, "I don't understand. What would Naamah want with a useless cook?"

"It is not my place, or yours, to question Naamah's commands." He laid a hand on the pommel of his sword. "Where is the girl?"

"Trulian," he yelled, "our guests request your presence."

Trulian entered the workshop, drying her hands on her apron. "What can I..."

"No," Shylah interrupted, bolting to the kitchen entrance and tucking Trulian behind her.

Trulian rested a hand on Shylah's back and whispered, "I'll be alright," then stepped out from behind her sister.

Abaddon grabbed Trulian's arm and pulled her toward the front door.

Shylah darted around the opposite side of the table nearest the herb shelves and gripped his other arm. "You can't take her. I'll do anything. Take me. Just leave her alone." Her fingers slid down the slick leather until she yanked off his glove.

He turned on her. "As tempting as that is, little bird. I have my orders. Naamah demands her orders be followed."

Looking over his shoulder, he said, "Take her," and pushed Trulian to the guards behind him before adding, "I'll be needing my glove."

Time slowed. Shylah didn't think. She reacted. She grabbed the bundle of stinging nettle from the herb shelf. Ignoring the pain, she lept at Abaddon, smashing the leaves against his face before he could fully turn back around. It was a mistake. The back of his bare hand, aided by the momentum of his turn, connected with her cheek.

The force sent her to the ground. She used her right arm to brace herself. Another mistake. Her wrist snapped. She whimpered and cradled it.

Abaddon grabbed her wrist, yanking her to her feet.

Pain seared through her, and everything flashed white. Her whimper turned to a howl.

"Oh, little bird. See what happens when you try to fly." He snatched his glove from her hand. "Sweet dreams," he said, twisting her wrist.

Pain pulsed through her entire body, escaping on the wings of her scream.

He released her, and she dropped to the floor in a heap. Shadows circled her vision, and everything pulsed in time with her heartbeat, pushing the shadows further into her vision. She reached her arm for Trulian. Her final mistake. Another wave of pain shot through her, and the shadows consumed her.

CHAPTER THIRTY-THREE

DURMAD

Durmad popped another blackberry in his mouth. Yesterday, he'd spent the afternoon collecting dried blackberry fruit left behind by the birds and other wildlife, the leaves still clinging to the canes despite their lack of life and honeysuckle blooms from the bushes that cradled the blackberry brambles. He'd also collected enough fresh leaves and flowers to fill a medium pouch next to a basket of fresh berries for Trulian.

He opened the lid and smelled the dried honeysuckle and blackberry tea he'd collected. The sweet earthiness reminded him of Shylah. In truth, most things reminded him of her. Every animal stepping on twigs or dried leaves at his family cottage made his heart skip until he remembered Shylah wouldn't know how to get back there, so it couldn't be her walking around.

Every alley reminded him of kissing her when he'd returned late last night. He'd reimagined each kiss, each touch, each look in his mind when sleep eluded him. Instead of the goodbye kiss on the forehead, he imagined kissing her lips again as he lifted her off the ground. The alley disappeared, and when he set her down, she sat, not on a stool in the workshop but on the fence outside his family cottage. He'd finally fallen asleep, picturing Shylah standing at the cottage door as he returned from training.

But now, it was time to deliver the box to Shylah. He tied a piece of string around it, securing the lid closed, then placed it and the pouch of fresh flowers and leaves in his satchel. He tossed one more blackberry in his mouth and headed out.

The market was in full swing, and the crowded streets slowed his progress. Children darted between people, and he nearly flattened a bladesmith avoiding two boys playing wyvern tag. Helping the man collect his knives, Durmad picked up an herbalist sickle with two feathers carved into the handle. "How much for the sickle blade?" he asked the man with stormy gray eyes that seemed to swirl around the center.

The man grinned. "Yours. A thank you for your help."

"No. You should be paid for your handiwork." Durmad fumbled for coins in his satchel. "How do ten sovereigns sound?" he asked, producing ten silver coins the size of a small fig, but the old man was gone. For a moment, Durmad would have sworn that he was just ahead of him in the crowded market, but every time he tried to follow the bouncing gray head, another young boy would knock him just enough off course that the old man slipped away. He returned the sovereigns to his satchel pocket and added the herbalist sickle beside the box.

Standing at the back door, Durmad took a deep breath. He hoped his uncle would be sleeping for another hour so he'd have time to talk to Shylah alone, but he was prepared with a story about delivering a message from Naamah in case he wasn't. Walking into the kitchen, he expected to find Trulian preparing lunch. But the room was empty. He would have thought everyone was still sleeping if not for the biscuits on the counter with butter and an open jar of jam beside.

"Trulian?"

No response. He set down the basket of blackberries and tightened the beeswax cloth on the top of the jam. He'd never seen Trulian leave food out like that. Something didn't feel right.

He thought, smirking, that maybe Trulian was sick and Shylah had been in charge of breakfast. That would explain the haphazard mess. Shylah was very neat and organized with her elixir ingredients, but her dedication to designing meant she was easily distracted.

He stepped into the workshop. "Shylah, can we? That's strange. Nothing's on the table. It's as if she hasn't started designing yet." He turned toward the hallway. "Uncle? Anyone?"

A moan came from the floor behind him, and he spun to see Shylah crumpled on the ground. In one swift movement, he pulled the satchel strap over his head, set it on the elixir table, and knelt by Shylah.

"Shylah. What happened?" He grasped her hands to pull her up. She screamed and pulled her hands back. A bump protruded from her right arm, two inches above her quickly swelling wrist. "Your arm is broken. Let me help."

She twisted her arm away from him. Standing, she said, "No. I'm fine. I need to..." Wavering, she almost fell back down, but Durmad caught her shoulders. She hissed through her teeth.

"You are not fine. Let me help you. I will heal it, but I need a closer look."

She hesitated.

"Please."

She leaned against the table, nodded, and gingerly stretched out her arm.

Durmad rested his hands beneath it. "Bones are different than the skin. I will need to feel where the break is." He wiped a tear from her cheek. "This'll hurt, but I'll try to work fast." He pulled the herbalist sickle from his satchel, ensuring the blade was secured in the handle. "Here. You may want to bite down on this."

He watched her place the sickle between her back teeth and nod. Taking a deep breath, he hovered his fingertips above the bump, barely touching her skin. She inhaled sharply. He pressed a little harder. The bump was too hard to be swollen tissue.

She whimpered, and his heart clenched.

He had to reset the bone before he could heal it. Setting it with only his ability would be less painful but prolonged. He could focus all his energy on knitting the tissue and bone back together if he manually set it. The faster he could do that, the faster the pain would stop. He'd seen grown men pass out on the training field when he reset bones.

He lifted her onto the table and moved his satchel out of the way. "You need to lie down."

She nodded, still gripping the folded knife in her teeth.

Durmad lifted her ankles and gently swung them onto the table as she laid flat, resting her right arm across her stomach. He placed one palm beneath the break and one over the bump. "Shylah, this will hurt, but I need you to fight the urge to pull your arm away."

Shylah closed her eyes.

"Do you want me to count?"

She shook her head no.

He squeezed the bone back into place. A muffled scream escaped her clenched teeth as her midsection lifted off the table. One second, her entire body was ridged, and the next, it was slack. She'd passed out.

Glancing around the workshop, he wondered where his uncle was. Surely, he'd heard the noise. Shylah's breathing grew ragged. Durmad pushed the thought of his uncle from his mind and focused all his energy on healing her arm.

CHAPTER THIRTY-FOUR

SHYLAH

"Shylah," Durmad's voice caressed the darkness. His hand brushed against her cheek, and she turned toward it. Her eyes opened against the resistance of crystalized tears at the corners. His blurred face took form. Smiling, she breathed in the dream of him, and raised her arms to pull him to her. The throbbing in her right arm and stiffness in her back brought his face into sharp focus as the memories flooded into her conscious mind.

"You have to be careful with your arm. I healed it, but it will be sensitive for a few hours."

"You!" she said, pushing him away and jumping off the table. "What have you done?"

Durmad frowned. "Your arm was broken."

Glaring at him, she demanded, "Where is Trulian?"

"Trulian? I don't know. I came in, and you were in a heap."

"Where did they take her, Durmad?"

"Who? Shylah, what are you talking about?"

"Abaddon. Where did he take Trulian?" She stepped to move around Durmad, but he blocked her. "I have to get her." She stepped again.

Durmad gripped her by the shoulders, holding her in place. "Shylah, what are you talking about?"

She glared at him. "Abaddon took Trulian." She squirmed, but he gripped her tighter. "But you already knew that, didn't you?" She pushed against his chest, but he didn't move.

"I have no idea what you're talking about."

"Do you think I'm daft? The only reason half a dozen Green Willow Guards would come for Trulian is if you told Naamah. I can't believe I trusted you. Maybe I am daft to think someone like you could change."

Durmad flinched. "I didn't tell anyone about Trulian. I wasn't even in Morena until early this morning. I went back to the—"

"I don't believe you. I should have known you'd manipulate me. I'm still just some toy to help you pass the time, aren't I?" Shylah twisted more violently, but his grip only tightened.

"I don't think—"

"Let. Me. Go," She raised her knee to his groin.

Durmad immediately released her and turned, bracing himself on the elixir table.

She pulled her apron off and tossed it on the table.

How long have I been passed out? Trulain could be anywhere.

She had to find her sister before Naamah did anything to her.

Shylah unceremoniously pulled out the bottom drawer of the elixir cabinet. Ripping her money pouch from its hiding spot, she discarded the drawer, letting the contents spill onto the floor.

"What are you going to do? Try to bribe Naamah?"

"Yes." Shylah jumped up. Durmad stood within inches of her.

"She doesn't need your money." He pulled his satchel from the table. "She's the ruler of Dimmet. Shylah, you're not thinking straight."

Shylah squared her shoulders. "Then I'll promise to design whatever elixir she requests."

Durmad huffed. "You already have to design whatever she requests."

Shylah's jaw clenched. "Then I won't design for her anymore."

Durmad held up her left arm. Her sleeve slid down, revealing her bonding mark. "You don't have a choice."

She yanked her arm free. "I don't care. I have to find Trulian."

"No. I will find her. You have to stay here." He reached into his satchel.

Taking advantage of his distraction, she shoved him. "I will not." He remained an immovable wall between her and the front door. She'd have to go through the kitchen. She darted to her left between the table and herbs.

Durmad launched himself over the table and gripped her left arm inches from the door. "Fine." He pulled her down the stairs. "You are leaving me no choice."

They reached her bedroom door. She would not be locked away. Before he could completely open the door, she flung her entire body against it. He yanked on it, and she flung her back against it again. "I will not stay here."

"Won't you," he said, releasing the doorknob.

She smiled. She'd beat him, but her smile faded as he grabbed her waist and hefted her over his shoulder. "Put me down," she yelled, slapping his back and flailing her legs. "I'm not a child."

"Then stop acting like one," Durmad said, throwing her onto her bed.

The impact knocked the air from her lungs, and she gasped. She pulled herself to her knees, ready to spring off the bed and out her door but stopped. Durmad stood in the doorway, a silver box held in his right hand.

"After you left yesterday, I filled this for you." He slammed the box on the small dresser beside the door and retrieved a pouch. "I am not the one who told Naamah about Trulian," he said, tossing the pouch next to the box and closing the door.

Shylah heard the click of the lock and sprang to the door. "Durmad! Let me out of here." She pounded on the door.

"I did not betray you."

"Then let me out."

"No."

"Durmad." She hit the door.

No response.

"Durmad," she yelled and hit the door again.

Still no response.

"No," she screamed, "let me out." She pounded on the door. "Durmad!" Tears burned her eyes, and her arm ached, but she didn't care. She had to get out of the room. "Let me out!" She heard the floor creak above her head. "No. Durmad." Grabbing the silver box, she threw it at the wall. It broke open, spilling dried honeysuckle flowers, dried blackberry fruit, and leaves over her bed and floor. She turned her face to the ceiling. "Durmad."

The workshop door slammed.

Shylah screamed, collapsing onto the floor. Tears streamed down her face.

How could I have trusted him?

The Green Willow Guard never kept their word.

Why would Durmad be any different?

Her tears slowed as her despair gave way to anger. She clenched her skirts in her fists. She was not some vulnerable child incapable of protecting herself. She was an elixir designer and a damn good one. She'd kept herself and Trulian safe for three years without his help. Everything was fine until Durmad came back. The anger boiled over. She angled her face to the ceiling again. With as much venom and disdain as she could pull forth, she spit out, "I will kill you!" She knew exactly what elixir would do it.

CHAPTER THIRTY-FIVE

DURMAD

The workshop door slammed behind him, and Shylah's scream reverberated through the small lower-level window of her room. He squeezed his eyes shut. He hated locking her in the room, but she had to stay put. If she went tearing into the castle, she'd make things worse. It would have been helpful if she'd calmed down enough to tell him how long they'd taken Trulian or where his uncle was.

With a shake of his head, he started jogging down the street. She may not have been able to tell him anyway. Time moved differently when someone passed out. He'd seen knights lose whole days while healing. The time didn't matter. He had to get to the castle as quickly as possible. Ducking into Castle Alley, he broke into a sprint.

The fastest route was behind the stables, but his anger flared as he turned the corner, and the stables came into view. Abaddon leaned against the stable wall, helm under his arm, surrounded by several adoring guards. Shylah collapsed on the workshop floor with a darkening bruise on her cheek flashed into Durmad's mind. He willed his legs to move faster, clenching his fists tighter as he closed the distance between him and Abaddon.

"You bastard!" Durmad yelled. Before Abaddon could do anything more than turn to face him, Durmad punched him square in the face. Abaddon flew back, and Durmad straddled his chest, pinning him in place.

"Where is she?"

Blood was flowing from his nose, and Abaddon coughed. "What in the blazes?" He swung a fist at Durmad, who blocked it and followed with another punch.

"Where did you take her?" Durmad punched again, but his fist stopped inches from its target as a guard grabbed each arm and pulled him off Abaddon.

Durmad shook them off. "Release me."

Abaddon rolled over and lifted himself to all fours. He touched his nose and inspected the blood. "She's with Naamah." Pushing himself back until he sat on his heels, Abaddon spit blood near Durmad's feet and smiled, blood outlining each tooth. "Naamah wanted you to be the one, but you were missing. Probably bedding that little designer." He spit again and drew one foot up as if proposing to Durmad. "So imagine my surprise when that little morsel tried to stop me." He chuckled and bent over his knee to stand as he said, "Of course, she couldn't."

Durmad kicked Abaddon's head, knocking him flat. He leaned over the unconscious man. "That's for Shylah."

The guards stepped toward them. Durmad glared as he turned. "No one touches him. Do you understand?" The men glanced at each other. Durmad stepped forward, and each man stiffened. "If any of you touch him, move him, or help him in any way, your next training bout with me will be your last. Do you understand?"

The guards backed away in silence. Once they all dispersed, Durmad turned back to Abaddon and spat in his face before taking the castle steps two at a time.

Dodging servants and more soldiers, he shoved aside the guard just outside the throne room and burst through the doors without an announcement or permission. It could mean death, but right now, all that mattered was returning Tru and proving to Shy that he hadn't been the reason for her sister's abduction. He could stand Shy's anger at pranks and leaving, but the vacant loathing he'd seen when she woke up and remembered that a Green Willow Guard had taken her sister was more than he could take.

Six of his fellow guardsmen surrounded him within ten feet of the doors. "Let me pass. I am sure she knows I am here or assumed I would be," he said, pushing through the ring of guards. One happy side effect of his ability was that most guards feared he would use it on them. He wouldn't, but their fear and doubt served him now.

Durmad's steps faltered, and he held his breath as he saw Trulian. She was not alone. Jorden sat beside her. The two sat on a chaise lounge beneath one of the massive stained-glass windows depicting an indigo wyvern perched on a cliff. The winged beast's gaze focused directly on Trulian as she sipped tea beside Jorden with two Green Willow Guards behind them.

"Durmad, I expected you sooner."

Naamah's voice snapped his attention back to the throne, and he closed the remaining ten strides in two breaths before taking a knee.

"Durmad," Trulian's voice floated to his ear. Glancing at her under the guise of his bow, he saw Jorden holding her back. He knew she wanted to run to him, but he dropped a hand to keep her back. She relaxed, and Jorden removed his hand from her forearm.

"I came as soon as I could. One of your guards damaged your Elixir Designer, and I had to heal her."

Anger pinched Naamah's eyes briefly. Liam had reacted similarly to the threat of Apollyon causing Shylah harm at dinner. Durmad couldn't reconcile their personal treatment of Bonded with the apparent anger of anyone else doing the same.

"I will have Liam take care of the guard," she said, relaxing her eyes again.

"It's already been done," he said, standing.

"Good," she responded before sitting in silence. Her breathing was the only sound for several agonizing minutes.

Durmad let his focus drift to the corner of his gaze. Trulian appeared to be unharmed. "Why have you collected Trulian?"

Naamah picked at the fabric of her dress. "You may go see her if you wish."

He didn't need another invitation. Quickly kneeling before Trulian's feet, Durmad asked, "Are you alright?" He inspected every inch of her he could see. "Did they hurt you?" he asked, glaring at the two guards behind her while searching with his ability for internal or unseen marks of harm.

Liam leaned forward. "I know what you're doing, and you won't find any. I told you, we don't harm our Bonded."

Durmad stood with clenched fists and glared at Liam. "Why did you need Trulian?"

Naamah walked to Trulain's side and tucked the strand of hair that had fallen from Trulian's braid behind her ear. "Jorden requested that she come."

"Let her return to her sister, and we can talk. She offers no value to you."

Naamah clicked her tongue. "Each of my Bonded has value simply because they are bonded to me." She ran her hand down Trulian's red braid. "Just look at how Jorden appreciates a companion his age. It has been hard on him to have Liam gone for so long."

Durmad wasn't sure if Naamah really knew her son. He watched Jorden's smile tighten like a mask under his mother's doting words. Naamah faced Durmad again, and every muscle tensed as her fingers gently wrapped around Trulian's braid.

"Besides, she does make for a grand bargaining chip."

CHAPTER THIRTY-SIX

SHYLAH

After screaming herself hoarse, Shylah paced her small room, contemplating the best poison to use on Durmad. She could use thelyphonid venom. He'd be weak from vomiting for a week. Or she could knock him out for three days with fennec blood slipped into the Fire Onion Juice.

No. Not strong enough.

He'd betrayed her sister, betrayed her, and then locked her in her room to go galivanting through Morena.

She kicked the silver box across the floor. It hit the leg of her bed, and the lid broke off, sliding under Trulian's bed. Sick and weak were not enough. The Green Willow Guard had taken Trulian. There was no going back.

She stepped on a dried honeysuckle flower and squished it into the ground as if killing a bug.

No. He doomed Trulian.

He deserved much worse than being inconvenienced, but most poisons would do just that because of his vacuole ability. She needed something she could hide and would work fast enough that the damage would be done before he could counteract it. He'd told her about Liam's attempt to kill him in training camp, so it had to be something he didn't see coming and something stronger than the sap of a Cartwheel plant.

But what?

Whenever an elixir puzzled her, Shylah cleaned. She swept the spilled honeysuckle and leaves into a pile and put the broken lid and box back on her dresser. There had to be something that would cause him as much pain as he'd caused her. It had to make his heart shatter like hers. She straightened her blanket and lifted her pillow. That's it. Grabbing the vile of Biting Strobilus Milk, she sat on the edge of her bed. She could hide it beneath the sticky sauce of honey cakes. By the time he realized the sweetness was more than honey sauce, it would be too late. The Biting Strobilus Milk would eat away at every cell it came in contact with, too many cells for him to fix, she was sure.

A smile crawled across her face as she tipped the bottle and watched the thick white liquid slowly slide down its neck. It was poetic, too. Sliding the bottle into her waist pouch, she stood. She had the what; now, she needed the how and the when.

The door flung open with a bang.

"You bastard, how —" she stopped mid-sentence. Aidan stood holding a metal bar. Her fury shifted to relief, and she hugged him around the neck.

He pulled himself free and turned, saying, "There's no time. Hee—she said to bring you to the forge."

Shylah gripped his forearm as he turned. "Who?"

"Josephine. She told me where to find you," Aidan said, gripping her wrist and pulling her into the hallway.

She dug in her heels and yanked him to a stop. "I haven't seen her in over two years. How did she know? How do you know her?"

"Do you want to save Tru or not?" He released his hold and jogged down the hall, turning back at the base of the back stairs. "Are you coming?"

He knew about Trulian. No matter who told him to get her, he might know where they took her sister. Shylah broke into a run, and he scaled the stairs two at a time. Aidan darted out the back door, and it was all she could do to keep up with him. Standing at a table pulverizing and mixing ingredients didn't build running stamina, and after darting around a few corners, the first cramp sent a knife stab through her core. It took all her will to stay upright and keep pace with the firesmith apprentice.

Questions burned in her mind, and she used them to distract from the pain permeating every breath.

How did Aidan know Josephine, and if she'd been in Morena this whole time, why hadn't I seen her? Had Aidan seen Trulian taken to the palace, or had he overheard someone?

So many contradicting scenarios played in Shylah's mind that she skidded to a stop just beyond the door when they finally reached the forge.

What if Trulian had traveled to Josephine—to Aidan? How can I cover that up?

A man's hand grabbed her wrist and yanked her through the doorway.

It took her eyes a few seconds to adjust from daylight to the forge lit by two coal forge fires and a single window. The large barn doors that slid open during working hours remained closed. Shylah scanned the forge floor for Josephine, or at least what she thought Josephine would look like after three years. Josephine wasn't there. Aidan stood just behind the older man with stormy gray eyes who pulled her through the door.

Shylah yanked her hand free and backed away. "Where's Josephine?"

Aidan stepped forward. "He told me to tell you she wanted you. He didn't think you'd come if he sent for you."

"He's right." She turned to leave only to find the old man standing in her path with hands raised. "How did you?" Shylah's chest tightened as she took several steps backward. She had to get out of here, but she'd only been to the forge a few times, and the barn doors had always been open.

Where was the back door? Was there even one?

Her breathing shallowed until her back ran into Aidan.

He wrapped her in a hug. "It's okay. I trust him."

Shylah squirmed, but one thing being firesmith apprentice did was make a boy strong. The more she squirmed, the tighter his arms pressed around her. "Good for you, but I don't trust him." The old man nodded, and Aidan released her. She turned to face both and quickly scurried behind an anvil. "Now, I don't trust you."

"Thank you, Aidan. You may leave."

"Now, wait a minute. Just because I don't trust him doesn't mean I want to be left alone with you," she said, pointing at the old man.

"If I remain over here, will you listen to what I have to say?"

Shylah glanced between Aidan and the old man. The idea of being alone with a strange man, let alone one who was bonded, was unnerving. "I need to find my sister."

"I am here to help Trulian."

She glared at Aidan. "Did you tell him my sister's name?"

The old man stepped into her line of sight, placing Aidan behind him. "The young man told me nothing. I came to him and elicited his help in retrieving you, so we could keep Trulian safe."

"I can take care of my sister. I don't need your help."

The old man's gray eyes swirled, and Shylah was certain they glowed briefly. "Then where is she now?"

"With the Queen. Which is why I have to get out of here. Why I need to find her." The tightness from her chest crept up her neck and pulled at her tongue. She squeezed her hands into fists. She would not let herself panic. She would not give up. She would not cry. And she would not trust a stranger.

"I'm not a stranger."

Shylah stiffened.

"I knew your father. Like me, he was from the kingdom of Pith."

"You're lying." she glared at Aidan over the old man's shoulder. "Do you think this is funny? Are you so bored you need to play a trick on me?"

"He's not," the old man said and turned to Aidan. "Wait outside the door."

"No! Don't leave me alone with this lunatic," she said, but Aidan only nodded at the old man and closed the door behind him.

The old man walked to his left, and Shylah stepped to hers, keeping the anvil between them the entire time. He sat on a stool beside the filing table. "I'm not lying, although I understand the confusion. Did you never wonder why Pith was a real place to your father, but everyone else in Baylon treated it like a myth? A bedtime story for children?"

Shylah furrowed her brow.

No, I'd never thought about it.

It was just how her father talked about it. No one else pointed it out, so she never thought twice about it. Then, when she came to Dimmet, nearly everyone connected to the Queen treated it as a real place.

Why would I doubt that?

"I never doubted my father."

The old man smiled. "That's good, because he knew. I imagine that Pithian blood runs through your blood, through all the girls taken—Naamah can sense it. She only seeks to bond with those of Pithian descent."

Shylah shook her head. "Why would my descent matter to the Queen? I'm not even the strongest Distillate."

"All the more reason why it is your connection to Pith she is after and not your ability. Pithian blood is the only way she can return to the headwaters and," he stood, "she must not get there."

"I can't help her get to Pith. I don't even know where it is."

"You don't have to. She does. Our children were born there, but it will take more than them to help her return. Only those with Pithian blood can bear the key."

Shylah's anger shifted to confusion. "Does the Queen have secret children? Everyone knows the prince's father died from the infection before she became Queen."

"The people know what she tells them."

"That doesn't prove you are the dead would-be king. Not to mention the fact that you're standing in front of me right now."

The old man returned to sitting. "I am a powerful peripatetic and have been traveling through the memories and dreams of all Ethereal just beyond her reach."

Shylah snorted. "Right. That's even harder to believe than–" Before she could finish her comparison, the old man disappeared from the stool and materialized directly behind Shylah. She jumped over the anvil, but her skirt caught on the horn, and the large block of wood it was strapped to fell with her. She yanked her foot from beneath the edge of the anvil, grateful it had only hit her two smallest toes, and scrambled backward.

How had he disappeared and reappeared so quickly?

She'd never seen Trulian do that. The cave and shove at the cottage popped into her mind—*until three days ago.*

"You." She scrambled to her feet. "You're the one training my sister."

CHAPTER THIRTY-SEVEN

SHYLAH

A grin spread across his face. "I knew you'd figure it out before long." Her conversation with Trulian echoed in her ears.

He wanted Trulian to train the Queen in her peripatetic ability, but why? Why not train her himself? It made no sense.

"You say the Queen must not return to Pith, and yet you want Tru to train her to do whatever you just did. I don't have time to do whatever it is we're doing." She pushed herself to stand. "I have to get my sister before Naamah discovers she can travel."

"Trulian knows to train our child and no one else. The Queen does not want Trulian for her ability. Not yet, anyway. She is merely a pawn in the Queen's chess game with you and the guard."

"What guard?"

"The one you plan to kill."

Shylah froze. "How did you—I'm not planning to kill anyone. I can't protect Trulian if I'm dead, and the Queen would kill me if I killed a guard."

The old man walked around the anvil with the agility of some-one half his age. Of course, Shylah didn't know exactly what that would be. "That is why you must not do it. You will put everything in jeopardy if you try to poison him."

Shylah gritted her teeth and stepped toward him. "He betrayed us. He deserves to die."

"He did not betray you," he said, touching her left forearm.

She pulled her arm back, or at least her brain told her muscles to pull her arm free from his grasp, but her arm refused to move. Then, the tingling started around her wrist. The more she fought it, the more it turned from a tingling to a burning itch. "What are you doing?"

"I will show you."

"Show me what?" she asked, kicking her leg out before it, too, went limp and dropped back to the ground. Her heartbeat quick-ened as her neck tensed, pulling her ears back, and she flared her nostrils. "Let me go," she said.

"You must see."

The dark circles formed at the edge of her vision and slowly grew, blacking out her sight.

Breathe. Just breathe. Don't panic. Breathe.

She took deep breaths despite her racing heart. The blackness stayed for a split second, but at that moment, she felt her heart stop and the weight of her body evaporate. As the blackness receded and her vision was restored, she stood outside the castle stables—the old man still gripping her arm.

Abaddon leaned against the stable wall, laughing with other members of the guard. Shylah gritted her teeth.

"Abaddon! I'll kill you." She ran at him, hands finally gripping his neck, but before the life left his eyes, she was ripped back. He remained casually laughing.

A guttural scream ripped from her gut. "Where is she?" Gripping the pouch tied to her waist, she pulled out the bottle of biting strobilus milk. She lunged forward, smashed it into the side of his face, and waited to see the holes begin to riddle his smug grin. But, again, she was ripped back. He remained unharmed and the bottle sat fully intact in her pouch.

"You are here, but you cannot interact. You can only watch."

"Watch what?"

The old man pointed down the alley as Durmad rounded the corner. In a blink, he closed the distance. As Abaddon's eyes flew wide, Durmad punched him square in the jaw with so much force that the stunned soldier's helm flew free, and he lay on his back in the dirt and straw.

"Yes!" Shylah yelled and punched the air.

Durmad dropped onto Abaddon's chest.

"Where did you take her?" He punched again, but the other guards dragged him off.

Shylah gritted her teeth and repeated the question in her thoughts as Durmad shook himself free. As Abaddon spat blood and responded, the Queen's name reached her ears, and Shylah's heart stopped.

Trulian was the one place where Shylah couldn't protect her.

The world began to spin. The old man's grip tightened, and he whispered, "Not yet. Watch and listen." With a yank of her arm, she focused again on Durmad, whose foot swung directly into Abaddon's head. The man flew back again, but this time, he lay motionless as Durmad leaned over him and said, "That's for Shylah."

The words made her ears tingle and her cheeks twitch as a grin spread across her face. He'd taken revenge for her and was searching for her sister. Her chest relaxed, and her breathing slowed until he turned toward them. She held her breath and turned as he ran past. Again, she told her muscles to move and to follow him. She had to be there when he found her sister; she knew he would. Something deep in her gut warmed; he would find Trulian.

Despite the lightness surrounding her soaring thoughts and heart, she felt heavy, as if she were melting into the ground like a block of ice left in the sun for too long. The darkness came faster, but she still tried to fight it until the moment her eyes flew open and the forge came into focus. The old man released her arm, and she spun to face him. "What sorcery was that? Take me back. I have to find Trulian."

The old man raised his arms. "You will find her when you let go."

"Let go of what? You aren't making any sense." She stepped back and ran into the anvil she'd been using as a shield. "What did you just do? How?" she asked, pointing behind her.

"We traveled."

Shylah squinted back at him. "Travelers can't transport people, so what was that? Was it even real, or do you have some ability to make me see things that aren't there?" She sifted through every-thing she'd just witnessed. It seemed real until she tried to intervene herself. Maybe it wasn't real. Maybe Tru wasn't really with the Queen. Maybe she was somewhere else, but when Shylah tried to imagine where the else might be, she had to acknowledge that the Queen was the only logical place for her sister to be.

"Why do you say a traveler cannot have a passenger? It won't be long before Trulian can do that for you."

The realization hit her again that the old man was training Trulian to overpower her elixirs. The man responsible for her nearly dying twice in as many days. She pointed her finger at him and said, "You are the problem –not the solution, you arrogant troublemaker. Tru can't train anyone to travel, and you're forcing her to fight my elixirs, my ability, to fight me." Dropping her hand to her pouch, she grinned and added, "Maybe you're the one I need to kill."

The old man raised his hands. "I am only here to help and protect. I see that has run its course with you, so I will leave."

"Oh no, you don't," she said and lunged forward, but all she grasped was air. The old man disappeared.

Her scream echoed through the empty forge, and Aidan flung open the door. "What's wrong? Where'd he go?"

Shylah darted at him and shoved him back against the wall. "You. You lied to me and for what —a stranger."

"He said he knew your father, and Trulian introduced us, so I figured you—"

"You figured wrong," she said and punched him in the gut. It barely phased him, but it made her feel better. Her fists really wanted to connect with the old man's stomach, but Aidan was there, and the old man was not.

"Shylah," he said, squeezing her shoulders. "You need to go back to the workshop."

"Not a chance," she said, ripping herself free of his grasp and sprinting out the door. The night had already touched the horizon, and the streets lay mostly empty. Everyone was either in for the night or headed that way, but she knew where Tru was —the castle.

CHAPTER THIRTY-EIGHT
DURMAD

Durmad, locking eyes with Jorden, asked, "A bargaining chip for what?"

Had he told his mother?

Surely, Naamah would not have been hinting at a bargain for her release if he had. Jorden only smiled and tilted his head.

Naamah grinned, "You surprise me. I thought you were much quicker," she said, walking to a window on the opposite side of the throne room.

"Quicker? Are you testing me again?" he asked, slowly standing. "Is that why you took her from her sister forcibly or why I had to heal Shylah, who was passed out on the floor of the workshop? If you send your Green Willow Guard to hurt defenseless female Bonded, I will never willingly give you control of me."

"She is hardly defenseless, but I did not give orders or permission to harm. They were only to bring Trulian here. Are you sure she didn't do it to herself?"

He spun and glared at the Queen's back. "Why would she—no, she did not break her own arm, punch herself in the face, or knock herself unconscious from shock. Your dog did that."

Naamah stared out the stained-glass window. "And who do you suppose is my dog?"

"You sent Abaddon to collect Trulain; who else would I assume was the only guard willing to do your dirty work?"

"I understand you are upset, and you have a right to be, but take care that you do not create an unhealable rift in your anger." She glanced over her shoulder, making eye contact as she lowered her voice. "Abaddon will be dealt with, and he will never rise above Knight Bachelor." Waving him over, she added, "Come."

Durmad glared at Liam, who quickly took a sip of his tea and glanced out the window, effectively avoiding eye contact.

That might save him now, but I will find out why Liam didn't tell me about the Queen's plans, or why he hadn't gone to collect Trulian.

He stepped to Naamah's side. The fading sun cast an eerie light through the colored glass, and slivers of green, blue, and red divided Naamah's pale skin into harsh angles accentuated by her sleek black hair pulled back and intricately braided down her back. The light made the black beaded veins on the arms and bodice of her gown look like fingers reaching for her heart.

"Did you deliver the payment?"

"What? Oh. Yes, my Queen."

"What did you fill it with?"

"What?"

"The box. What did you fill it with?" she asked, then began walking to another window closer to the throne room doors and further from the group sipping tea.

Durmad followed. "My mother's honeysuckle and blackberry tea."

"Interesting. And she liked it?"

"I don't know." Durmad thought back to Shylah, who was locked in her room. He wasn't even sure she'd speak to him when he finally released her, let alone appreciate tea.

"That's too bad," Naamah said, stopping in front of the stained-glass window depicting a black wyvern with blue eyes. It shot its icy breath toward a tree divided into five main branches that each grew different colored leaves. "I had hoped she would help you make your decision."

My decision? How could Shylah help me make my decision?

"I have not told her of your offer."

"I see. And what have you decided?"

Durmad looked over his shoulder. Naamah said Trulian made a good bargaining chip. Maybe she would accept a trade. "You could have sent for me. There was no need to take Trulian," he said.

"Ah, yes. You would have come, but you would not have given me an answer."

"If you demanded an answer, I would give you one. You are my Queen."

"An answer, yes, but not the one I desire."

Durmad furrowed his brow.

How could she be so sure I wouldn't give her the answer she wanted?

Until he walked into the throne room, he didn't know what answer he would give.

"I have my ways, and you should know that by now; however, you didn't know. You did not know how deep my desire went or how your Bonding would truly benefit you."

Did she just read my mind?

He glanced at Liam again.

What was the Queen's true ability?

Perhaps her own children didn't even know. He turned back to the smiling Queen. "I still don't think I see that," he said.

"As my Knight Commander, you can ensure no other guards harm your family because all those Bonded to the throne are family. You would also have the power and ability to punish anyone who went against any order you gave." She faced him. "I also knew Trulian would be the strongest leverage."

"Even you?"

She smirked. "Every family has a head, so there are limits, but I give you my word. But right now, I need an answer. A yes allows Trulian to go home safely."

He looked over his shoulder at Trulian, who reached for a pastry the size of her face. Jorden smiled and poured fresh tea into her cup. "And a no?" Durmad asked, watching Tru close her eyes as she bit into the flaky dough.

"Then Trulian remains with me and Jorden." The guards gripped their swords and stood straighter as Naamah touched Durmad's bicep. He fought the urge to pull it from her touch and use his ability against the looming guards as Naamah continued, "Still safe, but away from her sister."

He knew it wouldn't matter if Tru were safe or not; Shylah would never stop storming the castle to demand her sister's return. Eventually, she'd push the Queen too far, and he'd lose both sisters. "That will crush her sister, and you will lose a strong Elixir Designer. I'm not sure that's in your best interest." The memory of Trulian in the cave flashed into his mind, and he faced Naamah. "Am I the only reason you took Trulian?"

She chuckled and turned back to the window. "What other reason would there be?"

Durmad stared at the side of her face, trying to read her mind through her expressions. "I don't know. I have never presumed to understand why you do what you do. I don't know why you want me as a Knight Commander anyway. I can serve you well as a soldier, regardless of my position."

She walked toward the throne room doors, stopping before the window depicting her sitting on the throne, Liam standing just behind her, and Jorden sitting on the stairs in front. She pointed at the window and said, "Him."

Durmad glanced back at Liam, looking out his own window. "I don't understand."

"You will. Troubled times are coming. I need him protected. As you want Trulian and her sister protected. You can protect them all. You can heal him when he needs it."

"I can do that as a soldier. I still don't see the need to be—"

She lowered her voice and said, "I know you have heard him speak her name in his sleep."

"The mysterious woman he won't acknowledge. Yes, he says her name most nights."

Naamah nodded. "He is weak of heart, and when it comes time to fight her, which he will have to, he will need you beside him to do what he will not be able to."

Her statement echoed in his mind until realization clouded his face. "You want me to kill the woman he loves."

Naamah huffed. "Love? No. He does not know what love is. Infatuation, yes. She has placed a spell on him. You have seen it. He will not entertain even the idea of another woman. It is not healthy for him.

Brooding does not make for a wise or strong leader, and he must be both if we are to find our quarry and achieve our goals. The only way to break her spell over him is through her death. He will not kill her when the time comes." She reached her hand out and touched the stained glass. "But I am confident she will him. Many will want to help her in that endeavor."

He glanced back at Liam, who grabbed a pastry. "If I agree, I have conditions."

She nodded, clasping both hands in front of her. "As I knew you would. What are your conditions?"

"The first is that Trulian returns home with her sister. Unharmed."

"And the second?"

He drew a deep breath, letting his chest puff out and his shoulders rise. "Give her sister, Shylah, two replenish days. She is designing too many elixirs. You will burn her out. She almost died a few days ago from overuse of her ability. Had I not been there, you would have lost a valuable Bonded." And I would have lost— he thought but didn't know how to finish it.

Is Shylah my friend? A type of sister like I told Abaddon and Liam? Or is she more?

Naamah stiffened. "What!" Her face reddened, mixing with the dull beam of green-colored window light to cast her face in a sickly hue of brown. She gritted her teeth with such force that Durmad was sure she swallowed dust from her own teeth.

Maybe she does care for her Bonded, at least as long as they were useful to her, Durmad thought as he glanced at Trulian, who smiled and waved as Jorden offered her the plate of pastries.

"She will be fine, and her endurance is growing with her ability, but she needs ample rest between designing streaks. My uncle does not currently allow for that."

Naamah stormed toward the throne. "That dolt of a man will be my undoing. He was to train her to replace him. She is the only reason he is still of value to me." She stopped so abruptly that Durmad nearly collided with her back. "Regardless of what comes of the hunt, I have a replacement, and he knows it. Maybe he isn't so daft after all," she said, rubbing her chin.

Durmad glanced at Liam, who quickly looked away. *Coward.* This was going to be more complicated than he thought. "My Queen. Maybe it is better to have another train her. My family cottage still lies empty."

Naamah spun to face him, whipping the azure tips of her braids across his neck so hard that he was sure there would be a mark. "There is no one else to train her, and your uncle knows that. Perhaps I have treated her too kindly," she said, more to herself than anyone else in the throne room.

Durmad stood on the throne room floor while the Queen climbed the five steps to her throne. As she sat, she added, "I see I must harden more. I cannot have him suspect what I value. It will make him more desperate, and desperate men make stupid choices."

He climbed the bottom step. "You can't hurt her."

She cocked her head to the side. "Perhaps I was mistaken, and I chose the wrong sister."

Typhon Toes! Control yourself.

He returned to the floor of the throne room. "You just said she was valuable. Hurting her will most likely damage that. Weren't you just upset about others having done just that?"

She leaned back on her throne. "I agree to your conditions. Now, do you agree to the Bonding?"

He glanced again at Trulian before saying, "I have one more condition."

Naamah sighed. "Which is?"

"As I said before, my family cottage is empty. Let Shylah and Trulian stay there. She can come to Morena for training, but the cottage garden will give her ample access to the necessary ingredients to maintain her ability."

Naamah tented her fingers in front of her chin. "Interesting idea, but no. At least not now. She is not far enough into her training. However, I will grant your request under my own conditions: she must finish her training, and you must find our quarry."

Durmad squinted. "I don't know enough about the target to agree to those terms."

She smiled, dropping her hands in her lap. "Then you must trust me. Once you are a Bonded, you will have everything you need to locate it."

"My Queen, I must follow your commands, but I am unsure I *trust* you."

"It seems we are at an impasse," she said, nodding to the two guards who stepped one to each side of Trulian and lifted her to her feet.

CHAPTER THIRTY-NINE

SHYLAH

S hylah ran past the stables where Durmad had laid out Abaddon with a single punch, followed by a kick to the head. Or at least she hoped that's what she'd seen. No sign of a fight remained.

What if the old man was a type of manipulator or manifester like Naamah?

Everything he showed her may not actually be true. Her pace slowed.

What if Trulian wasn't actually at the castle with the Queen?

She searched her memory for proof that what the old man showed her was false. It seemed real.

Only one way to find out.

She blew past one guard before they realized what she was doing, and two Green Willow Guards grabbed her arms—one on each side.

Pulling against them, she said, "Let me pass. I am the Queen's Elixir Designer. I have the elixir she requested ready. Do you want her wrath directed at you if I don't deliver it to her in the next five minutes?" She focused on the facemask portion of the guards' helmets just below their eyes. To most, it appeared she was looking them in the eye, but if she did, she couldn't lie. She was a horrible liar, and her eyes always gave it away —or at least that was what her father always told her.

The taller of the two guards stepped back, looking her up and down, but never loosened his grip. "Where's the elixir then? I see no suitcase and no bottle in your hand."

Typhon Toes! Why did I have to be caught by the one observant and competent guard in all of the Green Willow?

Now, she had to stall. "It's right here," she said, patting her stomach a few times before feigning confusion and saying, "How'd you?"

"How'd we what? Go ahead. Tell us how we forgot to do our job."

The shorter one, who still had a good three inches on Shylah, smirked. "Neither of us has a death wish."

She resorted to straining her neck as she studied the ground. "That's exactly what will happen if you don't help me find my satchel and the Queen's elixir." She twisted, looking behind her. "It must have fallen off."

The shorter Guard chuckled. "Or you mistook us for someone born yesterday, which we were not."

"Are you going to help me find my satchel or stand there like fools?" she asked.

The tall one snickered. "Oh, we'll help you look alright." He and the shorter guard nodded to each other just before simultaneously lifting her just high enough that her feet barely brushed the surface of the ground and carried her back across the courtyard.

As they passed the stables, she kicked out. "Where are you taking me?"

"You said you left your satchel behind. We're helping you find it," the shorter guard said.

"You aren't even looking," she said, twisting her shoulders.

The tall one gripped her arm a little tighter. "I'm sure you just left it at home."

She looked over her shoulder. They carried her further from Trulian with every step. "But you don't know where I live."

"Of course we do. Everyone knows where the Queen's Elixir Designer lives with his upstart apprentice."

She gave one more twist and kicked to free herself, but the short one's last comment sucked all her fight from her, and she gave in. Her escorts carried her back to Apollyon's workshop, only setting her back on the ground once inside. The moment her feet hit solid ground, she bolted for the door.

"Ah, not so fast," the short one said, cutting her off. "You will stay here."

"I will do no such thing," she snapped and jumped around him.

"Oh, you will, or we'll come back with Sir Abaddon again."

At the mention of Abaddon, a shock of pain went through her arm, and she froze.

Again? Were these two with him when he took Trulian?

Heat bloomed in her chest, and her nostrils flared as she turned on the tall guard behind her.

He shifted his weight from one foot to the next. "You should be more well-behaved like your sister. She didn't fight one bit."

"You bastard. Where did you take my sister?" she yelled and sprung on the guard. Locking her legs around his waist, she clawed at any exposed flesh while the shorter guard yanked at her middle, trying to pry her off his companion.

"What in Typhon's name do you think you're doing?" Apollyon's voice cut through the chaos. "Shylah, get off that guard."

Unhooking her ankles from each other, she dropped to her feet, saying, "You." Turning on her caretaker, she clenched her fists. "This is your fault, you miserably, useless man. Why aren't you asleep already? Haven't I done enough work for you the last few days?"

Apollyon puffed up his chest and stepped forward. "Now listen here: I am the Master Designer. You're just the help that the Queen took pity on."

Shylah screamed, "Go shove your head in your treasure box if you're so valuable, and leave me alone." She hit her shrillest volume on the last three words.

"Why, you impertinent girl. I'll teach you a lesson." He grabbed the leather sharpening strap from the wall and stepped toward her.

Shylah backed into the elixir table while the two guards leaned against the wall, arms crossed. She hated the Green Willow Guard and all they stood for. They'd burned her home, no matter what tale they spun for everyone else. She knew the truth and would kill every last one of them.

"I should have done this sooner," Apollyon said, twisting the leather strap in his hand.

Shylah backed into the stool.

"It works best when you're young, like Durmad was, but I am sure it will sink into your thick skin—eventually."

She grabbed the stool and flung it at him with all the force of three years under his less-than-helpful teaching, with all the anger of being left to fend for herself first by her parents, then Durmad, and now Trulian. Everyone was gone.

Apollyon dodged enough for the stool to land only a glancing blow, but his heel caught on the edge of the receiving room rug and fell back.

Shylah stood over him, fists clenched and chest heaving when the two guards grabbed her arms again.

The front door burst open, and Trulian wrapped her arms around Shylah.

Shylah fought against the guards, who released her arms as Durmad's voice filled the workshop.

"Get out. I will deal with you later." The guards hurried out the front door.

Shylah smiled, imagining Durmad kicking both men like he had Abaddon. She squeezed Trulian.

Durmad reached down and pulled Apollyon to his feet. "Uncle, go to bed."

Apollyon huffed, brushing himself off. "Go to bed? Did you see what she was doing?"

Durmad's voice deepened, "Go to bed. Naamah wishes to see you in the morning."

"The Queen!" Apollyon says, smoothing his greasy hair down and adjusting his night clothes. "I must be rested for her." He glared around Durmad, pointing at Shylah. "And she will hear of this impertinence girl. I am sure you will end up in the—"

"Uncle!"

"Fine," Apollyon snapped and stormed off like an infant who had been told to go to bed without dessert.

Shylah brushed Trulian's hair out of her face and inspected her arms, neck, and face—any bare skin. "Are you hurt? Did she force you to take her anywhere?"

Trulian smiled at her sister. "No. We just had tea. I can't take anyone with me yet anyway." She hesitated. "How did you know I was working up to that?

"The old man training you. He took me to see Durmad storm the castle." Shylah lifted her eyes to Durmad. "And you."

He raised his hands in surrender and closed the space between them.

Shylah wrapped an arm around Trulian, hiding her sister behind her back. He would not get to her sister again—not ever.

"I am sorry I locked you in your room, but I couldn't have you storming into the castle and making things worse. You don't always think straight when you're angry," Durmad said, hands still raised in front of him.

She crossed her arms over her chest. "I think perfectly fine."

He raised an eyebrow. "Is that why you were about to murder my uncle?"

"I was not going to—" The thought of the strobilus milk and her plan to poison Durmad crept into her thoughts. She was going to kill in her anger. She'd vowed to kill every last Green Willow Guard. Now, facing him, knowing what he did to avenge her, not only to a friend but to a Green Willow Guard, she wasn't sure she could do it. He stood feet away, studying her. She would not give him the satisfaction of reading her feelings in her face. Turning her back to him, she took in her sister's doe-eyed grin.

Tru was so young, so trusting. She needed to be protected.

Wrapping her in a hug, Shylah renewed her vow to keep her sister safe. It was just the two of them now. She could kill to protect her family.

She kissed Trulian on the forehead. "It's late, and you have had a busy day. You should go to bed." She faced Durmad again. "Thank you for bringing her home."

His shoulders drooped as he picked up the stool and sat. "It's the least I could do."

Shylah tilted her head. "What do you mean the least you could do?"

He looked down at his hands. "It's my fault the Queen took Trulian."

Shylah stiffened, gripping Trulian's shoulders.

He had betrayed them, and for that, I will kill him.

"You should go."

He nodded. "I have more business with the Queen anyway." He kneeled in front of Trulian. "I will come by tomorrow for lunch and check on you." As he stood, he said, "Both of you."

CHAPTER FORTY

DURMAD

Durmad took a deep breath before entering the dimly lit castle chapel. Each feather wall sconce carved from a single morion gemstone swallowed most of the light before it could escape into the air. A chandelier of emerald feathers caught in a web of morion stones hung just above the dais at the far end. It cast splinters of green light around the room like elongated arrows pointing to where the Queen and Liam stood behind the altar carved of the same morion stone.

Durmad paused before walking up the aisle. He'd expected Liam to meet him at the door, but seeing him beside the Queen, beside his mother, made him feel less like Durmad's friend and more like the king he would someday be. Durmad wasn't sure he could trust everything Liam had said about his mother or the Bonding, but it was too late now. He'd agreed to this to bring Trulian home.

It was too late for regret. He steeled himself and plodded past the rows of wooden pews with black velvet cushions and green light splinters. When he reached the altar, he bowed and asked, "Is all this necessary? Most of your Bonded from the other kingdoms didn't have a ceremony." He remembered Shylah's story and shifted his gaze from the altar to Liam. "Many of them simply accepted your invitation to come to Dimmet."

The Queen set a green silk bundle atop the altar. "Yes, but this is not the same. I saved them from abandonment and isolation from the people. I brought them home. You do not need saving."

She unfolded the green silk, revealing an object carved from a single oval of emerald and a single oval of morion. The ovals intertwined to form an X, but Durmad couldn't see a seam or joint where the two gemstones were broken so that they could weave through each other.

Looking back at Liam, he asked, "Then why require the Bonding versus an oath?" He knew the answer but wanted to see if she'd admit it in front of Liam.

Naamah picked up the woven stones in both hands. "We've been over this, but your Bond will not be with me. It will be with Liam."

Both Liam and Durmad's focus snapped to the Queen. She'd said his Bonding was to protect Liam and do what she knew he couldn't or assumed he couldn't do.

How would being Bound to Liam even allow for that?

"Mother, what are you talking about? I do not want anyone Bound to me," Liam said.

Naamah handed him the X. "That is why you need someone you can trust. And someone I can trust." Her cold stare landed on Durmad.

Durmad's brow furrowed. "But I agreed to be Bonded to you, not Liam. How will that fulfill your request?" His mind spun.

If I am Bonded to Liam, will the Queen still keep her word? How can I protect Shylah and Trulian if my primary Bond is with someone other than the Queen?

His chest tightened each time his eyes darted from the Queen to Liam and back to the Queen.

"I do not want a Bonded," Liam said. "I do not need one." He pushed the woven gemstones back toward the Queen. "This is not why I came."

"But it is, my son," Naamah said, stepping back. "As your Bonded, Durmad will be forced to protect you no matter what happens."

Liam shoved the X again. "I already know he will protect me."

The Queen locked eyes with Durmad and said, "No matter what." With open palms, she guided the X and Liam's hands over the silk cloth covering the top of the altar. "He has agreed to a Bonding, but I never said it would be to me."

Durmad searched his memory for the conversation. She hadn't said her; she'd said he would be Bonded to the throne. He'd been so focused on saving Trulian that it hadn't occurred to him that she hadn't said the Bonding would be with her. When he thought about it, he preferred being Bonded to Liam. At least he trusted Liam more than the Queen.

"I'll do it."

Naamah chuckled. "You already agreed, and I have already fulfilled my end of the bargain." She reached across the altar and lifted Durmad's wrist. "Place your hands on the emerald and morion loops nearest you."

Durmad followed her instructions and nodded at Liam.

Liam stared at the stone X between them, but didn't move to grasp it.

Durmad took a deep breath. "This is better, Liam. I trust you with my life."

Liam nodded back. "And I, you."

Naamah backed away. "See? That's better. You both need to grip the morion stone."

Liam hesitantly reached out and grasped the emerald loop across from Durmad's hand.

The Queen wrapped a black ribbon around Durmad and Liam's hands, which gripped the emerald loops, before tying it around the center of the X. Then, she did the same with a green ribbon and their free hands.

"Durmad, given your ability, this will be exponentially more painful. The motion will absorb your ability, but it will not stop it. The emerald will amplify your loyalty and affection for Liam. Under normal circumstances, it makes the process quick and painless; however, your ability will actively fight against the mark."

"I understand," Durmad said, clenching his jaw.

"You don't, but you will," Naamah replied, pulling a bottle of liquid from her pocket. "When I pour the Frankincense on the center of the gemstone and ribbon knot, the Bonding will begin." She placed a hand on Liam's shoulder. "Are you ready, my son?"

Liam nodded, and his grip on the gemstone knot tightened until his knuckles turned white.

"Drink this," Naamah said, putting a small bottle of clear liquid to Durmad's lips. "I had the Designer create a painkiller for you."

Durmad drank the liquid and tasted the faint remnants of honeysuckle and green grass; he tasted Shylah.

Naamah uncorked the bottle, and the earthy scent of wood mingled with faint notes of citrus and spice filled the space between him and Liam. The moment the first drop of oil touched the ribbon, a shock of pain made every muscle in Durmad's chest knot. He closed his eyes, and light exploded on the back of his eyelids with every burst of pain. Between shallow breaths, he managed, "My. Chest. Why?"

Naamah's voice sounded like she was at the end of a tunnel as she said, "The frankincense. Your Bonding is sacrificial, so it's over your heart."

Liam howled, and Durmad's eyes flew open. "Liam?" His head snapped to the Queen. "What—"

"He is being marked, too. Your Bonding is a mutual connection, because you were both willing. You are connected and will keep each other safe. Now, breathe."

Durmad squeezed his eyes shut again and gripped the stone with all his might. He felt his ability pushing against the intrusive mark as it painfully and slowly crept across his chest. Sweat stung his eyes, and his knees buckled. If not for the altar between them and their hands being fastened to the stone, Durmad would have been writhing on the floor of the dais. He focused on his breath despite its shallowness.

Keep breathing.

He didn't know how long the Bonding took. The pain made the time bleed into itself as if he'd been asleep. At some point, he passed out, or the pain wiped his memory. He remembered stumbling past the stable, climbing wooden stairs, and a blurred figure dropping him on a bed.

Everything else was all darkness, flashes of lightning, and pain —so much pain.

CHAPTER FORTY-ONE

SHYLAH

Shylah tied her waist pouch to her belt the next morning and woke her sister. After breakfast, she designed the handful of elixirs and prepped them for delivery before entering the kitchen again. Trulian was checking the buns planned for lunch.

"I can finish those. There are some elixirs to deliver, and you can get more cheese and anything else you need from the market on your way back," Shylah said, handing Trulian the bag of elixirs and some coins.

"Are you sure? I can just tell you what to get, too."

"Last time I picked the cheese, I got the wrong kind," Shylah said. "The entire workshop smelled like feet for a week."

Trulian giggled. "We don't want feet cheese today." She wiped her hands and draped her apron over the back of the chair beside the hearth. "The sauce is in the bowl by the sink. The buns will be done in ten more minutes, then let them cool for fifteen before adding the sauce. If you put the sauce on too early, it will melt, and we'll have soggy buns instead of blackberry sticky buns."

Shylah tipped the bowl of sauce as thick as honey. Two other bowls sat on the counter: one with fresh blackberries and the other with a paste the same color as the berries. "What are these for?"

"Right. I almost forgot," Trulian said, pulling a tringle of brown paper from a shelf and quickly folding it into a cone. She filled it with the paste and folded the end. "Before you sauce them, but after fifteen minutes, pipe the blackberry filling into the center. Cut a small slit in the end of the bun the width of the tip of your pinky finger, then cut the tip of the paper tube off, shove it into the slit, and squeeze till you feel it push back on the paper. You don't want it to ooze out, so less is best."

Shylah's grin flattened. She'd helped make buns before, but she'd never filled them.

Trulian placed a hand on Shylah's wrist. "I will hurry. If it's too much, I can do it when I get back."

Shylah huffed. "I design complicated elixirs every day. I think I can handle filling a sticky bun. Don't worry."

"You sure?"

"Yes," Shylah said, shooing her out the back door. "Now, go. We don't know exactly when Durmad plans to come by."

Trulian nodded and ran out the back door and down the side alley.

"Don't be too fast, though," Shylah whispered.

Ten minutes later, she pulled the buns from the shelf above the fire and left them to cool on the counter. She couldn't put the biting strobilus milk on every bun, just Durmad's.

So, how will I know which one?

As she put the breadbasket on the counter, she thought about putting the sauce in a certain direction or flipping one over and saucing it flat-side up, but neither of those guaranteed that Durmad would eat the poisoned bun. Trulain would most likely eat the flat-side bun in an attempt to cover up for Shylah's mistake.

No, I have to make it seem like it was specially made for him. The blackberries.

She could put two blackberries on top of the one meant for him. They were his favorite, so Trulian wouldn't suspect.

When the buns had cooled, Shylah filled the buns and set them back on their cooling tray. She pulled the bottle of biting strobilus milk from her waist pouch, uncorked it, and let three drops fall along the top. The drops disappeared into the soft dough, and Shylah hoped they wouldn't burn all the way through. She sauced them and placed a single blackberry atop each, placing two berries atop the one marked for Durmad. She stacked the buns into the basket when the sauce set and placed Durmad's on the stack. Trulian burst through the back door breathlessly.

"You finished. Good," she said, setting a wedge of cheese and fresh herbs on the counter. "A messenger gave me this for Apollyon. After you give it to him, hurry back. I could use your help." Trulian returned the apron to her body without another word and began pulling out trays, cured meat, dried bread disks, and other items from the storage space opposite the hearth.

Shylah examined the note as she walked to Apollyon's study. It bore the seal of Naamah in red wax. She knocked on the study door.

"What?"

"A messenger brought this for you," she said, listening for movement. There was none. "It's from The Queen." Shylah heard the scuff of chair legs on the wood floor and hurried steps just before the door swung open, nearly hitting her in the side.

Apollyon unceremoniously snatched it from her hands and slammed the study door in her face.

"You're welcome, Sir," she muttered and returned to the kitchen.

Moments later, Apollyon hurried from the study, said, "I've been summoned," and left through the front door.

Not five minutes later, Durmad walked in the back kitchen door. Before he could say a word, Trulian hugged him around the waist. His smile looked forced, almost rehearsed, instead of the effortless smile he always bestowed on her younger sister.

"Lunch is almost ready," Trulian said.

They ate the cheese, cured meats, olives, fruit, and dried bread until crumbs remained. "I'll get the blackberry sticky buns," Shylah said, retrieving the basket from the kitchen counter. She paused just inside the kitchen and took several deep breaths.

Do I really want to poison Durmad in front of Tru?

Her wrist ached, and her throat went dry as she remembered her sister being ripped from her grasp.

Yes.

He'd betrayed her, betrayed them. No matter what the old man had shown her, she hadn't seen Durmad deny that he hadn't put Trulian in danger.

In fact, he'd said it was his fault, hadn't he?

She had to kill him to protect Trulian from The Queen, even if her sister didn't understand. "One day, you'll understand," she whispered, leaving the kitchen.

Durmad smiled as she set the basket on the table in front of him. "Tru said you stuffed and sauced the sticky buns. I'm impressed."

Shylah chuckled. "Don't be. I probably overstuffed some and understuffed others."

"The one on top with the two blackberries I made—" But before Shylah could finish her statement, Trulian grabbed the sticky bun meant for Durmad and shoved the entire thing in her mouth.

"No!" Shylah screamed and pounced on Trulian.

CHAPTER FORTY-TWO
DURMAD

"Shylah, stop," Durmad said, pulling at her shoulder as she flung chunks of sticky bun from Trulian's mouth.

"No. You don't understand."

Durmad grabbed Shylah around the waist and lifted her off her sister. She thrashed. As her back rubbed across his chest, fresh bursts of pain threatened to buckle his knees. "Shylah, stop."

Trulian coughed and spit soggy hunks of sticky bun onto her plate. Then her face went gray, and she slumped in her chair. His breathing was shallower, and he sat Shylah in his chair. "Tru," he said, cupping her face in his hands.

"You have to heal her," Shylah's command was pinched with desperation.

"From what?" he asked, looking over his shoulder as he searched with his ability. "What did you do?"

"Biting strobilus milk. It was on the sticky bun," Shylah said, voice shaking.

He found the acidic milk boring a hole near the back of Trulian's mouth, on her tongue, and on her cheek. He quickly knitted the cells together and pulled the blood cells to the locations so they could coat the acid, keeping it from doing more damage. There was a similar hole starting halfway down her throat, and he repeated the process again. With each second he used his ability to heal Trulian, it stopped killing his own pain. His chest burned, and his skin throbbed more intensely the longer it took. Luckily, Shylah had pulled most of the bun from Trulian's mouth before she could swallow it.

But why was it even on the bun?

Slowly, the color returned to Trulian's face as her cells fused. He searched the rest of her throat, lungs, and stomach but found no more traces of the acidic poison. Wiping sweat from his brow with the back of his hand, he stepped back. "That's all of it."

Shylah jumped up, kissed her forehead and cheeks before hugging her around the neck, repeating, "I'm sorry."

Durmad stumbled back and barely made it back to his chair before collapsing. "Why would you give that to your sister?"

"I need to get her to bed," Shylah said, carrying Trulian out of the room.

Slumped in his chair, Durmad tried to let his body recover, but he needed food. He reached for the sticky buns but stopped short. Shylah had been offering them to him.

What if there was more than one poisoned with biting strobilus milk?

There were a few grapes and a piece of dried bread still on his plate, so he opted for those.

Did she intend the poison for me? But why?

He rested his forehead on his forearms and fought the urge to fall asleep. Every muscle in his body ached for rest, but he couldn't. He had to ask Shylah what happened. She couldn't have meant to poison him. Sure, he'd locked her in her room, but that was for her own good, so he could bring Trulian back. Beyond that, he'd saved her, protected her, thought of her.

Why would she want to poison me?

"Durmad," Shylah whispered, hesitating in the doorway to the dining room. "Thank you."

"Why would you give that to your sister?" he repeated again, forehead still on his forearm.

"I didn't. It was meant for you."

Durmad forced himself up with a wince. "Me? Why would you try to poison me?" His chest thrummed. "You could have killed me."

She stiffened. "You betrayed us."

"I didn't. What are you talking about?"

"You said it was your fault Trulian was taken. You told The Queen," she said, anger clipping her words.

Durmad ran a hand through his hair.

How could she think I'd told the Queen about Trulian?

"Think about it. Trulian would have never returned with me if the Queen knew she was a peripatetic. She'd still be in the castle. The Queen was using her to get to me, not you."

Shylah crossed her arms and looked at the wall beside him before shaking her head and saying, "That makes no sense."

Durmad shook his head and stood. "You're not the only one who's caught The Queen's attention. I should go." He stumbled forward and caught himself on the edge of the table.

"You need to rest more," she said, pushing on his chest.

He howled and grabbed her wrist, flinging it down. "I'll be fine," he said, pushing past her and into the workshop. It took all his strength to reach the elixir table.

Shylah placed a hand on his wrist. "How did you get hurt?" He tugged his hand, but she gripped it harder. "I know it wasn't Abaddon. You laid that bastard out flat."

He looked down. "How did you—?"

She smiled. "I saw it."

His brow furrowed. "But. Your room. How'd you—?"

She chuckled. "You're just now wondering that? I was out of my room when you returned with Trulian, and you didn't let me out."

"But?" He looked down again. "How?"

"Aidan, the firesmith's apprentice, let me out after several hours."

His knees buckled slightly, and he barely caught himself on the elixir table again. "That's after I knocked Abaddon out. How did you—"

"I traveled," she said, pulling the stool to him. "Here. Sit."

"Wait. I thought only Trulian could travel."

Shylah stepped back. "She can."

"So how?"

Shylah sighed, waving his question away. "I found out who the old man with the gray hair is, and I know who's been training Trulian." She told Durmad about the strange interaction, traveling, and how the man claimed to be the lost king. "He said something about Trulian needing to train so she could train *their child*. She leaned back against the edge of the elixir table. "Do you know if Liam or his brother are peripatetic?"

Durmad rubbed his chin. "No. Liam is a powerful Distillate, and his brother can speak to animals." He hung a boot heel on the leg-rung of the stool. "The old man, being his father, would explain Liam's cryptic response when I talked to him about the male Bonded. It was like he didn't want to talk about it, but his own father? Wait. You just tried to kill me," Durmad said, crossing his arms over his chest and sucking in a breath.

Shylah stepped closer. "None of that explains how you got hurt."

Durmad stiffened. "I'm not. Besides, I can heal myself, remember." He frowned. "You tried to kill me. Why do you care if I'm injured anyway?"

"Because you saved Tru," she said just before slapping him square in the chest.

Durmad shot to his feet with a howl of pain and backed away, keeping the stool between them. "That's a strange way to show your gratitude," he hissed.

She crossed her arms and thrust her hip to the side. "See. You *are* hurt. What happened?" she asked, pulling the stool to the side and closing the distance between them. Grabbing the bottom edge of his tunic where it tucked into his pants, she gave it a gentle tug.

"What are you doing?" Durmad asked, pushing her hands away.

"I have salves and elixirs for pain."

"First you try to kill me, and now you try to help me?" He strode to the front door. "I'm fine. I don't need your help." He opened the front door and faced Shylah. "Not everything the Queen does revolves around you and Trulian. There are things...things you don't under-stand. Goodbye, Shylah," he said, closing the door behind him.

CHAPTER FORTY-THREE

SHYLAH

The following night, Shylah pulled the hood of her cloak over her hair, tugging it down over her eyes. It wasn't strictly frowned upon for a woman to enter the Even-tide Tavern after dark, but it wasn't common either —at least not for someone of her age or station. Pulling her neck into her shoulders, she melted into the shadows of the heavy fabric.

The new cloak had been delivered earlier with a note from Durmad apologizing for losing hers in the Kyselina Desert. It was nicer than the one she'd lost, almost too nice. Instead of a thin fabric worn from years of use before she'd inherited it, it was thick wool dyed a deep eggplant with a black fur lining. It was the most expensive gift she'd ever received. Well, besides the silver box of tea she'd broken, but Aidan should have the hinge fixed in another day.

Gripping the strap of her satchel as she slunk in the back door, she hurried up the stairs. She'd hoped Durmad would come by the workshop so she could apologize to him. She wasn't sure how she'd be able to make up for trying to kill him, but she had to at least try. In two more days, he'd be gone again. She'd thought helping him heal if he hadn't already done it himself would help, so she came prepared.

Her foot hit the top step as Liam stepped out a door. Her heart pounded in her ears. She'd assumed Durmad had his own room, but maybe he didn't.

What if they were all in the same one?

She ducked into the shadows, hunched her shoulders, and held her breath.

Liam knocked on the door across the narrow hallway.

Abaddon opened the door, tightening his belt, and a woman pushed past him, straightening her corset. As she passed him, Abaddon smacked her butt. The woman grinned back at him and dragged a hand across Liam's chest.

Liam frowned and pushed her hand away.

Shylah smiled at the woman's pout.

Maybe Liam wasn't so bad after all.

She held her breath, pressing herself against the wall as the woman entered the stairwell only a few feet from Shylah's shadow.

"Must you be so—"

"Manly? One of us has to. What will they think of the Queen's Green Willow Guard if I'm not?"

Liam shoved Abaddon's shoulder. "Crass. If you showed a little discretion, they might just think we are more than the Queen's unsatiable hired swords."

"Ah, but where's the fun in that," Abaddon said, turning to knock on the door next to his, but Liam caught his wrist before a single knuckle touched the wood.

"He's not coming."

"What do you mean—hang on." Abaddon grinned from ear to ear. "Did that bar wench finally snag him? That dog."

Abaddon turned to pound on the door, but again, Liam grabbed both shoulders and flung him into the wall opposite the door. "Let's go, or do you want to be the reason we're late to the Queen's meeting?"

"Fine," Abaddon said, holding his hands in surrender. "I'll poke the bear tomorrow."

"No, you won't. You'll leave this one alone," Liam said, stepping into Abaddon's space before leaning back and patting him on the chest. "Now, why don't we get to the castle before the Queen puts us both in the dungeon for being late."

Abaddon chuckled and stepped toward Shylah's shadow. "She won't put her son in the dungeon."

Liam clapped him on the back. "That's right. It would be you in the dungeons."

The smile disappeared from Abaddon's face, and Shylah bit the inside of her cheek to keep from laughing. As they passed, Liam glanced at Shylah's shadow and nodded slightly.

Or did I imagine it?

Shylah replayed the moment over a few times. There was nothing near her shadow. No reason for him to even glance her way, except for her.

Could he sense my presence because of my Bonding?

There was still so much she didn't understand about how the Bond worked, and Apollyon had been no help explaining it.

Does Liam want me to help Durmad?

The tavern's back door swung shut, and she crept out of the shadow. It didn't matter what Liam thought, what he wanted or didn't want. She needed to thank Durmad and check on his injury. At least now, she knew which of the twenty doors was Durmad's room. Standing before the door, she raised her hand to knock—unless the bar wench was in Durmad's room, and he wasn't injured. She lowered her hand.

No, Liam had to have seen me. He had to have nodded. He wouldn't let me disturb Durmad after stopping Abaddon, would he?

She didn't truly know what any of them were capable of, other than Abaddon anyway; him, she knew.

She pushed back the hood of her cloak until her bangs showed, took a deep breath, and knocked.

Durmad's muffled voice seeped through the door, "Not now, Abaddon."

She knocked again. This time harder.

The sound of boots dragging across the floor sent her heart pounding in her ears again. She sucked in a breath as the door flung open.

"I said I—" Duramd's mouth hung open as he looked down at her. "Shylah. What are you?" He stepped forward and looked down the hall. "Did they—"

Before he could finish the question, she pushed past him into the room and pulled her hood back. "I came to thank you for the new cloak and make sure your injury was healed. With your ability, it should not have been so tender yesterday."

He shut the door and ran his hand through his hair as he sat in a chair just inside the door. His clothes were more disheveled than usual, and his tunic hung half untucked from his pants. Two empty jugs of Fire Onion Juice lay on their sides beside the bed, and another sat atop the dresser. "I don't need you to check on me."

"No?" She closed the space between them and smacked her hand against the center of his chest. He sprang to his feet and flung her hand from his chest. The force sent her tripping backward over her feet until her legs hit the edge of the bed, and she sat with a thud.

He crouched down in an instant and kneeled beside the bed. "Shy. I'm so sorry. I didn't mean—"

Shylah placed her hand on his shoulder and smirked. "See. You need me." She unclasped her cloak, draping it across the pillow, and pulled her satchel over her head as she stood. "Now sit down," she said as she started removing items from the satchel and placing them on the dresser in the corner. "I brought several salves and elixirs for the pain and to promote healing." She turned around, but instead of sitting on the bed, Durmad was standing inches away from her.

He reached over her shoulder and grabbed a few elixirs. "Put these away and go back to the workshop. You cannot afford to be out so late. You need your energy for elixir designing tomorrow."

After snatching the elixirs from him, she said, "No. I don't," and forcibly returned them to the dresser. "Tomorrow is my replenish day."

"See," he said, collecting salves, "you are more exhausted than you realize. You still have one full day before your replenish day."

"Durmad, stop." She gripped his forearm and moved his hand away from her satchel and back to the dresser top. "Naamah gave me an extra replenish day. I'm not sure why—she's never done anything for my birthday before—but who am I to complain if she wants to give me an extra day."

He released the salve. "Tomorrow is your birthday? I hadn't realized. I mean, we never talked about that before..." He backed away.

"Before you left?" she asked, returning to emptying the contents of her satchel onto the dresser. "You were only there about six months. It doesn't matter anyway." Placing the last pouch of herbs on the dresser, she swiped the jug of Fire Onion Juice. The liquid sloshed—about half-full —she put the jug to her lips and gulped the room-temperature liquid. The few times she'd had it before, it was chilled, but at room temperature, it burned more as it slid down her throat.

Durmad snatched it from her grip, and the clear liquid dripped from her chin onto her top.

She wiped her sleeve across her mouth and chin. "You can spare some," she said, motioning to the empty jugs on the floor.

He slammed the jug back on the dresser. "I needed to dull—It doesn't matter. This is my room. My business." Their eyes met, and he deflated. "Just collect your things and go home, Shy." He turned, flopped on the bed, and set his arm across his eyes.

"I can't do that," she whispered, walking to the side of the bed.

"Yes, you can. You should spend your replenish day energizing your ability, not spending it on me. I'll be fine."

Shylah sat on the edge of the bed. "No, I can't leave."

He flung his arm to his side. "Get out."

Her chest tightened. She'd never seen him so in pain, so desperate. He needed her help whether he liked it or not, but she wasn't sure how far she could push him. She pointed to his pillow and said, "No, I can't leave. You're on my cloak."

"I'm what?" he asked, turning his head to the side before grabbing the cloak and shoving it into her lap. "Here. Now you can leave."

Shylah stood and draped her cloak across the chair. "Nope. Still can't." She heard him stand and cross the room. Her hand shot out and pressed against the door, keeping it shut.

He dropped his voice, and his breath caused her hair to tickle her ear. "Move your hand, or I'll move it for you."

She whispered, "Only if you don't flinch."

"If I don't—"

Before he could finish his question or statement, it didn't matter which it would be; Shylah thrust her flat hand into his chest again. He jumped back. Mouth opened in a silent scream. Fists clenched at his sides. "You flinched."

He spun and hopped a few times before whispering and yelling, "Typhon's Toes, Shy," and lying back across the bed. His fight evaporated.

Shylah sat on the edge of the bed again, took a deep breath, and lifted his tunic, untucking it the rest of the way from his pants. He half-heartedly pushed her hands back down. "Durmad, I have to see what I'm working with, so I know what will help." He lowered his hands and stared at the ceiling. A dark line surrounded by pulsing red and purple veins started three inches above his belly button and followed the line of his stomach up to his chest. At the joining of his ribs, she knew what it was—the tuft of downy barbs just before the afterfeather tugged at her heart. The Bonding feather was massive, crossing over the center of his chest before curving slightly so that the tip kissed the base of his left collarbone. The pulsing veins covered his entire chest.

She lowered her hands, letting the tunic cover most of his feather. His eyes still stared at the ceiling, but a track of tears ran from the corner to the curve of his ear. "Why did you—" she whispered but couldn't quite finish the question. She didn't know what to think or how to feel. He'd been so sure about remaining a boundless orphan only a few days earlier.

What could have changed, and why hadn't it healed?

"It was the only way," he said, sitting up. Gently gripping her waist, he lifted her off the bed and swung his feet around to the floor.

"Only way for what?"

"She wanted my commitment. Not Tru. She still doesn't know."

Shylah stood in silence, processing what he'd just said while he leaned his elbows on his knees and buried his face in his hands.

Naamah didn't know about Trulian's ability; she was safe, but Naamah wanted Durmad. Why?

Shylah took in the sight of Durmad sitting in a heap on the edge of the bed.

What did he have that the Queen...

Shylah gasped, and her eyes flew wide.

Power. Durmad's power. Naamah wanted to control it. Control him.

Squatting in front of him, Shylah placed a hand on his left forearm until he dropped his hands and looked at her. The bright emerald eyes that had mesmerized her from the first day they'd met were dulled by tears—not of pain, no, there was no grimace or clenching of teeth. These tears had an air of abandonment as if his very essence was relinquishing his spirit to all of Dimmet. He'd given up his independence—his freedom—*for what?* Her sister.

"It isn't your job to protect Trulian. You didn't have to—"

Durmad cupped her cheeks in his hands. "I didn't do it for Trulian."

CHAPTER FORTY-FOUR

DURMAD

Durmad searched her eyes for understanding.

How could she not know?

After all he'd done. After all the times he'd saved her. "Shy, I did it for you."

Her brow furrowed a moment before it raised, and her lips parted.

There it was.

Finally, she knew. If she understood, he knew he could bear the pain. He could do what needed to be done if Liam couldn't. Smiling, he kissed her forehead, relaxed his muscles, and dropped his hands.

Her eyes shifted back and forth between his eyes and mouth before she pushed off his knees and kissed him. In the suddenness, his mind and lips froze until she started to pull back. He pressed into the kiss. When her eyes closed, he wrapped his hands around her waist and lifted her to his knee. Cradling the base of her head, he closed his own eyes.

The scent of earth dipped in vanilla filled his senses, and stars burst in the darkness of his eyelids. Cupping her cheek with his other hand, he traced every curve and crease of her lips with his, memorizing their softness. It was only a few more days until they left for the last year of training, and then he'd be on the hunt until they found whatever the Queen was searching for. He didn't know how long it would be before he'd see Shylah again; before he'd embrace her, before he'd smell her, before he'd kiss her again.

Her hands rested on his shoulders and flitted up and down his arms, sending goosebumps across his bare skin. He pressed deeper into the kiss. Her lips parted—a soft moan escaped her throat as he tasted her kiss. Her mouth wasn't enough. He wanted to taste more. She squeezed his arms as he kissed her neck, inhaling the rich vanilla scent floating from her skin. His hands drifted down her back, pulling her closer. She wasn't close enough. Kissing the bone just below her neck, she arched her back. Her chest pressed against his, and the pain exploded.

He pushed Shylah off his lap and flung himself flat against the bed. His fingers clawed at the air around his chest as if ripping away the skin that burned and needled between each stab of pain as the Bonding mark etched each barb into his skin. Shylah said something and moved around, but the pain dulled all his other senses. All he could feel, taste, smell, hear, and see was the burning of his own skin.

As cool pressure hit his chest, his breathing felt as if he had been sparing for an entire day. The air entered in lungs, but disappeared so quickly it felt like he was suffocating. *Shock.* He squeezed his eyes.

Don't panic. It's just pain. It will end. You're getting air.

In his head, he repeated all the phrases he'd told fellow guards on the training field. He couldn't pass out, not in front of Shylah.

Focus on your breath. Breathe in through your nose and out through your mouth. Just keep breathing.

The cool glass of an elixir bottle rested on his lower lip. Opening his mouth, Shylah tipped his head to the side and poured a bitter elixir as thick as honey that pooled inside his cheek. He swallowed and coughed. It was almost as strong as Fire Onion Juice and burned the entire way from his throat to his stomach.

His breathing deepened as the pain lessened, and his back relaxed. As she applied a cooling salve, each gentle caress of Shylah's hand pulled the pain to the surface until the only sensation left was an itch he couldn't scratch. Opening his eyes, he focused on her face. She stared at her left hand as she moved it around his chest. The further her hand moved from the center of his chest, the deeper the pain shot into his muscles. When her hand rested on the center of his chest, the pain completely disappeared for the briefest of moments, making its reappearance much more intense. Her brow furrowed, and she tilted her head to the side.

"What's wrong?"

"Nothing. Well, not exactly nothing. I'm not sure." She moved her hand around the side of his chest to his ribs, and the pain cut into his lungs. He sucked in a breath. "They move," she said as she continued running her hand over his skin.

"What moves? Why do you keep—" a flash of pain as her hand moved to his ribs on the other side

"The red and purple veins. They," her brow furrowed deeper, "they follow me."

He gasped for breath. "Then... Stop moving."

Her hand crossed back to the center again. The instant the pain stopped, he grabbed her wrist and pressed her hand firmly against his chest. "There. That doesn't hurt," he said, sighing.

Shylah stared at her hand. "They're gone."

"Shy, what are you talking about?" Durmad asked, still pressing her hand against his chest. It was the first true relief he'd experienced in two days, and he wasn't about to give that up.

"The veins. They were following my hand, but now they're gone. Look," she said, tipping her head toward his chest.

He glanced down; the red and purple veins no longer pulsed. "Did you see your bond mark? It's glowing." She pulled her hand back, and the pain radiated through his chest. Sucking in a breath, he squeezed his eyes closed until the pressure of Shylah's hand pushed away the pulsing pain again.

"It's my mark. It's drawing in, or I think it's drawing in the veins." Their eyes locked. "And your pain."

He grinned. "Are you treating me like a plant?"

"Am I what?" she asked.

He watched as her eyes darted back and forth as she searched her memory for the context of his comment. Her mouth dropped open when she found it. "Maybe."

"You won't bury me in acid dirt, though, right?"

She leaned in, a smirk creasing the corner of one eye. "Maybe."

"I guess I'll have to figure out how to break free," he said, poking her in the ribs with a chuckle. She instantly giggled and folded in on herself, pulling her hand from his chest. The shock of pain swallowed his laughter as he tried to suck in a deep breath.

Shylah quickly returned her hand to his chest. "I guess I have to stay," she said, looking over her shoulder. "My cloak is over there, though. Think you can bear the pain while I grab it?"

"I've handled it this long. I'm sure a few seconds won't matter much."

"Okay. Ready?"

He nodded.

"One, two…"

On three, she jumped up and grabbed her cloak from the chair. He sucked in another breath and scooted to the outside edge of the bed.

"What? Why did you?

"I can't have you rolling off the bed. The pain would wake me up," he said, flashing her a shaky grin as the pain deepened again. She immediately put her left hand on his chest and gingerly climbed over him. He stretched out his arm, and she rested her cheek just beside the tip of the feather. Covering her with the cloak, he kissed the top of her head. "You really are remarkable. My uncle is a dolt. Even the Queen thinks so."

She exhaled a half chuckle. "Someone should tell him that."

"Maybe I will," he said, rubbing her back. "We should both get some rest while we can," Shylah grunted in agreement and nuzzled into his side. He closed his eyes and absorbed her scent and the feeling of her lying next to him. There would be many nights where the closest thing he had to someone lying beside him was his armor laid out in case of attack.

"Durmad?"

"Uhmm?"

"What if it never gets better? What if… What if we have to stay like this?"

He brushed hair from her face as she stared up at him. "I doubt that will happen. The Queen would find a solution. She can't lose her most treasured weapon," he said with a grin, "or her best soldier." He kissed her forehead as her sigh tickled the hair on his chest—this he could get used to.

CHAPTER FORTY-FIVE

SHYLAH

The room was still dark when her eyes opened, but she knew right where she should be: Durmad's tavern room. She flexed her left hand and grabbed sheets, not Durmad's chest. She pushed herself up, and every muscle screamed from the stiffness that comes from laying for hours in the same position. No one was in the bed beside her.

"Durmad," she whispered.

No response. Her chest tightened, and her heartbeat in her throat.

Where was Durmad? Was he in pain?

The night before, she'd fallen asleep with her boots on, but stocking feet touched the wood floor.

Where are my shoes? What time is it?

Durmad's room had no window, so there was no way to tell until she left. She had to find her shoes first.

Grabbing the candle off the dresser, she knocked over several bottles she'd brought.

Matches.

She needed matches. Her fingers nudged a small box, and she quickly lit the candle. Her cloak lay on the chair near the door, and her boots were set neatly in pairs on the floor beneath. Scanning the room, she saw the spars furnishing, Durmad's armor, and saddlebags, but no Durmad.

She sat on the chair, frantically sliding her boots on. The faster she tried to go, the more the laces slipped out of her grasp.

Would Liam know where Durmad had gone? Was there a meeting I didn't known about?

There had to be. Maybe Naamah knew how to heal his Bonding mark completely. Standing, she tried to remember the night before.

Which door was Liam's? Which Was Abaddon's?

The last thing she wanted was for Abaddon to know she'd slept in Durmad's room last night. She could only imagine the intrusive thoughts he'd push into her mind with that information. Liam's was across the hall. She was sure of it.

Shylah pulled the door open and ran right into Durmad's chest.

"Whoa, careful," Durmad said, balancing a tray of two steaming mugs, pastries, and fruit. "Morning, birthday girl."

"What—where were you? How is your pain?"

Durmad walked into the room and set the tray on the bed. "I was getting breakfast. I figured you didn't want to eat with Abaddon and Liam, so I brought it to you." He grinned. "As for the pain, it's gone."

"Are you sure?" she asked, smacking him in the chest's center.

He looked down at her and nodded.

"How?" She rested her hand on his chest. Last night had been like a dream; she didn't want to wake up, and here she was, awake. Her Bonding mark no longer glowed, but it hummed. A slight grin pulled at her cheeks.

What was going on?

The longer she rested her hand on his chest, the stronger the hum grew. She looked up, and their eyes met.

His grin broadened to a smile, and he placed a hand over hers. "I feel it, too. I felt it this morning when I woke up." He leaned down and nuzzled his cheek against hers as he whispered, "Looks like you have a healing touch, too." He kissed her cheek before backing away and clapping his hands. "Now. Breakfast."

She stood staring at him. She wanted more than a kiss on the cheek. She wanted his arms around her, to— "Wait. Did you say birthday girl?"

He nodded. "I've planned a trip for us."

She pulled her head back into her neck. "When did you have time for that?"

He grinned. "Well, think of this more as a brunch and less as a breakfast."

"How late is it?"

"Almost noon," he said, handing her a mug of tea.

She stood holding it and staring into the air between them. She'd never slept so late. She didn't even know she could. He tipped the mug to her lips. The warm steam on her skin brought her back to reality. "How? Even as a child, I never slept in. My mother used to always complain about it."

"My guess—I think pulling the essence of the Bonding mark through you drained your distillate ability, and you needed to recover."

"Pulling what through what?" She'd never pulled the essence of anything through her own essence. She was only an amplifier. She lowered the mug. "But you're not even a plant."

He shrugged. "I don't really know, but it's the only explanation I have."

She sat on the edge of the bed, dazed.

What does this mean for my elixir designing? Could I do it with plants, or is it only something I could do with people?

She absently took the pastry Durmad set in the palm of her hand.

Or can I only pull Durmad's essence?

She took a bite of the flaky dough filled with blackberry jam.

"I'm not sure either," he whispered.

"Huh?"

"I'm not sure how it's possible or what it means, but we have the rest of your replenish day to think about it." He grinned again, "Or should I say, the rest of your birthday."

"The rest of my what? How did you know it was?" The night's conversation when she insisted that he let her stay and help him came flooding back into her mind. She'd told him it was her birthday, and he'd remembered. What's more, he'd planned something. She hadn't done anything special for her birthday since she was ten. Her eyes brightened. "What are we doing?"

He raised his eyebrows and looked at her over his mug. "I guess you better hurry and eat so you can find out."

She spent the next five minutes shoving pastry and fruit into her mouth while drinking scalding hot tea. She'd never eaten or drunk so fast her entire life. Once the last sip of her tea was gone, she wiped her mouth, set the mug down, and jumped to her feet. "Ready." She felt like a little kid again. "Where to?"

A sly grin crossed his face, and she stepped back a half step. "Well, we have to see a man about a horse."

CHAPTER FORTY-SIX

SHYLAH

When they turned the bend in the trail, Shylah heard the waterfall before she saw it. Water plummeted over a hundred feet, crashing on massive boulders worn flat by its continual pounding and bouncing off the surface of the plunge pool as if it were stone. The roaring of rushing water and the thunder of its impact echoed off the canyon walls, overwhelming her ears and pushing her ribcage as if the sound was jealous of her breath.

Rainbows sprouted from the waterfall's spray, only to fade into the air. It reminded her of the water-filled bottles her father used to position on her windowsill. They painted splintered rainbows across her bedroom wall. The joy of dancing with her father in the middle of the rainbow shards lifted her heart and cheeks.

When her father had died, she'd given up on rainbows, on joy. Like the protective bark of a tree chard by flames, a hardness settled over her when she stepped on that boat deck. It slowed the deterioration of herself, but it hadn't stopped it. She had to think about Trulian and protect her only family. It had made survival bearable.

Tears inched from the corners of her eyes. She hadn't realized how much of herself she had lost. Everything had become about survival, about Trulian. Shylah had stopped venturing out into nature simply to feel its essence surround her. As an elixir designer, her interactions with nature had become the completion of a task. Her shoulders grew heavy as the lightness left her body. She'd thought more about her home in the last two weeks than she had in the previous two years.

A weight pressed on her leg, and she flinched. She'd been so lost in the heaviness of her memory that she hadn't noticed Durmad hopping off Atlas or tying Eclipse to a nearby tree.

"I didn't mean to startle you," Durmad said.

Shylah forced a weak grin and dismounted, saying, "It's all right. Just lost in my memories." When she turned away from Eclipse, Durmad stood inches from her.

He wiped the tears from her face, and she fought the urge to lean into his touch. She pressed her hand on his chest. Stepping past him, she shook her hand. The momentary touch made her wrist hum. "It's beautiful here. I didn't know this place could even exist in Dimmet." Looking over her shoulder, she added, "How did you find this place?"

He pulled the saddlebags off Atlas and stood beside her. "The cottage is just over a mile in that direction," he said, pointing to the forest to the left of the falls. "When I was a boy, my mother would bring me along when she collected ingredients. There's a special kind of turquoise algae that grows along the shore in the shaded tide pool. She used to—"

Shylah raised her eyebrows and gripped his arm. "Wait. Turquoise? What was it called?"

He shrugged. "Something like sio...siobel...sion, I'm not sure."

She gripped his arm tighter, "Cyanelle?"

"Maybe. I was just a kid," he said.

Shylah scanned the shaded area between the plunge pool and the cliff. One of her mother's first lessons was harvesting and drying the algae to create a vibrant turquoise powder. The elixirs designed with cyanelle powder not only fetched a higher price but required less of the designer's amplification. It extended the life of any elixir it was added to. There was only one pool near Baylon where it could be harvested in all of Castigation. It had been that single ingredient that established and grew Baylon.

It had a darker side, too. The Baylon elders always told the children the story of the old woman who drank from the waters infested with the turquoise algae. She thought she'd heal faster by going straight to the source, but instead, she began to wither away. Within twenty minutes, she'd been reduced to a pile of dust and turquoise-tinged bones. The tale was a cautionary warning to keep nosey children from swimming in the pool. As a further layer of protection for the cyanelle—and the children—only a few people had even known where it was.

And now she knew Dimmet had a turquoise pool. It could change the way she designed elixirs. They'd be more potent, and she'd be able to design more before the headaches came.

Still scanning the shade, Shylah asked, "Can you show me?"

"Yes, but you should eat first. Last night was long. Join me."

Tearing her eyes from the waterfall and cliff, she smiled. Durmad had laid a blanket out with a round loaf of bread the size of a two-handed river stone, a wedge of cheese, two oranges, grapes, and a medium brown jug. Laughing, she joined him. "Is that Fire Onion Juice? Are you trying to get me drunk again?"

He flashed a toothy grin as she sat. "No, although that would have been smart."

Shylah shoved his shoulder.

"It's cool blackberry and honeysuckle tea with a little bit of lemon fizz."

"I've never had that." She folded her legs to the side, sitting on her hip.

He opened the jug and handed it to her.

Taking the jug, she cast a sideways glance at him. "A cup?"

His grin faltered. "That probably would've been a good thing to add. I haven't put together many picnics, let alone meals for more than just me," he said, running his hand through his hair.

Shylah sniffed the open jug. Fizz tickled her nose, and she giggled before taking a sip. Bubbles danced on her tongue and gently pricked her throat. The slight lemon flavor added another layer to the sweet, tangy, bitter flavor of the blackberry and honeysuckle tea. She tipped it back and drank several gulps.

"Careful. It might—"

But before Durmad could finish his warning, Shylah knew what he was about to say. The gentle prickling turned to a burning feeling like she had swallowed several grapes whole. She wiped a drip from her chin and opened her mouth to say, "Sorry," but a belch escaped instead. She quickly covered her mouth. Durmad's deep laugh was contagious, and soon, Shylah laughed so hard that she started crying.

"That belch rivaled any Green Willow Guard," he said, tearing the bread in half and handing one to her.

"I don't know. I've heard your uncle's belches in the kitchen through his shut study door," she said, ripping off a small piece of bread and popping it into her mouth.

"I did say rival, not beat." He flashed her a grin. "I can beat it."

He reached for the jug, but she yanked it out of his reach. "Don't you dare."

Chuckling, he plucked a grape and tossed it into his mouth.

After they finished eating, Shylah meandered toward the falls as Durmad cleaned up. The closer she got, the more her mind focused on the roaring water. It sounded so angry and harsh, yet the moist air softened her hair. The same water that could cradle a child could wear away something as hard as a stone.

She kneeled beside a patch of flowers growing near the edge of the plunge pool. They flourished, because the water gave them life—nutrients, but too much water would kill them, and their soft petals would turn to a dried, crusty skin. So much of nature had two sides: soft and hard, strong and weak, life and death. Too much of one side and nature's essence became twisted—she became twisted. She'd spent so long fighting everyone else, building a shell around her and Trulian, that she saw poisoning as her only option. She tilted her head, stared at the clouds, and asked, "How did I get here?"

"On a horse," Durmad said over the sound of the falls and bumping into her.

She sucked in a deep breath and faced him. She saw the Green Willow Guard in the angles of his jaw, the muscles the sleeves of his leather jacket tried to mask. The training had given him the hard exterior of the fiercest soldier, but his eyes testified to the softness she'd seen in stolen moments the last two weeks. She'd been too young to see it before, and her own protective hardness had almost twisted her ability to see him.

But can my edges even soften? Maybe.
She had last night.

Exhaling, she said, "I'm sorry." His grin softened, and he tucked stray hair behind her ear. His hand skimmed the edge of her ear, sending tingles down the side of her neck. "I don't know what I was thinking. Well, I know what I was thinking, but I was wrong. I never should have—You didn't betray me. I mean Trulian. It's just been so long since my parents, and with your uncle, the Queen, and you leaving—but that wasn't your fault, well it kind of was, but I don't mean—what I do mean is I focused on the wrong thing, I closed you out—I closed everyone out. I shouldn't have—"

Durmad's lips crashed into hers as he pulled her close. Her hands flew to his chest and quickly slid around his neck. The tingle in her neck expanded until her entire body felt like fire trapped in a jar, and its only escape was through the heat in their lips, their tongues, and their mouths. Giving herself over to the fire, she put every regret, every desire, every unspoken apology into her kiss and welcomed his in return until they were breathless and gasping for air.

CHAPTER FORTY SEVEN
DURMAD

The next morning, Durmad sat in the dark of his uncle's kitchen holding a box until the back stairs creaked under Shylah's footsteps.

She emerged and started the fire.

He smiled. She hadn't even noticed him. "Shylah," he whispered.

She jumped, swinging the wrought iron poker in his direction.

"Whoa," he said, stepping into the faint light spilling through the window and setting the box beside the sink. "It's only me."

She relaxed. "I nearly skewered you. Maybe you shouldn't lurk in dark kitchens," she said, turning back to the meager fire she'd started and prodding it a few times before hanging the poker back on its hook.

Quietly closing the distance, he wrapped his arms around her waist. She leaned into him, and he buried his nose in the top of her hair, inhaling her earthy scent. It reminded him of spring green plants smashed against rocks sitting on fresh garden soil with a hint of vanilla. He never wanted to forget the way she smelled or the way she felt in his arms.

She swatted his wrist. "I need to get back to the fire."

He held her tighter as she half-heartedly tried to pull away. Nuzzling into the side of her neck, he said, "I'm surprised uncle lets you anywhere near a fire after his chair."

She spun in his arms and hit his chest. "You know that chair was hideous."

While the firelight made the red in her hair glow, the pale morning light spilling through the window ignited her eyes, and they shone like polished sapphire gems. She pressed against his chest. He smiled as she shifted her weight in his grasp. She was beautiful, feisty, and still awkward. It was bewitching—she was bewitching.

His knuckles caressed her cheek, and she stilled, her hand still resting on his chest.

"I have things to do," Shylah said in a ragged whisper.

Their connection thrummed through his mark while her feather gleamed pale blue around the edges. "Those will still be there later today." He lifted her hand to his mouth. "I will not," he said, kissing the vein under her wrist. Her body shivered against his, and he grinned, holding eye contact. "I want to remember what it feels like to get lost in the blue waters of your eyes, the smell of your hair, and the feel of it against my cheek." He tucked the stray hair that always framed her face behind her ear, and it twitched at his touch. "Or how your body shivers beneath my touch," he whispered, running his fingertips along her chin. "I don't want to forget the feel of your lips." He ran a thumb over her lower lip, tugging it down slightly.

Shylah stood on tiptoes, wrapped her hands around his neck, and smiled up at him. "We can't have that," she said.

His lips pressed into the warmth of her lips—gently at first. Her fingers slid through his hair, and the thrumming of his chest intensified. He didn't want to leave her—not now. They'd just connected.

He picked her up, set her on the counter, and kissed her neck. A soft gasp reached his ear as her chest lifted.

How can I leave her? I can't, but I must.

She pulled his lips back to hers, and his desperation took over. The thrum turned to electricity as he deepened the kiss. He would dream of her, of this kiss, until he returned.

The sound of the wrought iron poker clanging on the stone hearth severed Durmad and Shylah's connection. He wiped his mouth and spun to see Trulian frozen mid-tiptoe.

"Sorry. I tried to sneak past, but my skirts," Trulian said.

Shylah slid off the counter and straightened her skirts. "It's alright, Tru. I have things I have to do if I want to see the parade."

The parade. The box.

Durmad gripped Shylah's wrist. "Wait. I have something for you." He grabbed the box from the counter and motioned for her to sit in the chair he'd waited in. She sat and he placed the box in her lap before kneeling before her.

Glancing at the box and then at him, she gingerly untied the twine bow before removing the brown paper, revealing a blue box embossed in a pattern of black flowers. She slid the lid off with a soft pop. Her brow furrowed at the paper he'd packed on top.

"It's a map. A crude one, but it will take you back to the waterfall. We ran out of time to collect any of the siagel—"

"Cyanelle," she said with a smile.

"That," he said. "This way, you can go any time you want."

She smiled and caressed his cheek.

Placing his hands on her knees, he leaned forward.

Her eyes darted over his shoulder, and she dropped her hand.

Trulian.

He exhaled and sat back on his heels. "The rest are bags of—"

"Tea," Shylah said with a dreamy grin as she held up a bag.

"It's the honeysuckle and blackberry tea I made you with a little comfrey for good measure. There's enough for six months."

"Why six months?"

He took a deep breath and rubbed his hands down his thighs. "I hope to return in six months. That is when I will bring more tea." He rested his hand on the box. "Drink a cup a day."

She blinked back at him.

Taking her hand, he said. "Shy, promise. You must drink one cup a day to keep the side effects of your distillate ability at bay."

"I promise."

He nodded and stood. "I must go prepare for the procession back to the training grounds."

Trulian said, "We will wave to you."

"No. We mustn't confirm the Queen's suspicions that we are close. If anything, we must leave her wondering if she made a mistake." His heart clenched at the thought of what he must say next. His thoughts about how to insulate Shylah in his absence had kept him awake most of last night. He pursed his lips. It was the only idea he'd come up with, even if it still felt half-baked. "You must forget me."

"What?" Shylah shot to her feet.

He laid a hand on her shoulder. "Everyone, especially the Queen, must think you have forgotten all about me. Dote on Aidan," the name of the firesmith's apprentice stuck in his throat. "Make it appear that he has your affection."

Shylah's mouth dropped as she pulled her shoulder from his touch. "I will not."

He ran a hand through his hair. "You must. It is the only way I can think of to keep the Queen from trying to use you against me like she did Trulian. She already suspects our connection, though I don't know how. We cannot give her any more confirmation."

Shylah's shoulders sagged.

"As soon as we have found our quarry, the Queen will be more amicable to our connection. I'm sure." He saw the doubt tilt Shylah's head, and he repeated it to himself.

I'm sure. She will need nothing else from me.

He took a deep breath. "It must start as soon as I leave this kitchen."

Her eyes widened, and Trulian took the box from Shylah's hands.

"I will not be able to wave or even acknowledge you or Trulian," he said, glancing between the sisters. "The Queen will be riding behind me. She will see everything."

The look of pain on Shylah's face gnawed at his stomach. He'd just found her, and now he had to lose her. He tightened his hand into a fist.

This is the only way.

"I must go, but remember," he said before kissing her one last time. "No matter what happens, my heart is yours."

CHAPTER FORTY-EIGHT

SHYLAH

Shylah finished designing the three elixirs in an hour but sat on the stool staring at the bottles until Trulian brought her a cup of tea. "Thank you," she whispered, holding the tea inches from her lips without taking a sip. She held her breath, letting the steam curl before her eyes. Exhaling would force the faint white curls to fade into the air around her, disappearing like it had never existed—like Durmad.

"Shy, you have to drink it for it to work," Trulian said, gently touching Shylah's arm.

Smiling, Shylah exhaled, bringing the cup to her bottom lip. The steam dissipated, but a moment later, it warmed the tip of her nose, bringing with it the earthy scent of dried leaves and honey.

Today, the whole city would say goodbye to the Green Willow Guard recruits. She would have been glad to get rid of every last Willow Guard two weeks ago, but now it was different. Now, it meant saying goodbye to Durmad. Part of her wished she still hated him. Hating him for two and a half years had been easy. If she hated him, she could

351

forget him. Now, that very thing terrified her more than she'd thought possible.

Taking a sip of tea, she closed her eyes and traced the warmth as it coated her mouth, traveled down her throat, and spread through her core.

Six months. He'd be back before six months. Right? What if it was longer? No, I can't think like that. He will be back sooner.

Opening her eyes, she took another drought of tea.

"Should we deliver your elixirs on the way to the procession?" Trulian asked, pulling Shylah from her thoughts.

"Apollyon won't do it," Shylah said, taking a larger drink. The gentle warmth of a single sip increased tenfold, burning a path across the roof of her mouth and down the inside of her chest.

Apollyon was the last person she wanted to see this morning. She didn't have to worry about seeing him at the procession—he never attended. He hadn't even attended when his nephew left the first time.

Shylah's chest clenched.

Do I still call him Apollyon's nephew, or is he just a Bonded like me now?

A shiver ran down her spine at the thought, and she was back in Durmad's tavern room. She gripped her left hand around the cup, and she finished off the hot liquid. Her heartbeat echoed in her ears like his Bonding mark had pulsed beneath her fingers. She'd been able to take away his pain—to use her Distillate ability to pull the essence of his mark through her own blood, but she had no idea how she'd been able to distill his essence through herself. She needed more training, but there was no chance Apollyon would explain what happened—he probably didn't even know himself.

I may not know how I did it, but distilling his spirit means he will never really leave.

The thought made her smile as she took the empty cup into the kitchen. Parts of him were left behind in the process. Her fingers brushed his hand-drawn map. She folded it and grabbed her satchel. Today wasn't really a goodbye; it was merely until we meet again. He was part of her now.

Shylah took solace in the knowledge that the Queen would follow the Willow Guards to the training grounds for the expected two-week supervision. Life would return to normal. Tucking the folded map into a small internal pocket, she stood a little straighter—there was a waterfall to explore and cyanelle to collect.

Trulian hugged her from behind. "It will get hard, but everything will be okay, Shy. I promise."

Shylah sighed and hugged her sister back. "I wish you wouldn't say things like that. I don't mind a little bit of ignorance every now and then." Shylah's mind drifted back to when Trulian had pushed her into Durmad, thinking they'd kiss. "Besides, you don't always interpret it correctly."

"I'm just trying to help," Trulian said, pulling back.

"I know you mean well." She squeezed Trulian, and they left for the gates of Morena.

The closer they got to the gate, the harder it was for Shylah to breathe. She barely understood her emotions and the thought of pretending that they didn't exist and that she felt them for someone else overwhelmed her.

Should I tell Aidan, or would it be better to keep it secret?

They'd helped each other before, but this felt different.

Shylah and Trulian stood along the South side of Castle Lane like any other citizens of Morena as the procession of Green Willow Guards clad in full leather armor with helms atop their heads began. The last two horses were always the highest-ranking guards, with the highest riding on the North side, like the North Star. Liam would be the North Star, and Durmad would be just below him to the South, followed by the Queen's entourage.

Shading her eyes, Shylah looked east toward the castle. The morning sun highlighted the sharp edges of the green feathers adorning their helms and cast each guard's face in shadow, making each blend into the next. They marched in four evenly spaced columns. Every step sent a quiver through the feathers in unison. It reminded Shylah of a bird rousing its wing feathers to sluff off excess water and debris after a bath.

Trulian squeezed Shylah's hand as two guards atop horses turned the bend in Castle Lane. Shylah touched her fingers to her lips; her heart soared and plummeted all at once. She fought the urge to reach out and run a hand along Atlas's shoulder in the hopes of touching Durmad one last time.

He wasn't even gone yet. How am I going to do six months—or longer?

Durmad's left hand rested on his leg, and as he passed her, he raised his fingers an inch off his leg, sending a hum through her Bonding feather. It was the slightest of movements meant only for her understanding. It was supposed to be a final goodbye—one final connection and reminder between only them. But it crushed her heart. Every fiber of her being longed to jump into his arms, hug him, hear his voice, and kiss him one last time.

As the Queen's carriage came into view, the crowd pushed toward the street. The parade seemed to move in slow motion while the crowd jostled Shylah, pushing her forward. She fell in step behind the Queen's carriage. Slowing her pace, Shylah let the distance grow until she passed through the gate and stepped off the road. The crowd continued passing her as they took part in the traditional Vale Mile.

Gradually, Shylah slid along the city walls. She needed to feel close to him, but the idea of trailing behind his back for a mile, hoping for a backward glance she knew would never come, felt like torture. It would be second only to the silent walk back to the city. Feeling the weight of his absence would break her.

Her body ached to feel connected to nature—to herself. There was only one place where the memory of her mother had filled her with hope instead of pain, one place where Apollyon or the Queen did not taint her memories of Durmad.

Unfolding his map sent a wave of peace through her. She didn't know how long he'd be gone or how she'd fake her feelings, but he'd given her the gift of an escape where she could simply *be* without any expectations—without any one to protect. He'd given her back herself.

EPILOGUE

TRULIAN

Unlike her sister, Trulian didn't watch the procession of soldiers; she watched her sister. The pain of finally finding hope after three years of sacrifice only to lose it days later cast her sister in shadow. Even the glowing red strands in her hair dulled despite the morning sun.

Trulian squeezed her sister's hand.

The shadows sank to Shylah's chest, and Trulian's heart stopped. When it started again, it beat so fast she thought her chest would burst. The procession of guards and crowded streets were no longer before her. Instead, the wind stung her eyes as she ran through the alleys around the firesmith's forge.

She entered the market, and her pace slowed. People filled the market.

Not procession day.

Trulian squeezed her eyes closed as a wave of guilt pinched her throat, and Durmad's name echoed in her mind. She fought to open her eyes but only leaned back against the bakery wall before bending

357

over to catch her breath. Her fingers grasped a leather apron, and her eyes finally opened.

Her fingertips were dyed various shades of green and purple, with dirt jammed beneath the nails. She tried to turn them and inspect them, but they refused. Instead, her fingers spread across a pale green skirt with a hole stitched closed by black thread. Trulian remembered repairing the acid burn hole after Shylah had nearly given her a black eye with the herb pot, but it hadn't been her skirt. She'd repaired it for Shylah.

These weren't her hands. She'd traveled to Shylah's memory. *But when?* Visions were the most disorienting part of her peripatetic ability. Instead of the straight line most had for their lives—their memories—Trulian's twisted, curled, branched, knotted.

Shylah wiped away tears as her fear—no, grief—washed over her. Trulian heard her own name on the edges of Shylah's thoughts, but Trulian's training was incomplete—her focus broken. The overwhelming emotions threatened to drown her.

Did Shylah always feel this weight, or had something happened to her? Is that why she heard her own name?

Focus.

There was always a reason for her impromptu travels; Droweht called them visions. She could see through the person's eyes, feel their pain, and hear their thoughts, but she was helpless to change anything. It was always that person's past, no matter where it happened in Trulian's timeline. Droweht promised that keeping everything straight would get easier, but she hated visions the most—another thing she couldn't control—yet.

This vision was a memory for Shylah. Somewhere, some-*when,* Shylah was remembering this experience.

So, why am I seeing through Shylah's eyes?

Shylah gained her composure, bought a fresh cardamom roll, and wove her way through the market crowds. As the warm, spiced dough slid across her tongue, Trulian heard her sister think, "I need another cup of tea."

Why did she need another cup? Durmad had left enough for one cup a day. So, how many cups had Shylah consumed?

Shylah left the market and crossed Castle Lane.

She must be heading back to the workshop. *Was she on a delivery? But why was she running away?* Trulian tried to quiet her own questions and listen to the emotions coursing through Shylah's body and mind.

"Keep it together. You must stay strong for Trulian," the thought made Shylah's body suck in a breath, and Trulian wasn't sure if it was Shylah's breath that caught or her own. She needed to get a better handle on the disorienting visions; she needed to make sure Shylah knew she didn't have to be strong all the time.

The beat of horses' hooves sounded behind Shylah; her throat tightened as she darted down a side alley, running directly into Apollyon. The force knocked Shylah back.

Trulian felt the shock of pain run up her tailbone and her sister's strength drain from her hands—Shylah's hands—into the dry dirt as she tried to stand.

"You think you can run around all day?" he spat as he grabbed Shylah's left wrist and yanked her to her feet.

"It's my replenish day," she said, pulling on her arm, "I—"

"Have a workshop to clean and reorganize," Apollyon said, squeezing her wrist tighter.

Shylah whimpered.

Apollyon dragged her around a corner. "I thought the past two months would have squashed your defiance, but I see now it will take more."

"The Queen said—"

Apollyon yanked Shylah's wrist, and Trulian felt the stab of pain as Shylah's shoulder dislocated, preceding a scream.

"The Queen is still traipsing around the training grounds. She's so worried about what she hunts that she has no time for the likes of you."

Dread seeped into Shylah's mind, muddling her thoughts, and Trulian felt her body weaken as Shylah grasped for anything to divert Apollyon's attention.

They turned another corner, and Apollyon swung Shylah to face him. His upper lip pulled into a snarl. "Shall we see how well you can heal yourself now that he isn't here to do it for you?"

Fresh pain shot up Shylah's arm as Trulian watched him twist her sister's wrist.

Shylah gasped for breath and whispered, "What do you think he will do when he returns?"

Apollyon leaned closer—Trulian felt the heat of his breath on Shylah's cheek as he said, "If he returns."

Trulain's heart shattered as she felt the fight leave Shylah's body.

"Fight back," Trulian screamed as her own desperation doubled the dread she felt from her sister. But for Shylah, this had already happened. Trulian's sense of time braided and flipped in on itself. This was her sister's memory, and she couldn't change a memory. She felt herself giving up along with Shylah.

Apollyon flung Shylah against the building, and her breath evaporated.

Trulian's eyes flung open. She sucked in deep breaths as the crowd passed her. The Queen's carriage was just clearing the gates, and Shylah walked with the crowd a few feet in front of her.

No longer a memory.

She watched Shylah disappear beyond the city gates. Trulian rubbed her shoulder. It was never dislocated, but her muscles still ached from the memory of it. Her chest felt hollow, as if what should have been there had left through the gate with her sister. Part of her had resented Shylah for insulating her—babying her, but now Trulian felt protective of Shylah. The only way to protect her sister was to master her ability and that meant more training.

Most people were distracted by the procession and would be until the evening meal, giving her time to slink through the streets unnoticed. She pulled her cloak over her head, tucking her fiery red waves beneath the rough brown fabric. Backing into the shadows, Trulian darted through the back alleys until she reached the fourth battlement in the city wall; the castle's Pithian tower hovered over her as she pushed the tip of her finger against a small carving of a circle divided into four heart-shaped knots. The slight pressure caused a pop to sound to her left. Pushing with her left hand, the rock slid just wide enough for her to slide through sideways.

As the sliver of light died and the shadows enveloped her, Trulian gritted her teeth as the vision of Shylah being dragged through the alleys of Morena played across her mind.

I will give you back your fight.

BE ONE OF THE FIRST TO HEAR ABOUT BOOK 2

THE ELIXIR OF THE QUEEN

JOIN HER NEWSLETTER:

www.aduhlar.com

TO BE CONTINUED IN

THE ELIXIR OF THE QUEEN

The Queen has met her match,
but it takes more than a few
clever moves to win a game.

ACKNOWLEDGEMENTS

So many people have contributed directly and indirectly to the creation of this story, these characters, and the of world of Ethereal. This is my small way of saying thank you for the love, support, and encouragement of my crew of treasure hunters who continue to help me find my own hidden gems.

If it weren't for my parent's support and encouragement to continue learning and adapting, I might never have considered this new venture. I am truly blessed to have a mother with unwavering love and support and a father who always pushed me to try new things and keep moving forward in my career.

My family and friends helped lay the groundwork for this story. My husband Michael cheered me on while giving me the flexibility to sit and write after my day job, and my four amazing kids, Jonah, Arianna, Elijah, and Hannah, always matched my energy and excitement.

The inspiration for this story began after reading Lyndsey Franklin's The Story Peddler just before challenging my creative writing students to write a novel in a month. I never ask my students to do something I'm not willing to do, so I wrote the first story in the Kingdom of Ethereal, which landed me acceptance into the University of Nebraska at Omaha's MFA program. If it weren't for amazing mentors and creatives like Kevin Clouther, Jim Peterson, Jessica Hendry Nelson, Terri Youmans, Michael Oatman, and Charlene Donaghy, my writing would have stopped with that first story. In my final semester, I was awarded UNO's Graduate Research and Creative Activity Grant to conduct research, which meant learning to blacksmith! Because of that experience, I changed my entire magic system to what it is now.

My time at UNO kept on giving even after the program finished because it produced my critique group. I am forever indebted to Tacheny Perry, whose minimalist prose continues to teach me how and when to pull back in my own writing, to Kristine Ganoung, whose pacing and syntax continue to teach me how to keep a slow-moving scene from dragging, and to Patti Jones, who's action pact prose and attention to detail continues to teach me when to lean into the action to generate energy within my prose, and, most recently, when to expand a rushed ending into a book 2. (Dear reader, it is she you have to thank or blame, depending on your view, for the upcoming release of *The Elixir of the Queen*.) These ladies have been there from the beginning, and I can't wait to help them share their own stories with the world.

If it weren't for my newsletter subscribers and social media followers, Shylah's story would never have taken shape. After all, they were the ones who said, "I want more Shylah!" Well, ask, and you shall receive. Shylah's story was made available to the masses through the wonderful supportive community created by CJ Redwine and Mary Weber. Thank you for creating the Red Herring Society and taking a chance on a new writer.

I had the space and place to write in large part because of two amazing local businesses: Healing Pines Recovery and Hidden House, a wonderful local coffee house. Thanks to Paul Leafstedt, I spent hours during long breaks drinking coffee and writing away or spreading out in the quiet solitude of an empty office.

The marketing and artwork are thanks to two particularly wonderful and encouraging students who you could say have been there since the beginning: Peyton Christensen and Sarah Breed. Peyton helped breathe life into the characters through her artistic gift and I look forward to seeing the rest of my characters in the world of Ethereal through her eyes. Sarah not only served as a beta reader, but helped design social media layouts, served as a sounding board for ideas, created pros and cons lists to help me process information, and let me feed off her excitement at seeing the process of publishing when burnout and frustration reared their ugly heads.

Finally, I have to thank the rest of my beta readers, who helped me get this book ready! Caleb Nava, Marlise Eshleman, Deanna Gibson, Lucy Schoel, Patrick O'Dell, Claire Tourangeauca and Martrice Endres. This book is where it is because of your contributions!

A.D. UHLAR

About the Author

A D Uhlar is a treasure hunter at heart. She seeks out the hidden gems forgotten in all the dark corners of the world. It started with school and pushing through setbacks, but the pressure only made the gems more valuable when she finally uncovered her love for the creative extended to writing.

Any true treasure hunter knows that you have to learn a few things before you can become successful. So, she completed a secondary teaching degree followed by a masters in reading instruction, but on that journey she took a college creative writing class. It was challenging, but in the best kind of way. You know the ones—they leave you energized, awake at night with ideas, and excited for the next challenge. As much as she enjoyed the class, she let the *practical* side of her brain take over. Although her treasure hunting and creativity never truly left; it simply emerged in other ways.

As a teacher, she looked for ways to keep English, writing, reading, and literature study fresh, but mainly she helped students see their potential and supported them as they explored the dark corners within themselves and their world. Dark places can be scary, but many of the best treasures are there hiding just below the surface.

In 2019, her creativity resurfaced and she took on the challenge of Nation Novel Writing Month with her creative writing club. She never challenges her students to do something she isn't willing to do herself. So, she wrote 57,000 words of a fantasy novel featuring a female blacksmith as the lead character. It was the perfect exploration into AD's own independence and inner strength.

That following January, she hit a closed road that didn't hurt as much as she thought. She wasn't a research match for a PhD in secondary education. AD has never been so grateful for a *NO* in her entire life. She knew she wanted to learn more, to dig deeper into herself and the world, so she explored other learning options.

Enter the University of Nebraska Omaha's low residency MFA in writing program. With some encouragement from her fellow treasure hunter and husband, she sent in her GRE, transcripts, and fifty pages of her newly minted story. Then the call came; *she was in!*

At the height of COVID, she began the journey of juggling teaching, parenting, and an MFA—oh, and a move two days before her program started. She completed her MFA in Writing at the University of Nebraska Omaha in August of 2022. As part of her journey, she applied for and received UNO's Graduate Research and Creative Activities Grant to engage in experiential research.

She learned blacksmithing. That's right. She even made the sword from the novel she wrote in 2019! And thus the Kingdom of Ethereal was born. The research enriched her magic system allowing AD to dive into the complexities of the world. Her 2019 novel draft changed.

Enter short stories. Writing novels is time consuming to say the least, so to explore some characters and elements of Ethereal, AD wrote short stories about the people inhabiting it. In December of 2023, her short story, "A Tooth for Trulian" arrived in *Meet Me At Midnight, an R.H.S. Anthology.* Then the anthology became a best seller on Amazon, giving AD the title of best selling author!

It didn't stop there. That little story kept on giving and AD's newsletter readers wanted more Shylah. So, she asked them what type of story they wanted and with a resounding 92%, they clamored for Romance. The original plan was to write a novella, but then Shylah, Durmad, and Trulian demanded more. It became The Elixir of the Green Willow Guard.

AD thought she had a winner and was ready to move on to the five book series featuring her female blacksmith, but again The Kingdom of Ethereal had different plans. Shylah and Durmad's story wasn't done, and Trulian's was just beginning. So a book two is currently in the works!

AD Uhlar's other stories include a group of college roommates living in a world where their traumas manifest on their skin as literal cracks and the history of Aimedaca is a well guarded secret. This world and series still in its drafting and discovery stage, also grew from a short story and ultimately became the creative work of AD's MFA thesis.

Another short story, she hopes will branch into additional stories and worlds was an exploration of her own Slovak heritage. "Red" in *All the Promises We Cannot Keep, an R.H.S. Anthology,* is a reimagining of the Czechoslovak tale "The Nickerman's Wife." She has barely uncovered the magical world of Slavic stories, and can't wait to continue uncovering hidden treasures.

When she isn't writing about the world of Aimedaca, The Kingdom or Ethereal, or exploring the stories of her Slovak ancestry, she continues to guide the creative ventures of her four children who still keep her on her toes. Roughly nine months of the year she coaches students in their own creative and academic writing pursuits, but really she sees herself as their coach even beyond the walls and desks of her classroom.

When not parenting, writing, coaching and teaching, she helps out with her parents' farm, plays canasta, and expresses her creativity through various mediums including her hair.

AD Uhlar can be found unearthing treasure at or @aduhlar on Instagram, Threads, TikTok, Facebook, YouTube, and Tome (tome books.com). If you want to get to know more about her, be in on early news, and get early access to her future novels, join her newsletter.